I0788122

BELVIDERE.

VI

X
Sans Nom

Title: **Belvidere.**

Summary: *A mysterious man is sent to a dead-end town; to do what, and to whom, he simply doesn't know. It's all part of a game he neither understands, nor controls. He befriends those he will likely betray; there will certainly be trouble if he does not. A fantastical, mysterious journey; an ephemeral olla podrida of raw erotica, graphic violence, racism, heathenism, bigotry and vulgarity, all buoyed by the providence of friendship, love and kindred souls.*

1.   Fiction-General.   2.   Fiction-Fantasy.
17 18 19 20 21   j i h g f e d c b a
First Edition - American

A Special Note To The Reader Who Is A Self-Appointed Observant Orthographer:

To this special group, the spelling and grammar police, please put your pencil down; I will save you the suspense.

This novel may be a grammar and sentence structure nightmare to people who obsess about such things. The pages that follow are vaguely, or not so, reminiscent of Beat literature, which can be described, by some, as a rejection of standard narrative and linguistic values, including, but not necessarily limited to, syntax, punctuation, sentence structure and morphology. The writing style is idiosyncratic; it is how the author thinks, and how the author believes this fictional account should be told. And just as important, it's how real people speak and communicate in the real world, which is rarely textbook or *correct*. It is real, or at least how this author perceives reality, which is all that matters between these end-papers.

In any event, there **will** be mistakes. And all the mistakes in this book were purposeful, and will be defended as such, even if they weren't. After two long years of editing, this writer simply got tired of re-reading and proofing. So what you see is what you get, whether it's *right* or not.

My suggestion is to take the broader view: simply enjoy the characters and enjoy the ride they take you on. Along the way, if you feel the need to get enraged, do so at the abject violence, the graphic sex, the racism, the bigotry, the coarse language, the heathenism....but for God's sake, don't get enraged at punctuation....leave the poor periods alone.

TABLE OF CONTENTS - VI

CHAPTER 211 – READY TO GO FOR A WILD RIDE?

The *almond rocas* were long gone, and Mae was onto soda crackers and sour cream, another childhood treat she somehow found at this nutty, cheesy Fair. She was in a crazy, funny nostalgic mood; if she still had that yellow frilly dress, she surely would have put it on, with hair done-up in a pair of floppy ponytails.

C smiled at the thought, a sixty-six year old, eleven all over again.

The two stood in line for a bracelet at the ticket booth; you could buy individual tickets, a rip-off, or just get a paper bracelet for unlimited fun on all the carnival rides, all night long. It was still a rip-off, but a bit less-so, and nary a Fair-goer passed by without a paper ring on their wrist.

As the two stood in line, C reached over and held Mae's hand; it was warm, and it felt good, rubbing and feeling it in his. And he didn't mean anything by it other than showing he was happy to see her, happy they reconciled; she squeezed back in kind.

And both of them were happy at the same time, for once. For a bit.

The two stood in silence, playing with each other's hand, fingers entwined, as they eavesdropped on a group of five, three girls and two boys, all in their early twenties, standing in front of them, smiling at the goofy adolescent banter, remembering how they undoubtedly had the same inane conversations as kids. Twenty-something was still *kids* to them.

The girls were certainly not thin in C's book, but to anyone else, they were slim and athletic, but a bit wide, loose and sloppy in the thighs, the hips, the rump; they gave off a collective, slightly butch-but-not, softball player vibe.

Each girl was wearing baggy, cartoon pajama bottoms over men's boxer shorts, with loose tee-shirts over tight jog-bras; flip-flops finished the look. All had the mien of a recent roll out of bed, the tallest not even bothering to pull what appeared to be yesterday's ponytail knot, crooked and mussed, along with a flattened bed-head that she apparently wore all day. Surprisingly, all three had a bit of acne, none worse than the other, but their complexions were still attractive enough for two good-looking guys to hang with them. The boys were put together fairly well, thin, wearing trendy shorts and loose tees, well groomed, except for faces sporting a hangover drag. They were a better looking duo than the trio of girls, and C was sure the girls put out gladly and often, otherwise these guys would have, and could have, easily farmed elsewhere.

As the five milled together in line, they passed around a greasy paper dish of chicken fingers, slathered in honey dip sauce, and a single egg-and-bacon on a roll for a group-eat; the girls yipped over one another about nonsensical shenanigans, as the boys half-listened, never attempting a word edgewise.

"Oh my God!"

"No music…."

"Creepy, creep me out!"

"Icing on the door; icing fight! Charlie started it!"

The one boy shrugged his shoulders in resignation.

"Of course, I was wearing my hair down!"

Screamed the ponytail girl, much louder than necessary.

"Sarah had it all over her!"

"Cake fight!"

Two of the girls chimed in unison, as the boys shoved the last of the fried fingers and egg down the hatch, followed by a sloppy, methodical finger-lick, a top-to-bottom ritual, with extended tongues, like dogs cleaning their balls.

C had to turn away from that one.

"Like it was so obvious!"

The one girl screeched.

"There was chocolate all over me!"

After some giggles and a lull, and a final finger-lick by the boys, along with a hand-wipe on the pants, talk somehow turned to travel, with no introduction or apparent tie-in, just a stream of twenty-something jumbled thoughts. And C and Mae stood silent, captive in line, listening to the wonderful nonsense, smiling, still holding hands.

"When we used to drive to N.C...."

"Drive cross-country to Arizona, like every summer!"

"Did she have, like, an RV?"

"What time is it?"

The first word edgewise by boy number one.

"8:10"

"Like my mom said: *what did you do all day?*"

And, for some secret reason, shared by all, the five of them laughed aloud.

"Like…."

"Drunk-sledding is so much fun!"

"Did I ever tell you about drunk-sledding with my broken wrist?   I just went down, like this ramp, I flew off!"

And just like that, the stories of icing fights, cross-country trips and drunk-sledding faded away, as the group of five checked out their new paper bracelets, and dissolved into the crowd, taking their stories with them.

"Good God."

Was all C said; Mae nodded silently in agreement, smiled and squeezed his hand.

"Being young, once, was okay, but never, ever would I want to do that again; once is *way* more than enough."

C said.

"I don't know, it would have been nice to know you when I was that age."

Mae said, dreamy.

"Are you kidding me? You wouldn't have given me the time of day; you were such a *hottie*, according to you."

"You're right, and I *was*. I would have blown you off **big time**! Oh, for the chance to do that, to blow you off! What was your name, back then, your real name? So I know what I would have called you when I told you to get lost!"

Mae said, smiling at him. And C just smiled back, and held up his bright green bracelet.

"Ready to go for a wild ride?"

1800

CHAPTER 212 – NO TONGUES, NO TEETH, NO NOTHING

They were both having a blast, they really were.

They had run a half-dozen turns on the *Fun Slide*, the *Tilt-a-Whirl* and the goofy *Funhouse*, all fairly tame and pre-teen. It was both silly and nostalgic, wrapped in the warm blanket of an August night in Jersey farm-country.

Surreal.

They stepped off the *Tilt-A-Whirl* one last time and that was enough spinning for C; his stomach couldn't take those sorts of rides. Mae could spin all day, and laughed at him for being such a wuss. She suddenly had a hanker for cotton candy; gotta have some cotton candy.

"Hey."

Mae said.

"Give me back the letter."

C reached in his pocket and pulled out the folded envelope. Mae took it, unfolded the crease, and proceeded to rip it into eighths, tossing it indignant in the next garbage can they passed.

"Thanks."

C said.

"I was just thinking about it; it served its purpose, and now I feel foolish even writing it, so I want it, and that chapter to go away, old news; agreed?"

"Agreed."

C said, and he kissed her lightly on the cheek.

"Good, no more talk about that stuff; let's get some cotton candy."

Mae announced, decidedly happy. And with that, she hooked her arm in his, and the two walked through the trampled grass corridors, searching amongst the food vendors for spun sugar, weaving through throngs of people. And amongst the crush of people, they spied, just ahead, Marty and Ji-Sue, at a carnival stand.

Marty's face was contorted in a serious stare, concentrating hard, his tongue tip sticking between his lips as he aimed his pistol at the clown-head, trying his best to fill the balloon with a stream of water before the ten-year old to his left beat him to the stuffed animal he just *had* to win. Head to head. Ji-Sue stood by his smile, smiling, and then smiling some more. C smiled, and poked Mae, pointing at the spectacle.

Just then, Ji saw them.

"Hi guys!"

She yelled, wildly waving.

And the momentary distraction was all it took; Martin shifted his eye off the prize, and the little pudgy boy to his left, through a concentrated squint, shot the last gulp of water that burst the red balloon atop the clown head, and with it came the bounty and the swagger, the *Pink Panther* beanbag, half the size of your palm. Marty had been eyeing that loot for Ji-Sue through no less than ten dollars in quarters.

"Hah!"

The little fat kid huffed, the remnants of pink cotton-candy sugar stuck to his lips, holding it up to Marty and waving it back and forth, a ruthless *in-your-face*.

"I woulda had it."

Marty whispered under his breath to himself, as he hit his fist against his leg, foiled again.

"Thank you trying; you almost got it!"

Ji-Sue said, encouraging her new-found date to cheer up.

"I can try again! Look!"

"As two little girls, seven years old and barely big enough to hold the pistols upright, searched for precious quarters."

Ji-Sue just whispered in his ear and giggled.

"Really? Okay."

Was all Marty said, blushing a bit as he walked away from the plastic clown heads. *Stupid clown-heads* he whispered to himself as he parted.

Wow, never saw that coming C thought to himself about the lightning Martin/Ji-Sue hook-up; he was happy for the both of them, and it made sense. But even now, he would still bend her over, one-off, given the chance. No harm, no foul.

The four chatted a bit, talking about deeds done and people seen. No one had seen Lilly or Buck, and Marty said Earl and Carol were eating funnel cakes at the pavilion the last time they saw them, sugar powder smeared across Earl's face. They all laughed as Marty told about Carol trying to hold Earl's hand, and Earl trying to make pretend he didn't know she was, and kept moving his hand away....their own little shell game. Carol kept it up, smiling, hoping to wear him down.

1803

"Let's all go on the *Fireball,* or the *Pharaoh's Fury* or the *Starship 2000,* or the *Octopus!*"

Mae shouted out each one, as she pointed down the line of rides, a mash of flashing lights and loud music. There was a hearty roar of yes by three; C just shook his head.

"No way, I'll get sick, no way. You guys go; I'll watch."

"Oh come on, Jesus; I can't believe you're such a baby!"

Mae prodded, but C held firm.

"Insult me all you want, but I won't change my mind; I don't do peer pressure. I know I'm a wuss, too bad, not doing it. I'll watch."

So the four made their way to the *Octopus,* the closest of the four rides.

"What about the *Ferris Wheel,* can you do that, grandpa?"

Mae taunted.

"Yeah, grandpa can do that. Grandpa can do lots of *other* rides too; want me to describe those rides, in detail?"

C said matter-of-fact, as Mae put her hand over his mouth in mock protest. The three then squeezed into one cab seat on the *Octopus,* surrounded by raucous teens, filling the other tentacles.

Cord made his way around the perimeter fence, to the exit gate for the *Octopus,* which was opposite the exit for the adjacent *Scrambler,* the next ride down the line. That was another one he wanted no part of, full of its own screaming fanatics, who just couldn't get enough.

The *Octopus* started up and quickly was writhing and spinning in all directions; it was hard to follow the cab the three were jammed in. C would have *so* puked on this fucking ride, for sure. Just watching it was bad enough. Every fifteen seconds or so, the *Octopus* arm would wriggle his way, and he saw the three revelers crammed to the left, or to the right, laughing, or screaming, or both. And the scene repeated itself, over and over, for a dozen times, until the ride wound down, and the octopus tentacles became lethargic. By fluke, like a lucky roulette spin, the ride ended with their tentacle extended right at Cord, nearest the exit. But rather than the smiles and laughs he expected at the end of a thrill, he saw three frightened faces, with wide eyes, looking right at Cord, right through Cord....right *past* Cord.

He spied them curiously, followed their stares, and turned around, eyeing the *Scrambler*, in wicked speed, full of screaming teens, the cars each taking turns thrusting toward him, like a boxer's jab, coming, it seemed, within inches of the fence he leaned against, before just as quickly receding, waiting for the next car to queue.

Each jab was a Polaroid of smiling faces, teeth flashing and tongues wagging, hair flying in all directions, one after another. Cord looked at each set of strangers, searching for the source of the *Octopus* stare....finding nothing special.

He was about to turn back at the *Octopus,* to look to his friends for some help, some explanation, when the last *Scrambler* punch shot toward his face, the last car of the lot. And this one had no screaming teens, no wagging tongues, nor flashing teeth.

This one had a Lillian....and a Button.

No tongues, no teeth, no nothing.

CHAPTER 213 – HE TOOK MY UNDERWEAR

C stared blank at the now-empty space, as the car recoiled into the heart of the *Scrambler*, rotating and moving on to punch a different hole in a different direction, away from him.

He simply stared, his limbs numb; shock, mixed with anger, disbelief and impotency settled in.

He didn't realize the other three had joined by his side; no one spoke, waiting for the *Scrambler* to slow to a stop, and the happy occupants to disembark.

Lilly and Button ended on the far side of the perimeter fence; Cord's view was obstructed by machinery and appendages, so he couldn't see how they exited the car, if he helped her off, if they talked, if they smiled….nothing. No clues to go by. They were mostly obscured by the throng of laughing, gabbing riders exiting the gate; he caught glimpses as they made their way toward him, toward the foursome.

Then he caught a first good glimpse.

Lilly was expressionless, and was changed. She no longer wore the ecru chino-style shorts, sandal flats and short-sleeve white cotton top she came in, twin to Carol. Now she was fitted with a gaudy, gold mini-skirt, imitation leather, alligator-pattern, which barely covered her crotch, and a black fishnet top, a mid-riff which revealed her stomach and navel, with a deep neckline. She wore no bra, and you could clearly see her breasts through the knit holes, and if you stared, and got not-that-close, you could clearly see the pink of her nipples.

C looked away.

She had cartoonish, five-inch silver slut-stilettos, laced partly up the ankle; even in the trampled grass and hardpan soil around the perimeter of the rides, flattened by thousands of Fair-goer feet, there was no way to walk in them, so she had to hold onto Button's arm, lest her ankles twist and buckle. Her face was caked with hastily-applied makeup; bright red lipstick and heavy mascara half-ringed her eyes, which had run, the start of tiny raccoon rings. She wore large, costume earrings; they were gold-colored plastic hoops. The slight tinge of a red ring circled her neck; the remnant flush of a recent choke-hold. Her right eye and upper lip were slightly swollen.

"Hey, Wanker, enjoying the Fair?"

Button said, smiling, as he exited the gate. He let go of Lillian's arm, leaving her to wobble on her own, and walked right up to Cord, nose to nose.

And C's first reaction was amazement; Button's face was almost fully healed, just the faintest trace of injury remained, as if he never endured the vicious beating that Cord had given him. Most men would have died in that assault; survivors would have been scarred and bruised for a month or more. But not Button; he had healed. It was uncanny, not unlike Cord's ability to heal, quick and almost, but not quite, absolute. Billy Bone's side tooth was back, replaced as if new, and the yawning gash above his left eye was reduced to nothing more than a faint shadow; you had to stare close to even notice a remnant. His nose was fine, no evidence is was broken, or even mangled. He showed no adverse signs of being beaten close to death; it was as if it had never happened.

Button was so close, he was exhaling stale beer into C's face. Cord's first instinct was to snap his neck; a quick headlock, drop to a knee, a heavy jerk and twist – all one motion. Less than ten seconds and it would be over. He had done it before, many more than once; quick, simple and over.

In less than ten seconds, it will be all over; the words rang in Ay's head. His muscles began to tense, to ready for the quick move to end it....to end him. And he knew Button wouldn't be able to stop it; he was as good as over.

He could have done it, easily, right then and there. But he didn't.

And for the second time in much less than a month, Cord inexplicably spared Button's life. It wasn't out of civility, or goodness, or fear of repercussion; none of that mattered to C. Rather, it was as if killing Billy Bones, somehow, at that moment, wasn't allowed. That's how it felt, inside, right at the moment he was about to spring and snap his neck. It was as if someone in his head put on the brakes, put up their hand, and stopped the thought cold. And it wasn't the puppet, the crickets, the flies or anyone else living in his head; this was a different feeling, a different voice, one he hadn't felt before. It wasn't even a feeling or a voice; it couldn't be described that way; it was simply a *something*. And as quick as it came, it was gone....fleeting. But the point was clearly made, and the decision was final.

Apparently, a different play was in the works.

Lilly walked like a zombie into Marty's arms; he hugged her, and both Mae and Ji instinctively sandwiched her, to hide her from view. Mae took off her light sweater, and wrapped it around Lillian. Ji-Sue took off her sandals and gave them to Lilly, who stood in silence, holding them in the air, oddly, while the girls unlaced the stilettos and tossed them in the trash can.

Lilly didn't cry, or sob, or complain, or anything, she just stared blank with raccoon eyes into the distance, into the darkness, at nothing.

Then, she said just one thing, monotone, without any hint of emotion, and she didn't say anything more.

"He took my underwear."

Button slightly turned his head and spat tobacco juice onto the ground, just to the right of Cord's shoes.

"Button, this is over, I'm taking you…."

Marty started, but Billy raised his hand in mild annoyance.

"Goober, stop right there; let me talk to your friend here for a brief moment, then you can play in-charge, okay little-doggie?"

Martin pulled out his phone to call for back-up.

"I wouldn't do that."

Button warned, laughing.

C waved Marty down, talking in a low, controlled tone.

"Take care of her; I'll be right back."

He followed Button, who had walked a dozen steps away, under a nearby telephone pole, sporting an overhead amber light. He pulled the balance of his chaw and tossed it in the grass, even though there was a trash can less than a foot away. He popped a cigarette from a crumpled pack in his pocket, lit it slowly, and took a long, slow, enjoyable drag. The smoke lazily circled his face, and disappeared into the night.

Cord stared at Billy Bones again; other than some faded bruising and a general bit of a puff along the left side, almost imperceptible, Button's face had largely recovered from the beating at the boat ramp….it truly was impressive. He sported a neat goatee; he wasn't sure if that was there the last time he saw him, he couldn't remember. It must it not have been, since C was noticing it now. Billy's head was clean shaven, which only accentuated how thick and bushy his eyebrows were. He was tan, with a clean, smooth complexion, and deep blue eyes, which seemed to glow in the amber light.

Button *really was* a good-looking guy, C thought, and he understood, looking at him, *really* looking at him, how the ladies easily queued for him, including the ones on C's team.

"Did you really think you could protect her? Really? I could have come and taken my little Chiquita anytime I wanted, whenever, wherever."

C stared at him, and Button snorted a laugh.

"You got a week 'cause I had other business to attend to, nothing more, and I had to figure a way to deal with you, that would be....appropriate. And now that's pretty much taken care of."

Button took a long drag, and blew the smoke into the air, above C's head, some sort of strange courtesy, like a favor. Then he flipped open a phone, pulled from his pocket, hit a single button and a high-pitched negro voice answered.

"Yeah, now; quick in and out."

Billy flipped the phone shut and pulled a miniature pair of binoculars from his shirt pocket and tossed them to Cord.

"Look up on the ridge over there, the white van that's flashing it's headlights; yeah, that one. Just watch, and meet the *Drin*."

C held up the field lenses and pinpointed the van, about a hundred yards away, just as the side door opened and out spilled a posse of black men; they seemed to keep coming, like ants. There must have been over a dozen that exited the panel door, milling around the van, under diffused light, enough to make them out, and what they were carrying: guns, chains and machetes....lots. There were pistols and semi-automatics of all shapes and sizes; one had what looked like a miniature machine gun - that guy held it aloft, pumping it in the air like a touchdown dance.

"Who woulda figured, a nigger posse working for me; I'd just assume *Mandigo*-cook all the fuckers, burn 'em alive, but they listen and do what they're told....domesticated....fucking livestock *[Button smirked]*."

Button tossed his cigarette in the half-tall grass and crushed it under his boot heel; a man in complete control.

"Anyway, they're on edge. And a dozen edgy monkeys, with guns and bad intent, is *not* a good thing, trust me; you have to throw them a treat now and then."

He could just snap his neck right now....quick and done. Cord's mind raced as Billy continued to speak, wondering if he should break the rules. But he couldn't do it; not with that feeling he had; he just couldn't.

"You know what they told me? They don't like the *smells* around here. Can you believe that? They say it smells! That from fucking *Nacas* who smell like shit themselves! And they're itching to hurt something, anything. I told them we're here to pick up some Opies to fuck with, or just fuck."

Button smirked. But Cord was done listening to this nonsense.

"Cut to the chase, I'm tired of hearing you yap like a little dog; you're a fucking pussy. I can snap your neck right now, and you can't do a thing to stop it....*nothing.* Your only balls are a truck full of niggers a hundred yards away; they can't help you here, pussy."

C said, shoving Button hard in the chest with an open hand, knocking the cigarette out of his grip as he bum-stumbled back a step. And the smirk left Billy Bones face, and he got dead serious.

"You touch me again, fuck-head, just once, and she's done....you understand? *Cut to the chase?* Is that what you said, mother-fucker? Okay, here it is."

And Button grabbed his phone, and the high-pitched nigger was back on the line.

"Show it, and do it...."

And he kept the phone open, to his ear.

"....and if I hang up, you know what to do."

Button looked up at the van. Cord followed his sight, and watched the van door open again, and the same dozen-plus niggers piled out, standing in a loose half-arc, this time sans weapons.

All except the last one, who stepped into the middle of the semi-circle, sporting a weapon much more ominous than guns, chains or machetes.

It was Carol Crowe, bound and gagged.

CHAPTER 215 – THE COUNT STOPPED AT SIX

"Now I have your attention?"

Button said sarcastically, as he knocked the last cigarette from his pack and relit, crumpled the pack and again, threw the trash on the ground, beside the waste basket.

"Now this is my last one, so be careful, don't you go knocking it out of my hand."

Button said, pointing his finger at C like a father scolding a child. He took a long, deep drag, staring at C.

"Bad habit."

Billy said, shaking his head through a slow exhale of smoke. Cord looked over to Marty and the group; they saw the commotion, but they hadn't seen Carol.

"Hey, Marty, take her and Ji-Sue home; Mae, do me a favor, go wait over by the ticket booth and I'll be over shortly, okay?"

"But…."

Came a collective retort; Cord shook his head hard in the negative and waved his hand to cut any debate, and they obliged.

"Funny, you were so fucking smug when those big niggers set on me, like dogs, in your house; not so funny now, is it?"

Button said, taking a long, slow drag and then talking to Carol just above a whisper, looking up at the ridge-line, Carol bound and helpless, a sheep surrounded by a pack of hungry wolves. Button flicked what was left of the butt on the ground, and let it smolder in the green trample of grass. He stretched lazy, reaching up to the night sky, like he just woke up. He spoke to C, but never took his eyes off the ridge. The boys had shoved Carol back in the van, and piled in behind her; once the cargo door shut, the van sat quiet, engine idling in the distant field, serene, with the happenings inside best left to the imagination.

Button smiled to himself, and assumed a comfortable pose, to spin his *own* story, his *own* travel tale, to C.

So began Billy Bones.

"We, the *Drin*, control a meat-packing plant, right down by the river, on the river. That place runs twenty-four-seven dude, all year long; a dirty, dirty place....disgusting *[Billy shook his head as he spoke]*.

First, the boys will gag and gang-rape her for the two hour ride south; based on seniority, Kreme-King will go first. I'm sure he'll rip her good; they call him Kreme cause he brags the girls all cream for him, and he stuffs 'em with big loads. Stupid nigger-stories, that's all these animals talk about, all they care about, big dicks and tight pussies, and they like the tight, white pussies the best.   Anyway, from there they'll go right down the line; Burr next, then Bogs, all the way to the fourteen-year olds....I don't even know their names. God knows what pool of fucking disease they're sticking their pricks in by that time. Then it starts up again, from the beginning, this time in her ass. A full round, top to bottom. These guys live for these night trips, fucking animals *[Billy turned to C and snorted a laugh]*. If they're lucky, they'll get a couple rounds in before they drop her off at the plant, stripped naked and gagged. They'll beat the living shit out of her too, after the fuck go-rounds, just for fun; nasty, nasty business.

It's amazing how much meat they run through that plant, non-stop, day and night; it's fucking unbelievable. Gets you kinda sick, watching it, and you know, the smell; you wanna fucking puke *[Billy shook his head]*.

They'll throw her in the feed-hopper alive, by the way — it's usually feet first, or sideways, sometimes head first, and the poor fucks always try to hold themselves up, against the walls, but they're coated with meat-grease, fat and shit from all the livestock, slippery as a pig, and down the chute they go. She'll only scream for a second or two; I've seen it, those fucking meat cutters and grinders are some scary shit, let me tell you, industrial-size, and loud. You can't even see the blades and choppers, it all spins so fast, like a big-ass blender. And everything gets ground up dude, I mean *everything;* bones, teeth, hair, shit and piss....*everything.* Right to mince meat....puree....meat diarrhea.

I shit you not, less than ten minutes after she had a line of nigger-cock pumping her ass, she's fully mixed into the dog-chow line; I've seen it, man, fucking amazing, watched it go from a person to *Premium Grade Wet — Slow-Cooked With Gravy [Button smiled],* canned, labeled and boxed. Less than an hour later and she's bouncing along on the forklift, shrink-wrapped on a pallet, to be loaded on the truck and delivered to the grocery store, stocked on the shelf by morning. I kid you not; dogs will be eating her for breakfast tomorrow, and she'll be shit out on the lawn before the end of the day. In less than twenty-four hours, she's a soupy dog turd, stinking up the front lawn, covered in flies.

Amazing, and true. Amazing.

And I'll make sure she gets delivered to Sam's and I'll buy a dog, and shit her out on her own fucking front porch, just for fun.

Just wanted to explain that, so you understand just how important it is, that I have your undivided attention."

Cord stared at him poker-face, deciding what to do. But he knew it would probably be nothing, unless he was to sacrifice Carol. There was no doubt in C's mind that Billy would do as he said, no doubt at all; he might do it anyway, regardless, for revenge, or just for fun. So for now, C remained still. The players in his head stayed behind the curtain, spectators, for now, seeing how Cord would play the situation.

"Well, comments….*nothing?*"

Nothing from Cord.

"Okay, well, enough talking, the time has come. *Nolens-volens;* know what that means? You're supposed to be so smart; *nolens-volens?*"

Nothing from Cord.

"*Willing or unwilling;* that's what it means. Pretty cool huh? I just learned that one, you know, trying to expand my vocabulary. Dealing with niggers all day gets you stupid. Anyway, that's what you're gonna do to save your little girl from the dog chow line, whatever I say….*nolens-volens.* I'm tired of playing silly games, and I'm tired of seeing your face. So, tomorrow morning, we end this."

"Why wait? Why not now, right here?"

"Because I said so, that's why. My game, my rules; *nolens-volens.*"

Button went to grab for his pack of cigarettes, forgetting he finished them. He snorted in disapproval. He reached into his front pocket, and pulled out a slip of paper.

"5:30 am, here's where you go *[Button passed him a carefully scripted, hand-written note, with directions]*;

walk or take a bike, I suggest a bike, it's a bit of a hike. No cars, solo, and I'll meet you in an old red hay barn, about thirty yards off the pavement; you can see it, barely, from the road. It's abandoned, safe….no one around. It's right on the edge of a big state park, but it's wooded; no one's ever around. Give yourself about a half-hour on the bike, maybe longer for you; be solo, and don't be late, or there will be trouble."

"Solo for you too? Or are you too scared to come alone?"

C mocked him.

"Solo pal, just you and me."

"Like I should believe anything you say."

C said, deadpan.

"I could give a shit what you think, or believe, just be there, *nolens-volens,* or that cunt gets a one-way south. No weapons, nothing, just you and me; we'll see how tough you are. But you had better be there; you'll be….I got faith."

Button sneared smug.

"No weapons, just you and me? I already humiliated you in the Cemetery and at the boat ramp; no way you're coming just you."

"Last I remember, you were out cold in the Cemetery, asshole, or did you forget? And you got lucky at the ramp; you only get lucky once. No weapons, or she's done; I see a weapon, and she's done, you understand me? Dog-food done."

C forced a laugh in disbelief; no way was this guy coming unarmed, *no way.*

1818

"I'll be there, unarmed, let her go."

C tilted his head toward the van on the hill.

Now Button laughed.

"I'll be there, unarmed, let her go."

C said a second time, rote, without a hint of emotion, and Cord stuck out his hand, once again, trying to impart some honor, some honesty to a man who didn't understand the term. Billy looked at Cord's extended hand oddly, like some sort of freak-show.

He didn't shake.

Then Cord made a fateful decision; one he would come to regret. He defied the *something* in his head.

"If you *don't* let her go now, right now, then I don't believe you *ever* will, regardless of what happens tomorrow morning; she's as good as dead anyway, then there's no reason to show up at all, no reason not to kill you right *now*, which I will, which you *cannot* stop, and you *know* it. Do you understand? I think you do. Let her go; if you're so good at what you do, you can pick her up anytime you want, said so yourself; no one's safe from you, right? So let her go now, and I'll be there; if not, I snap your neck, right here, right now, and you're done. You got ten seconds. Understand? I'm gonna start counting. Ten...."

Button just stared at him, unsure what to do; this wrinkle was not in the playbook. He took out his phone, flipped it open, but didn't hit the button for the Creme King. He just stared at C, with his finger resting on the digit....processing, as C counted down; he got to six.

Suddenly, from nowhere, the scenario hit Cord; he was amazed he hadn't thought it before. If Carol was in the van, then where was….?

"Where's Earl?"

C said, with new-found alarm. Button just smiled.

"I'm sure he's *hanging* around, somewhere."

Billy Bone's smile was pure evil.

And C's first thought was Earl was dead, lynched, hanging from a tree, and he didn't see anything else. There was no other outcome; he couldn't shake the vision, Earl dangling dead, swinging slow, as the rope chafed on the limb.

The count stopped at six.

CHAPTER 216 – THIS CAN'T HAPPEN, NOT HERE, NOT NOW

"If anything happened to Earl, *anything*."

Cord clenched his fists as the blood immediately flushed his face. He felt his vision start to narrow, the beginning of a blackout. He fought it, gritting his teeth; once they started, it was hard to stop it....*real* hard. If he blacked out now, he knew he would attack, he always did in those situations, and Button would quickly be dead, and then Carol would be dead. Earl was probably already dead, of that he was certain.

He stuttered the words, fighting the darkness as it enveloped him. The edge of his vision had already blurred out....gone, and it started to tunnel on Button's forehead, a quickened dimming of the lights.

He had about a half-minute, maybe less, till he was unconscious. As his mind raced, he swore he heard the puppet laugh.

"I'm fucking *done!* I need to see Earl, and I need Carol back....*now,* then we'll meet and be done with it, or, I break your neck, *right now*, and I don't give a shit what you do to her, don't care, she's dead anyway in my book; they're probably raping her as we speak. This is ending *right now;* you got three seconds to make a fucking decision, or you're mine. One....*[Cord pointed at Billy, right at the spot on his forehead where his vision was tunneling, fast; there was no way he was stopping it now, and Carol, he knew, was all but dead]."*

C took a menacing step forward and Button was caught off guard. This was not part of the game, or the plan.

Billy Bones had to think fast, because this can't happen, not here, not now.

CHAPTER 217 – WAKING FROM THE DEAD TO A NAIL RIPPING APART HIS FACE

"Why's *he* here? Where's Lilly? Where's Carol?!"

Cord heard the words, but they sounded muffled, spoken far behind him, football fields away, at the far end of a long tunnel, an abyss. But he knew the voice.

There was no answer from either C or Billy, and he knew it was trouble. He immediately started to hyperventilate, his enormous chest heaving, like he couldn't suck in enough oxygen. He became agitated and his eyes grew wide, and wild. A runaway freight was about to barrel down the tracks; he said it again, this time in a hysterical, guttural scream.

"Where's Lilly?! Where's Carol?!"

It was unlikely there would be a third request.

And the last time Billy Bones saw those eyes, he remembered being thrown headfirst through a wall, waking from the dead to a nail ripping apart his face.

CHAPTER 218 – SIMPLE. KILL HIM

The black tunnel simply disappeared, vanished into thin air.

Just like that, like it *never* had before, *never* in his entire life, in countless situations *just* like this. It was gone instantaneous. And C's head was crystal, and he was calm. Like he needed to be, right here, right now. To prevent a disaster.

And Carol smiled.

"Lilly's fine, Earl; I sent her home with Marty and Ji-Sue; she was just tired. And I just saw Carol, she's around here somewhere….she was fine too. I'm sure we'll find her in a couple minutes. Make that call, *now*, and I'll see you in the morning."

C said nonchalant to Billy, who's eyes darted back and forth, between Cord and Earl. He wasn't sure what to do, a Marine unprepared.

Cord tried to make small talk with Earl, who was resisting, and coaxed him to turn, away from the ridge, lest he spy the van, and ask questions. Billy hit the button and a muffled few sentences later, the van quietly drove away; Carol was left sitting on the ground in the far field, still bound and gagged….and clothed.

"Earl, go on over to the ticket booth; Mae's waiting for me. Let me go try and find Carol, okay? I'll find her and meet you over there; you go wait with Mae, okay?"

"You aren't answering me; *you aren't answering!* **Why is he here?** What were you talking to him for? *What are you doing tomorrow morning?!*"

"Earl, please just go, and let me go find Carol, okay? Trust me, I'll find her for you; she's fine."

And C laid his hand gently on Earl's chest, which was still heaving heavy, and he rubbed it back and forth, without saying a word. And as he did, the heaving slowed, and Earl's eyes returned to normal.

"I *don't like* him; I ***don't like*** him! I don't...."

Finally, Earl dropped his head, exhausted, and acquiesced. He quietly turned and made his way to the booth, and C sighed in relief.

C turned to deal with Button; in the mere moments that passed, he had decided to snap his neck, kill him right here and now, over and done, and deal with the consequences. This *had* to end and end *now*. As he slowly spun, he assumed a position to best spring, attack quick, without warning. Button wouldn't expect it....and Button would quickly, and quietly, be done.

Cord tensed rigid as he finished his spin, but there was *no* Billy Bones to kill....he was gone, simply vanished, nowhere to be found.

Cord exhaled long, the adrenaline slowly sapped. He looked up and could faintly see Carol laying in the grass, just inside the perimeter glow of a remote power-pole lamp in the fallow farm field, struggling on the ground. Cord sprinted and soon was by her side, out of breath, full of relief.

He unbound her, hugged her tight and held her, gently rocking as he whispered in her ear, and she answered, back and forth they went in hushed tones. She had a short, shallow gouge on her left cheek, her nose was a bit bloody, and she was generally disheveled, but other than that, nothing had happened, nothing really, except the fright of the experience and a handful of animal gropes and insults. Cord never told her what Button said, nor would he....ever.

1824

He studied her long and hard, and given the horror, she seemed mostly okay; she had composed herself, she never cried....and she seemed okay. She was strong, stronger than C had expected, and that was good, and it was necessary.

Cord told her about what happened to Lillian and how they both would be staying at the police station with Marty tonight. Ji-Sue and Mae would both go home, until after the meeting in the morning, which *no one* was to know of but her. He would take Earl's phone, and if he didn't call Carol by 6:30 am, an hour after the meet, she was to tell Marty, and send him out to the barn, with plenty of support, because by that time, with no call, it wouldn't be good. C told her he had to deal with this, and to resolve this, alone; it was the only way.

They agreed it was safer to never discuss what happened to her tonight with anyone, no one, *especially* Earl.

She composed herself the best she could, they fashioned a story for her bruises, and the two made their way to the ticket booth in silence. C lightly held her hand for a bit, till she was ready to let go, which she did, before they even made it back to the *Scrambler*. And he knew then, she was going to make it through this.

He could see her jaw set hard, and the last words of the discussion they would never have again were hers. And, as they passed the *Scrambler,* her last words were simple.

Kill him.

CHAPTER 219 – LIGHTLY TOUCHING THIGHS, HER NAME SLIPPED IN A WHISPER

August 6th, early Sunday morning, day one-hundred-nine.

Still no one visited, but maybe, this time, no one would. Maybe this trip would finally be different; maybe this one would finally be his last.

It was a mix of sounds that filled his ears: the metallic crank of the pedals, the chain-links slipping in and out of the sprocket, the kick of gravel from the tires and his constant, steady breathing. A hoot-owl called out, a solo three-hoot, about a half-mile back; that was about it.

The rest of the trip was eerie quiet.

The night air was heavy, full of moisture, and his shirt was damp with sweat; it was going to be another hot summer day, he could already feel it. The thought didn't cross his mind that he may never see it.

The moon looked full; it wasn't quite, three days shy, but to C, that's the way it looked. The soft light was enough to cast an ethereal glow, illuminating in grays the uneven edge of the broken pavement on the simple country lane, the tips of jagged rock outcrops here and there, buried icebergs in the soil shoulder, crooked signs-posts, stuck haphazard along the way, and, in the background, the outline of a never-ending row of close-packed sentry trees, lining each side of the desolate road ahead – the front line of a dense, deep and very dark forest, crowded right behind. And God knows what hid in there, watching him slowly pedal by, and disappear into the ink.

He was an intruder to this place.

There were no driveways, no houses on this stretch of narrow, broken pavement, just endless, nameless woods, intermixed with scattered, lonely, farm fields. But it was mostly woods. And although, in the grays and blacks that stretched before him, nothing looked familiar, he had a strange feeling he'd been this way before, some kind of re-do.

The road was steep, a rolling series of hills, each steeper than the next, like he was climbing some never-ending mountain, the ribbon of pavement always curving just out of sight to the left, or to the right, but always *up*. C figured Button picked this route to tire him; it was something that jerk-off would certainly do, and he was succeeding….C's thighs were screaming. Along the way, he heard water running, unseen, rivulets draining the steep slopes along the road, running through culverts under foot, heading downhill, to the Pequest, and onto the Delaware, far, far below, and many miles away.

He wore his typical running outfit; striped black and gray Spandex biker shorts – to just above his knee, his favorite navy tee-shirt, ripped, with a hole in the chest pocket, held together for years with a safety pin, and his familiar worn-out sneakers, his two companions for more than a decade. Those shoes had seen a lot, and they deserved to see this, whatever *this* turned out to be. He was dressed as if he was out for a regular jog; he half-laughed at the prospect. But he knew the encounter would be physical, and he figured it was better to be flexible, comfortable; but to die in Spandex? He wasn't too happy about the prospect of that.

He didn't bring a weapon; he thought long and hard about that one. Knife, gun, both, something else? But what? He got no help, no guidance, from the spectators in his head.

So in the end, he decided against the whole prospect, just about an hour earlier, in bed, staring through the darkness at the ceiling.   Lying there, he came to the conclusion he must have wound up in Belvidere, somehow, specifically for *this* night; it all seemed to make perfect sense, or at least he convinced himself it somehow did.   It was the culmination of a series of disparate events that led him down this lonely, country road, alone, in the early morning hours of a summer Sunday: the fourth dart; the last three-plus months wandering around this strange little Town, with all its quirks dings and nicks; meeting Lillian, and Earl, especially Earl; kindred spirits, angels; and, of course, meeting Carol….the dead one, who didn't seem quite so dead.

It must all be about this night, everything seemed to lead to this night; why, he didn't know, but there must be some reason, at least to the ones who controlled the strings.   And bringing a weapon didn't *feel* part of the plan, so he didn't.

The decision was as simple, and illogical, as that.

He figured, finally, there would be no more dreams with Jenny, no more mind-jaunts right before the cold of the gun barrel touched his temple; he was long-convinced that was the ultimate bus ticket out, but it was a ticket that he could never seem to punch.   Maybe he guessed wrong.

He figured if the ride was gonna finally end here, so be it.   He wasn't scared; to the contrary, he was relieved. He had been waiting a long time for this day, too long; it should have happened many times before, when all odds said he was done, should be done, *has* to be done.   But he never was; there was *always* a rabbit pulled from the hat.

Always. He was tired of always.

So if it *was* tonight, he was okay with it, regardless of what plans Button had. His only regret was not saying goodbye to Earl; that bothered him. He looked up at the slew of stars, at the moon, and asked Carol to tell Earl goodbye for him. Why do you always look *up* for requests like that? Why not right or left, or down? He wondered. For just a second, he had the faint hope Carol somehow would finally talk to him, to tell him *yes,* and not to worry, Earl would be fine.

But she wasn't around, not this morning....probably still asleep.

The only thing C knew, that *had* to be a certainty, was that if he was going to die, he had to bring Button along for the ride; right now, that's all he cared about. Cord couldn't die and leave him behind; he couldn't leave him to terrorize Lilly and Earl....never. He couldn't do that to either of them, or to Carol. Regardless of voices in his head, or feelings to the contrary, Button had to end, one way or another, this morning. There was no other option, and Cord would listen to no dissent, regardless of the source.

So far, there was no dissent to note.

And without any more of a plan than that, it somehow seemed plan enough; he just felt it, deep inside. He wouldn't say it was in his heart, he didn't know where that feeling actually sat, but it was in there somewhere. It was the kind of feeling he would get whenever he knew things would worked out, especially when it came to him, and killing people.

And that was enough.

He was surprised he didn't dream in the hour or so he slept; he was sure he would see his mother, hints of her, wafts of a familiar fragrance, snippets of memory, had been infiltrating his dreams more regularly. But for tonight, she too stayed away.

And so did the puppet. For sure he expected a visit last night; what night would have been more appropriate? But no, he too, hid.

So Cord spent that short nap, maybe, likely, his last, all alone.

How appropriate.

He hadn't passed a single car since he got on his bike. He thought that strange, even at the early hour, someone is always about, on their way somewhere. But not on this Sunday morning. He left the house at 2:11 am according to the stove clock; eleven minutes later than he wanted, but he was petting Chicken as she slept beside him, and she was purring loud, and he felt bad leaving so fast, without a last belly-rub.

He would miss Chicken; he hoped she would miss him, but C knew she wouldn't; cats simply move on.

He figured arriving at 2:30 am, now probably closer to 2:45 am, although later than he hoped, was still plenty early to get a lay of the barn, see if any traps had been set, and find a good place to hide, waiting for Button to show, so he could see how many people he brought, what weapons they had, and assess the likelihood of killing him before C was cut down by the rest of his posse.

He pedaled on in the darkness, figuring he was maybe five minutes away, maybe a bit more, since he passed the bent signpost on his right, a clear marker set in Button's handwritten note. He heard the hoot-owl again, maybe it was following him, or maybe it was a second owl.

He figured the last part of the ride would be a good time to take one last journey, and he smiled as he let his mind wander in times past. It would probably be the last good thoughts he ever had, and he wanted to relish them.

This one started at sixteen, his mom by his side, teaching him to shift manual in the old, gold, *Volkswagen 411 Fastback;* he looked over at her, seeing her profile, and smiled in his mind. And he gladly hitched a last ride in that VW, weaving in and out of a childhood full of memories; one last happy jaunt. And this last spin ended like all the ones before it did, in the same place, sitting on the same school bus, looking at her in profile, and smiling, as Kristine sat beside him, lightly touching thighs, her name slipped in a whisper.

CHAPTER 220 – THE MARK OF A RED DOT DANCING

The closest front corner of the barn was barely visible from the road, shrouded in greenery; without the glint of moonlight, he would have surely passed it by.

He walked the bike a good twenty feet off the shoulder, and propped it against a sapling; the scene was silent, except for the sound of his jostling.

He took a deep breath and slowly made his way to the barn, carefully weaving through a web of pickers - barberry and thickets of wild rose. The roses were deadly, clawing his thighs and midsection. There was no direct path, no worn trail; the barn was close, but seemed impenetrable. He slowly picked his way through the maze, ensuring he left no trace, no broken branches, belying his presence.

After some time, he found himself in a small clear aisle, about five feet wide, running along the front of the barn, which was weather-beaten, a dulled red from the bits of remnant paint that somehow hung on. He gazed at the facade and roofline, brushed with silver from the moon. He was facing an oversized pair of barn doors, pulled almost-shut, maybe three inches of space between them, much too narrow to squeeze through. He leaned his face into the crevice.

And immediately yanked back, caught by surprise.

A thick mat of cobweb ensnared his nose and mouth; he quickly brushed it off, spitting and wiping the gluey spinning on his shorts. He carefully approached the opening once again, and wiped his hand vertical in the space, ensuring it was web-free. He leaned in afresh, till his cheek was pressed hard against the rough, crackled paint on the edge of the door, and tried his best to survey the scene, with one wide eye.

It was pitch-black; he saw nothing.

He stood there, silent, face pressed hard against the door, for a good half-minute, waiting for his eye to adjust. During that time, he heard nothing, not a thing. And the space inside the barn was the color of midnight; there didn't seem to be any space between the clapboards, no openings in the roof, no window panes to let in the moonlight....nothing.

Complete darkness, and complete silence. Old barns are always full of cracks, splits, spaces and gaps, but not this one, and he thought it a bit odd.

His eye slowly seemed to adjust, but the whit of light seeping in wasn't enough to make any sense of the inside. But one thing was certain, he was the first one there, and that was good thing; coming extra early worked out well.

Fuck he whispered to himself; why didn't he hide the God-damn bike? What was he thinking?

Now he would have to worm his way back through the pickers, which he did, killing a good twenty minutes out and back, including the time to walk the bike far away, burying it under a cover of last-years-leaves and loose brush.

Thank God he thought to come so early.

He tugged on the barn door gently; it didn't budge. He squeezed his arm partly in the crack and pushed hard with his chest and hand; the door gave him a couple inches, but that was it. And it was a loud give-up, the rusted steel roller-pulley creaking and moaning in protest. That door hadn't moved in years. He got pissed and gave it a series of hearty shoves, and it soon opened enough for him to barely squeeze and shimmy in. Barely.

He found himself just inside the door, standing in the abyss.

The longer he stood, he realized there must have been some sort of moonlight seeping through tiny cracks and holes, too small to see, because his eyes finally began to fill in the faint outline of the barn layout, in shades of gray and darker gray, fading to black around the periphery.

It appeared that mounds of dry hay filled the lower level; the smell of long-stale alfalfa filled the space, and it was comforting; it, that smell, somehow, made him feel grounded, and safe. But it also reminded him of Kansas, which, in the end, was neither.

There seemed to be an upper loft, covering a third of the barn on each end, with the center third open to the rafters far above his head. It was a huge barn, and it seemed to swallow him; he felt small. It looked as if that upper level was also piled with haphazard mounds of hay.

He could barely make out some large object before him, tucked in the far right corner of the barn, about fifty feet away; it must be some sort of farm equipment, but he couldn't make out what, the edges blurred into, and swallowed by, the darkness.

He didn't see much else, but he couldn't see much detail anyway. There didn't seem to be any windows or hay-doors overhead, but he was sure they must be there, long-since boarded shut. And he squinted to spot a ladder, or pegged columns, or anything, to get him up into the loft areas, since that certainly seemed the best place to lay in wait, but there was nothing - no obvious way to get up there.

And that became the near-task at hand.

He slowly crouched and felt his way into the center of the barn, waving his hands like a blind man, so he could better survey both loft areas. He quickly decided the one above the double doors was the better bet, to be able to look down upon Button when he came through the entrance - the only way in, it seemed. He had to shut the doors again; he had to remember to shut the doors to three inches, like they were.

He figured, from the loft, he could drop down on him, surprise him, and break his neck clean with a quick chin-snap; if it worked out, the deed would be done in seconds – he had done it before, with men much bigger and stronger than Button. No need to talk, no need to draw the process out; a quick drop and snap - the element of surprise would seal the deal. He would hide the body in the straw, come back the next night to bury him outside, behind the barn, and that would be the end of that.

Only he knew it was never that easy, never that simple; there was *always* the mess that got in the way, the part of the plan never planned for – that was the hump you had to get through to kill someone....the unknown always posed a wrinkle. He had been there before. Too many times.

But, in the past, in the end, it always worked out for him – he always came out on top. He figured he'd find out soon enough how this morning's plan would pan. But so far, so good.

How the fuck do I get up there? He whispered to himself, spinning slowly in place, looking for some way to hoist himself. He looked back at the oversized, dark object in the corner, and as it became a bit clearer in the darkness, it had seemed to take on the shape of some sort of dozing troll.

Let the wild rumpus start!   It jumped in his head, prompted by the troll, and he thought of Earl, and of *Where The Wild Things Are* and he smiled. Everything was going to be alright; he felt it.

He stared at the troll, figuring there might be some tool, some answer to the loft, hidden in that dark corner, by that contraption. He took a couple steps toward the troll, then froze.

Something in the blackness had just moved.

It was a shape-shift, a brief shadow; it was small, or at least it seemed to be small. Or maybe it was the small movement of something much larger.

Much.

He couldn't be sure, of anything. The hair on his neck rose, and tinges of adrenaline shot his spine.

He stood statue, squinting, trying to figure out if his mind was playing tricks, or if something was hiding, protected by the troll. If there was, it was surely watching him. He slowed his breathing and, instinctively, began to crouch; waiting for something to happen, something to spring from the ink.

But nothing happened, not even the slightest movement of hay, not a whisper. The barn air was eerie-still; it was like a standoff, him and some unknown in the corner, imaginary or otherwise.

It had to be an animal, a barn cat, something, probably a barn cat; likely a barn cat.

And, as he crouched, surrounded by silence, deciding whether to move forward, or to retreat, détente, the hair on both arms suddenly uncurled and stood upright, for no apparent reason.

And for a split second, without warning, his mind involuntarily turned to thoughts of the puppet. All he could see was that hideous face coming right at him, lightning speed, under the blanket, mouth open, nothing but sharp, yellowed teeth. He looked down and could see the hair on his arm still standing, defiant, and a tingle ran steady up his spine; a portend of something that simply wasn't happening.

Nothing was happening in that barn, nothing; it was just him, his imagination, and some scared cat.

But something *was* happening. And the puppet smiled as the scene unfolded.

Like the silent flip of a switch, it appeared stealth on the back of his right thigh, the starburst he couldn't see, he couldn't feel, the mark of a red dot dancing.

CHAPTER 221 – SMEARED IN RED; THE SCREEN WENT BLACK

He remembered hearing the air flux from the bolt-cutter leaving the crossbow, not that it mattered.

The arrow pierced the back of his right thigh at two-hundred-fifty miles per hour, just missing the bone; the black tip deformed the skin on the front of his leg in a grotesque bulb, but didn't exit, hiding just below the surface. After a little less than a ten second delay, the blood began to leak from beneath his shorts and run down the back of his thigh, a faucet cracked open.

Cord didn't scream, but rather belted a loud hiss through grit teeth and grabbed his leg with both hands, which burned a thousand degrees. Before he could react, a second bolt-cutter sliced through his left thigh, barely grazing the bone. This tip stuck through the front of his leg, a good half-inch, and a steady stream of red quickly poured from both ends, pooling in his sneakers.

C fell to his knees, his legs on fire; he was in trouble.

The spider quickly scaled the rope off the barn door balcony and headed for the quarry. There was no high-jinx, nor riddles nor idle chatter, nothing at all – this was a serious ops and Button was in full game-mode, sporting a backpack of tools and image-intensifying night-vision goggles, making it daylight in the barn.

"Face on the ground, hands behind your head."

Button mouthed matter-of-fact, about twenty feet behind C; far enough away, but close enough to count. Cord ignored the order, and slowly sat up on his knees, pain shot to all parts of his body, and he was trembling uncontrollably, trying to stand up.

Button didn't ask a second time.

The third bolt-cutter left the crossbow and skewered Cord through the back just below his right shoulder, the tip exiting his upper chest, a good three-inch pass-though.

Blood from the third assault quickly ran down his chest and back, and the pain crescendo spiked in his brain like nothing he had ever felt before; he remembered his chin falling to his chest, and seeing, peripheral, the arrow tip jutting from his chest, smeared in red; the screen went black.

CHAPTER 222 – WHAT A COMPLETE FUCKING WASTE OF TIME

His eyes partly opened, but it was still dark, too dark to really see. And his head was spinning, like a bad drunk. He didn't feel pain, just a general numbness, roughly from his ears down.

He had no idea where he was or what had happened.

He went to turn his head, but couldn't; he was cinched tight across his Adams apple to a wooden column – a thick leather strap wrapped his neck, making it difficult to breath, other than short, controlled breaths. He was on his knees, backed against the wooden barn column, his ankles were bound with tight nylon straps, cutting into his skin; the same with his wrists, behind his back. The three arrows still pierced him, but the entry and exit holes were treated around the bolt-cutter shafts with thick gauze bandaging, to stop the hemorrhaging.

It slowly came back to him, what had happened, and he wondered just how long he had been out….minutes….or hours.

In the darkness, to his right, he heard the crack and split of fresh flesh, and realized it must be an apple, a crisp one, when one first bites into it. And then he simply heard slow, methodical chewing. More bites, and more chewing, and nothing else; it seemed to go on forever.

He felt nauseous.

Finally, the empty apple core landed in front of him, in the hay, close enough to make out.

Button didn't say a word the whole time. He got up and walked into the distance, removed the improvised chocks, and easily pushed open the barn doors, a good four foot plus gap, to let the moonlight in, which illuminated the barn fairly well. The troll was behind him, so C couldn't see what it really was; he figured it must be a tractor, but for some odd reason, he wanted to know, had to know, as if it somehow mattered.

Button yanked the night-vision goggles.

"You surprised me. I knew you'd come early; I was thinking an hour, two at most, never three….never. Me, I came here right from the Fair; I've been here since then. That's the difference between a civilian, who *thinks* he's smart, and a Marine, an elite *SOI MOS 0311;* you know what that is? Huh? Stupid? Its *School of Infantry Military Occupational Specialty Number 0311,* a *Rifleman;* that's me, and I'm fucking golden. Camp Pendleton baby, California. *SOI,* the youngest mortality rates of any School in the military, any! Most die before twenty-five, some die in *SOI!* That's where you would have died, 'cause you're stupid. These jerk-offs, and these are some fit mother-fuckers, they *still* go crazy, commit suicide, can't hack the program. But me? I fucking *loved it;* combat training, a true grunt….a real ground-pounder."

Button spat into the hay, took in a long deep breath, and squatted down in front of Cord.

"Scared?"

Cord didn't say anything.

"I don't think you are, not yet; but you will be, trust me *[Button said, shaking his pointer lazily at Cord].* You'll be scared you're still alive, and wishing you were dead, begging me to kill you. That's where this is going, where it's gonna end up….you know that, right? But we're hours away, trust me; we got plenty of time to chat. The best kills are the ones I can stretch….enjoy. How's the pain? You look pretty good for having three bolts in ya *[Button laughed]!* You know, lucky you make a lot of noise; I was concentrating on shooting that fucking cat running around the barn. It did better than you; I couldn't get a clear shot at that little fucker, wasted two bolts fucking around. But it was quick, and smart, smarter than you. But I'll kill it before we leave, cut its head off; it can't stay lucky forever, and we aren't going anywhere for awhile. I can't believe you came without *anything*; did you think we were gonna have a fist-fight? Arm-wrestle? What? You *that* stupid, or just have some sort of death-wish? Well, you'll get your wish, trust me."

Button flipped open his rucksack and took out a turkey-baster and a mason jar full of a brown, viscous liquid. He sucked up a wad.

"Open up."

He said; but C didn't.

"Listen, ever had *Mace* shot in your face? It sucks, trust me. Open up and I'll give you the shrooms nicely, no *Mace*; don't, and you get shot with *Mace*, and when you open up, which you will, you'll still get the shrooms down the hatch. Either way, *nolens-volens*. So open up, and we'll do this civilized, but we're doing it, and the brew is going in….either way."

C wouldn't.

Button sighed, and like lightning, hidden in his left hand, he *tasered* Cord on the side of the neck, drive-stun mode, burning the flesh.

C opened his mouth to scream, and in went the baster, shoved to the back of his throat, and emptied down the pipe. Cord tried to force a vomit, but couldn't; Button shoved his knee hard under his chin and forced his mouth shut. C bit off the edge of his tongue and swallowed it; his mouth quickly filled with blood; tongues bleed like a bitch.

"Chow it, that's it, take it easy, take it easy, medicines in; that should be enough for awhile. I'm curious to see, you know, how you react, part of the grand experiment. I'm hoping it'll help you endure the pain a bit, cause it's gonna get messy, starting real soon. I'm hoping to keep you alive for a couple hours anyway; that's the plan."

Button knocked a cigarette out and carefully lit it.

"Dangerous in here, whole place could go up in flames if I'm not careful. That'd be a shame; wonder if you'd make it out? Doubt it; you're not too mobile."

Button smiled at his own joke, then took a long, deep drag. He walked over to the knapsack and pulled out a little black book, the spine stiff from newness.

"Did me a favor, actually, tossing my old one in the river; got me all excited about starting new. Gonna start with cutting that fucking cat's head off, since that's how my old one started, when I was a little kid, you know, kinda nostalgia-like. And No. 2, that will be *you*, and there will be lots more after that, *lots*, starting with your retard-nigger boyfriend. I'm gonna lynch him from a big old tree; *you* gave me that idea - thanks. I'll watch him shit himself, the shit-skin that he is, while he swings and slowly chokes off. Then I'll skin him, cut him into fillets and feed him to our cage-dogs at the meat plant. Mean mothers, will chew your arm clean off. Next is that bitch on the Park; I'm still gonna do her dog-food style, but I'm gonna be the one to throw her in the hopper, myself, after the chain of filthy coons have their way on the ride down, just as I described. That one is simply too good to pass up. All thanks to you; you were what put the plan in motion; fast-tracked it anyway, so hey, thanks, for that. Way to protect your friends, keep them safe. Remind me never to put my chips in with you *[Button smirked]*. Oh, and the best part is Lilly; thanks for *saving* her. But I'm not going to kill her, no way....too valuable as a high-priced slut. Hundreds, thousands, of fucking slobs are gonna saddle up between her pretty legs and pound the shit out of that pussy and ass, and unload in her mouth, day and night, seven days a week, *non-stop*, paying and playing with what you *never* got to, and never will, see, touch or taste. And all that fuck-money will be coming to *me*, while she simply stays the whore she will become, and that her mother *always was*. Mother and daughter, together forever as two high-priced sluts; good for nothing else. Then, when I'm done whoring Lilly out, when she's shredded, stretched and broken, I've got *special* plans for her. She'll get what she deserves, thanks to her mother. All thanks, in part, to your inspiration. You helped bring it all together....the glue."

Button nodded in appreciation toward Cord, and took another long drag, eyes closed, savoring the nicotine.

And that's about when the mushrooms kicked in, and the barn began to morph, a television screen for a channel that doesn't quite come in, twisted like tie-dye taffy; fantastic bright colors streaking and mutating into amorphous shapes, with the drone of Button's muffled voice in the background, a record played a speed-too-slow. Every once and again, the picture and words would straighten, and the barn made some sense, but it was only for a second, till it tilted off-kilter again.

Cord couldn't keep his mouth closed; he lost control of his lips and jaw, and a drizzle-mix of drool and tongue-blood leaked from the lower right corner. He noticed it, but could do nothing about it; he had no ability to close his mouth....he somehow forgot how. Button continued to talk, but Cord couldn't really hear what he said, or it didn't make sense, or something. He had no pain and no idea of time, just numbness; that's all there was, for now.

1844

Amidst the fog, he seemed to focus on one constant thought, latched onto as it ran circular in his head, like water waiting to run down the drain. His whole life, all that happened, all the mess and confusion, violence and nonsense, the lows and lowers, the queue of forgotten faces of people that didn't matter, coming and going....all that, that endless line of pain and loneliness....it ended up here, like this? *Really?* This was where that God-awful road, over all those years, really led?   This was it? Jesus, he should have jumped off this train long, long ago.

And a general sense of fatigue seeped in, and a single thought flashed, like a beacon, over and over, forty-three years summarized in a sentence fragment:

what a complete fucking waste of time.

CHAPTER 223 – HE HAD CROSSED TO THE RIGHT SIDE OF THE LINE

Button's eyes lit up, dancing; he was getting excited, like he always did, right about this time. And this one was going to be extra special.

He was eager to explain, histrionic gestures belying his passion for the subject at hand, as he carefully squatted down and walked his prey through the process, face to face.

"You know, when you kill something, there's this imaginary line that you come right up to; there's no better way to describe it. It's very cool, actually; one side of it, whatever it is your fucking with, torturing, killing, whatever, it can live, or probably live, or maybe live, or should live, if you just stopped whatever you're doing, just on the *left* side of that line. You can hug the line, but you can't step over it *[Button held his hand vertical, in a slicing motion, for emphasis]*. But now, just a hair over the other side, the *right* side, of that line, well, that's kinda the line of no return; I call it the *you're-pretty-much-fucked* line. If you're on *that* side, well, things aren't so good, not good at all; in fact, you're gonna die, for sure, there's no stepping back, and now it's just a matter of when it happens, and how bad the slide is gonna be. And being the gatekeeper, you know, of the line, actually being the one *drawing* the line, deciding where it is, and when you get there, now that's a fucking rush, dude. And that's me, I'm the line-keeper, and you and me *[Button swung his pointer back and forth between the two of them]*, we're getting real, real close to that line, and that long, ugly, beautiful slide down, to the right. And I'm looking forward to seeing you on the other side."

Cord stared blankly past Billy Bones; he hadn't understood a single word. Button's sentences, the letters and sounds, made no sense whatsoever; they all ran together in a sticky hodgepodge of nonsense, molasses dripping off the edge of the table. A mushroom-induced hallucinogenic mess.

Besides, Cord was preoccupied with the dinosaur hiding behind the picker bushes.

The Tyrannosaurus was just barely peeking over the top of the roses, basked in moonlight; C could see his yellow eyes, and the top of his brown and green head, striped, and his little claws, but that's about it. He must be a baby; full grown he would be much larger, wouldn't it be? His eyes were oversized saucers, and it looked to be trembling, and Cord thought that odd, since a T-Rex shouldn't be afraid of anything. But maybe this one was, since he was so small, for a dinosaur.

C shifted his eyes from the dinosaur to the dimness in the barn, and the picture went to rainbow taffy – bright streaking colors shooting across his eyes; he looked back at the T-Rex, and it was crystal clear. Back and forth, back and forth C shifted his eyes, blurry then clear, then blurry again. And he tried to figure how that might be, and had no answer; so he simply stared at the dinosaur, since it was more pleasant, and it seemed nice enough, hiding in the pickers. But the dinosaur didn't pay much attention to Cord; he seemed to be looking, intently, at something else, leaning forward, like he was listening. Maybe he was going to eat the cat, but he somehow didn't seem to be a cat-eater, he didn't have that look, whatever that look might be. Ay watched the T-Rex intently, excited at the prospect of what would happen next.

Man, he had big teeth.

Button had gone back to the rucksack, digging for a headlamp and a canvas roll, tied with a soft, cotton string. He found them both, and laid the spotlight and canvas neatly on the hay covered floor, in front of C, untying the twine.

"You know, I found that magic mushroom shit on the web; can you believe it? You can find anything there….anything. This shit was some trail mix: *Magic Mint* and *Sally D;* figured mushrooms were good for you, since you're a vegetarian faggot. Supposed to make you hallucinate, you know, visions, like an Indian sweat. You getting those yet, you fucking queer? Huh *[Button finger-flicked C on the side of the head]*? You're sure drooling like you are *[Button snorted a laugh]*. Then, if you *really* overload, I read you get kinda schizoid, you know, like dementia – fucks your brain all up, light tattoos, fireworks, like an acid trip dude, or LSD, not that I ever use that shit, but seen plenty of it, for sure; spooks go through it like fucking water. Stupid niggers, they eat anything if it's free. I gave them some of your shrooms, not nearly as much as your mouthful, and they said it was some wacky powerful shit. So I figure, pretty soon you'll be talking to snakes and dragons, with faces sticking out of the woodwork, wagging their tongues at ya, dude; fucking scary shit. Anyway, I'm not sure I want you there, not yet anyway. I want to keep you alive, but you need to feel the pain. It's a delicate balance my friend; my job is not easy. This shit is supposed to last for four, maybe five hours, way past how long you'll still be on this planet, for sure."

Cord never heard a word Billy said, not one; it was all just an incoherent babble. Besides, he was still concentrating on that sneaky dinosaur, who seemed to be getting bigger, thicker, and meaner by the second. It didn't seem to be trembling any more, just a deep, steady breathing, heavy. It seemed as if it was breathing directly into Cord's ear; he could feel the warm, moist breath on the side of his head, and his neck.

1848

Then the Rex turned its head ever-so slightly, stared directly at C for the first time, eye to eye, and nodded it's head, almost an imperceptible signal, as if it was saying *Yeah, I see you, I know you're there,* but not in a bad way, not in an *I'm-gonna-eat-you* way at all. But then again, you can never tell with dinosaurs, they're pretty tricky.

"You know, I might as well tell ya what's gonna happen here, since it's just about time, and were at that little line. Like the cat, I'm cutting you're fucking head off, but just the top part for you, like the top of a soup bowl *[Button pointed to his own head, and drew a soup-bowl line around the perimeter].* And if I'm good, and *real* careful, I can pop that sucker off and you'll live through it, *all of it* – the shrooms should help you through. That's the plan, anyway. And if it works, that'll be fucking *awesome*! Then I'm gonna take a close-up of that fucked-up pussy brain of yours, first hand, you know, stick my fingers between the wrinkles and shit on it, spit on it, piss on it, maybe even take a forkful from my mess kit *[Button laughed]*, see what faggot brain tastes like, all while you're sitting there tripping, looking up at me, drooling, and I'm eating your fucking brains, all zombie-like. How fucked-up is that, dude? You watching me eatin' your fucking egghead, like a zombie? It took me awhile to think up this shit, trust me! And that's gonna have to hurt, don't ya think, me chomping your brains, while you're watching, all stupid-like? Of course, I wouldn't swallow; just chew and spit it back in your head; don't want to risk getting the faggot gene from you. You know, it's amazing how fucking easy this was to do; I was actually worried a bit, you know, that it wouldn't come off as planned. But you're just like the rest, stupid and easy. Frankly, I'm disappointed, expected more a struggle, but you didn't do shit, nothing, just rolled over....just rolled *[Button frowned and shook his head in disgust – another easy kill]*."

Button carefully, slowly, deliberately undressed – the ritual. First his black boots and socks, then the fatigues, then the tee-shirt and boxers, carefully folding the clothes as he went, the only time he was ever neat about such things. Naked, he moved the clothing away from Cord, toward the open barn door, out of any blood or body fluid spray zone; he hated the liquid on his clothes, and he liked to feel the spittle on his bare skin as he killed whatever it was he was killing. He liked to be naked when he killed....primal.

As Cord watched him undress, all he could think was that Button never did see that dinosaur hiding in the pickers, and that was a big mistake. By now, that wacky dinosaur had grown to *huge*. And it didn't look happy.

Billy turned slightly into the moonlight, arms extended over his head, like a Grecian warrior, and his chiseled torso revealed that beautiful, intricate tattoo, spread across his chest and extending onto his deltoids and upper arms, doves and songbirds intertwined in flower garlands, circled by butterflies. A large carp framed the edge, all set in a mural of red and blue hues....mainly blue. But in the barn, it took on various shades of gray. He looked down and admired himself, his body. Then he eyed the name *Lillian,* weaved across his shoulder, and the name *Carol,* intertwined across his chest, across his heart. His two little whores.

Carol? Well, that was unfortunately a whore he loved. But Lillian? He wanted to claw, dig and gouge her name from his skin, since he never loved the stupid, needy bitch; he just fucked and abused her to spite and betray Carol. And to add insult, he now knew, deep down, what Lillian, the slut, really wanted, and it was tied up in the barn, ready to die, in front of him.

"Like it *[Button said to C, as he eyed his rambling tattoo]*? Some people think it's faggie, so I figured I'd ask a real fag what he thinks? So, like it? Huh? Shows my sensitive side."

Button laughed at his stale, go-to joke, dropped his arms, and squatted naked in the moonlight, as he carefully unfolded the canvas roll. An assortment of ghastly stainless steel surgical tools revealed themselves, along with a portable bone saw, to cut off the top of Cord's head.

"You know, I was gonna buy one of those battery powered saws, like they use in autopsies on TV, you know, but I figured that might make too much noise. Besides, I like working with my hands, you know, a craftsman, so I brought my old bone blade I've used for years, sharpened it up real good, of course, figured I could take my time and feel it better, cutting through the skin and skull and shit, you know, cause that's important, to me, to feel it, while you scream. I'm gonna have to put a ball gag in you though, unfortunately, 'cause you screaming, yeah, that might be a problem. But I might let you scream just a bit first, just for fun; you know, for the first long slice."

Button grabbed the blade, stood up and held it aloft like a trophy; the moonlight caught the edge of the stainless blade and gave it a good glint.

"I think I'll start in the front, slice you open right across your forehead; what'ya think? Good enough place to start, right? Welcome to the right side of the line."

Button said, looking admiringly at the blade, held high at the end of his outstretched arm.

C's eyes were glazed.

Button then knelt quietly beside Cord and began to whisper, befitting the secret about to be shared.

"Oh, one last thing, figured I'd let you in on it while you can still use that noggin of yours, before I cut it open like a melon and make a big sticky mess. After I whore Lilly out, and she can thank her cunt-mother for that one, after she's drilled daily until she's a spent, bloody piece of meat, her disgusting, stretched snatch full of sores from filthy STD-cocks, I'm not gonna kill her, because I've got something *much worse* in mind for her. I'm just gonna let her in on a little secret. I'm gonna tell her *all about* her lying, piece of shit mother. I'll tell her about Earl, where that retard is really from, some retard family no one knows, with a retard mamma and pappy. And I'll tell her about me fucking her mommy for *years* in shitty hotel rooms, when I came home from leave, in secret. And how mommy swallowed every drop, and how she liked it in the ass the best, just like Lilly does. Like mother, like daughter. And how mommy liked to call the dirty act *Pump Time*, and it was *always Pump Time* with mommy and me. Oh, and that little part about why she killed herself, yeah, can't forget that little nugget. Ready? Drum roll....it was because she was knocked up, a baby on the way, *my baby*, Bibby's little brother, or sister – that's right, the first of *many* to come. And then Bibby could truly call me *Daddy*. Yeah, figure that will be a far worse punishment than anything I could *ever* think of doing to that bitch, and all I have to do is tell the truth! How beautiful is that! She'll end up in the loony bin for sure, which is where she belongs anyway, fucking wacko bitch. I'll drop her off and she'll rot in a rocking chair, drooling like you are, a stew of disease swimming in her mouth, ass and filthy cunt and wacked-out in the head to boot, all courtesy of mommy. And me and the *Drin*, we're gonna be fucking amazing, rich as shit."

Button rose from his whisper-crouch and again held the bone saw high overhead, fascinated, like a little kid, at how the moonlight caught the flat edge of the blade, tilting it back and forth.

Cord still hadn't heard a word Billy Bones spilled; the syllables were simply scrambled nonsense. He should have been thinking about Kristine, now was the time; but for some reason, he didn't. Maybe he didn't want her here, not like this. His thoughts drifted from the dinosaur, which kept growing ever-larger, to somewhere else, and his thoughts, for a moment, became lucid.

'Every man should keep a special place to retreat; a secret, somewhere to go and find himself, to heal, to be better.
For me, it's Bocas Del Toro, at least it is sometimes.'

He remembered telling Earl that, when he promised to bring him to Panama, Number Two on Earl's *List of Ten*. That's what came to him, and that's where C went, and he was disappointed he was going there, one last time, alone; he had hoped his friend would join him, his best friend, his only friend. But who really needs lots of friends when you have a *best* one; one is more than enough, especially a kindred one.

And just like that, C found himself swinging in that old hammock, one leg hanging over the edge, the silence broken by the swish of his ass scraping the wood decking, the water gently lapping against the wood pilings and the loose ends of the roof fronds rustling in the breeze. He was too sleepy to even open his eyes, the sun kissing his cheek.

But he managed to open one lid, barely, and he saw his best friend, Earl, barefoot and smiling that big toothy grin of his, walking toward him, with Jonesy resting quietly on his huge shoulder, the little dinosaur lizard, his friend and companion for years, and he was alive again, and happy to be back home.

Earl and Cord and Jonesy, in Panama....together, and happy.

And through the numbness, Cord managed to move his lips, barely, into the shape of a small smile. Button saw it, smiled himself, and knew the time had come to cross the line.

"Okay, time to put your big-boy pants on; time for the beginning of the end."

And Button, anxious for the ultimate kill, forgetting to strap on the head-lamp, dropped the blade to his side and took the first of the five short steps toward Cord, to cut off his head.

A blood-curdling scream filled the barn; he had crossed to the right side of the line.

1854

CHAPTER 224 –   THE CARNIVAL RIDE WAS FINALLY OVER....FOREVER

It was a muffled crack, like breaking a branch across your knee, but under a thick pillow, *that* kind of muffle. Through the bellowed roars, he was sure he was the only one who heard the snap, since it was inside his body, just below his ears.

And as quick as that, his backbone broke clean through, and he was paralyzed from the neck down. He knew it, since he couldn't feel a thing.

He laid quiet in the hay, face down, naked, straddled by the dinosaur; the bone saw had somehow spun around in the process and skewered his bicep clear through. Odd, it was the first time he had ever been stabbed, turned on by his own bone blade to boot.   And it was only the second real blemish on an otherwise perfect body; the other caused by a nail ripped through his face.

Both by the same dinosaur.

The gash bled badly, the stream of red quickly soaking and spreading through the dry hay on the barn floor. But he couldn't feel a thing; he just watched his arm bleed-out in a strange disconnect.

And just like that, that quick, he knew it was over. He was finished, done for good, just like that, and by a fucking retard to boot. And all he could do was laugh.

"You stupid fucking nigger!"

He kept laughing, now harder, repeating the phrase twice more.

"I'm still gonna kill him, and Carol, *and* your fucking sister! I'm taking them all away from you, forever, **all of them!** And you can't do anything about it; you or your cunt mother. And let me tell you a little story about her, and you, and your sister, you stupid coon! She….”

Earl’s heart was racing. He had stopped screaming that wild banshee bellow that started straight through the thicket of pickers, as he barreled into the barn in a full sprint; Billy Bones barely had the chance to turn his head into the moonlight before Earl crashed upon him, snapping him in two, like a fragile toy.

And now Earl was wailing.

“Stop it! Stop saying that! *Stop saying that!* **Stop saying that!”**

Earl was in a hysterical trance; he grabbed the sides of Button’s head and slowly twisted it counter-clockwise, as simple as turning the stem off an apple, to make the head stop talking.

And the skin, bones, muscles, tendons and veins in Billy's neck twisted, ripped, writhed, cracked and popped in a grotesque cacophony, until Button’s head corkscrewed, and his face was staring straight up at the barn roof, while his body still lay flat on its belly in the hay. A broken doll.

And somewhere along that gruesome twist and distort, the head in Earl's hands simply stopped talking. Billy Bones fell silent, and the carnival ride was finally over….forever.

CHAPTER 225 - HE KNEW, HE REALLY KNEW, IT WAS HER

Billy's eyes were spiderweb bloodshot, with a tinge of yellow; blood pooled and trickled from the corners of both sockets, along with his nose, mouth and ears; he bled from all of them, every one.

His mouth was partly open, showing his perfect white teeth, half-covered in a sticky film of saliva and blood. He was still smiling, the Plasticine grin of an automaton.

And Earl was quietly crying.

"I'm sorry."

He said to no one in particular.

He walked over to Cord, who was motionless, head down, choking himself against the leather cinch; tears were streaming down Earl's face.

"Please don't be dead, please, please, you're my best friend ever, please don't go away, please C....please."

Earl knelt before his friend, unhooked the belt from around Cord's neck and let C's head gently fall gently onto his massive chest. He was unconscious, barely breathing.

At the back of the barn, unseen in the darkness, the gray, feral cat silently hopped onto the farm tractor hood and watched the scene unfold; her new litter of kittens sat quiet, safe and snug in the hay, up against the dry-rot rear tire.

Two kindred spirits, kneeling, face to face, in the darkness, in silence; Earl sobbing quietly, his tears falling on C's cheek, lightly rubbing Cord's back, in a slow, light circle, over and over, since it was the only thing he could think to do to help his friend….it always helped when his mom did it to him. And he began to sing to C, barely above a whisper:

Amazing Grace, how sweet the sound;
That saved a wretch like me;
I once was lost, but now am found;
Was blind, but now I see

T'was Grace that taught my heart to fear;
And Grace, my fears relieved;
How precious did that Grace appear;
The hour I first believed

And as he whispered the hymn, as the tears streamed down his cheeks, he reached down and gently held C's hand, because there's nothing much better than holding the hand of someone you love.

And in his darkness, C felt it.

A tiny hand gently grabbed his from the abyss, and slowly led him out of the darkness; it was a long slow walk, but he knew, right then, he was going to make it. Once he felt the warmth in her fingers, how her hand felt so perfect, so soft, so safe, he knew, he just knew, that it was her….that he finally met her.

"It's you."

Was all C said.

No words passed, but he knew she heard him, because she squeezed his hand, just a tiny squeeze, the kind of squeeze that acknowledges, the kind that's special, the kind that says *yes, it's me.*

And he smiled, because he knew, he really knew, it was her.

1858

CHAPTER 226 – EARL SHOVED IT IN, AND CORD WENT BLACK

"Holy shit, holy shit, holy shit."

Martin whispered to himself, spinning around in the dimness, taking in the chaos, the carnage. He stared at Button, who was staring back, with that same creep-smile, frozen on his face, caked with dried saliva and blood. It was close to 4:30 am, and still dark, but not for long.

He couldn't believe he spent most of his life afraid of him, afraid of....*that*. And, for some reason, he noticed Button's ears, how small they were, and how they stuck out, just a bit. And it was strange that in all the years, he never once noticed that, never once. But now he did. He couldn't stop staring at those strange-looking ears.

He was surprised how fragile Button looked, the body of a limp, broken doll.

Cord was lying in the hay on his side, fetal, still dazed and mushroom-high, but beginning to clear, to better understand his surroundings. He only realized Button was dead, really dead, a few minutes earlier, although he must have known it sooner, but couldn't remember. And he remembered being shot, and seeing a dinosaur, and taffy, and he remembered her saving him, and her warm, tiny hand, slipped inside his.

But that was about it.

Earl, as best he could understand C's slurred direction, had cut the nylon binds on his ankles and wrists using the surgical tools. His tongue gash had coagulated, but it had swollen in his mouth to the point that it kept his mouth partly open, which worsened the drool.

And then there was the matter of the bolt-cutters.

They couldn't be pulled out, nor could they be pushed all-through. Marty fetched more bandages from the first-aid kit in his truck cab but wasn't sure there would be enough if C started bleeding again.

"Break it....off."

C mumbled staccato.

"How? We got nothing to cut them, it's carbon steel; we gotta get you to a hospital. Why are you out here? *What the hell happened?!*"

Marty spit, fast and furious.

C got agitated.

"Earl!   *Earl!*   Break....the   fuck....the   fuck....tip! Off....***break it***!"

Earl went to grab the bolt and snap the tip, but all he did was move the whole shaft inside C's shoulder, and Ay screamed in pain, writhing in the hay. Earl recoiled in fear, hurting his friend. Cord bellowed as he staggered, trying to get up on his knees.

"No....fuck."

He couldn't form the word *hospital,* not yet.

"Marty, how 'bout?"

And Earl pointed to the blade sticking through Button's bicep.

"Could, maybe, might work; but you know, can't touch the body, knife, pictures, um, forensics and...."

And as Marty fumbled, Earl quickly walked over, and without so much as a hesitation, stepped on Button's limp arm and gave the blade a good yank. Out it came, slicing the flesh fresh on its exit.

Earl walked over and knelt quietly beside his best friend, placing the knife gently beside him in the hay; Marty shook his head once, and, without speaking, slipped off his tee-shirt, roughly rolling it into a tight ball. He saddled behind Cord and wrapped his arms tight around his midsection, like a tight brace, and with his left hand, grabbed the shoulder bolt.

"Earl, now try and cut it nice and smooth….easy strokes, so you don't move it so much."

*"Fuckin….**do it!**"*

Cord was spitting the words through saliva from still-numb lips. He could feel his heart beat hard at the end of each fingertip, a constant throb, and the pressure on the back of his eyeballs was intense, like they were about to pop.

Marty shoved the shirt-ball into C's mouth, and the blade bit, and the shaft moved….and Cord screamed into the cotton, tears streaming down his cheeks.

Earl hesitated.

"Earl! Keep going, keep cutting, you're getting it, don't stop!"

And Cord's body shuttered with each stroke, till the tip silently fell into the hay. Marty pulled out his shirt, and Cord was crying in pain, as quiet as he could be. And the three knelt together, in silence.

"Whenever you're ready."

Marty whispered.

1861

And Cord shook his head angry-aggressive in the affirmative, and they all assumed their positions once again; this time, Earl placing the blade on the shaft exiting his left thigh. It only projected a half-inch, maybe a bit less, so Earl had to be careful not to cut C's leg. He jockeyed left and right, trying to figure out how to cut it, but he couldn't get the angle right, and was afraid to start.

"Earl, switch; you hold him, I'll cut."

And Earl got up, and as they switched, Marty whispered discrete in Earl's ear. C's head hung toward the floor, long spools of drool leaking from his mouth, quietly crying. Earl wrapped his massive arms around Cord like a cocoon, but his eyes were wide, and he was scared, but he knew just to wait for the word.

Marty knelt in front of Cord, and lifted him by the chin, gently.

"Hey, C, almost done; stay with me, okay?"

Cord opened his eyes and tried to smile. He shook his head, just a half-nod yes.

"*Now!*"

And with that, Earl shoved the bolt through his left leg another three inches, and Cord screamed bloody. Marty stuffed his shirt in his mouth to try and muffle the sound. Fresh blood ran thick from the exit wound.

"Mother….*fuck*….*fuck!*"

C mumbled, as he continued to cry.

"Had to buddy, couldn't cut it, sorry. Now, you know what comes next; hold on, and I'll get through it as quick as I can."

And the second one was worse than the first, since Cord knew it was coming. But Earl cinched him tight; Ay couldn't move an inch, and for that, he was grateful.

Two down.

"Okay, buddy, you know what we have to do….sorry."

Marty said, looking down at Cord's right thigh. The arrow tip never made it through C's leg, and the bulb of skin, blackened with blood leaked below the surface had grown to the size of an egg, and couldn't even be lightly touched without Cord screaming. The high from the mushrooms was wearing off quick, and the pain was reaching a crescendo.

"Fuck, fuck, oh man, I don't know….*I don't know*."

Cord babbled through his swollen mouth, looking down at the grotesque, blackened bulb on his thigh, flinching in pain every time Marty lightly pressed the balloon of blood below the skin.

"Hold him Earl, real tight….*real tight!*"

Marty picked C's head up under the chin, once again, with a single finger and whispered to Cord, so Earl couldn't hear.

"Okay, no tricks this time; the last one, it's gonna hurt like a mother, but we gotta do it, okay? Gotta get this through. I'm gonna count down from three, and Earl's gonna shove it through. Gotta do it, gotta, get ready; it'll be over quick."

C started to hyperventilate, like prepping for a fight, shaking his head up and down.

"Fuck, fuck, fuck, fuck!"

He kept saying, through grit teeth. And before Marty
even started the countdown, he yelled to Earl.

"Now!"

And Earl shoved it in, and Cord went black.

CHAPTER 227 – MAKE A DECISION….*CHIEF*

All three bolts were out.

Cord sat half-slumped in the hay, his back against the wooden pole, wrapped tight in fresh gauze. The pain was serious, and he was breathing heavy.

"How long….was I out?"

"Not long, but long enough to yank the bolts, and good thing; wasn't as easy as you'd think, pulling those fuckers out. Thought they'd bleed more, should have, but not too bad….kinda strange, like they just stopped bleeding, all on their own. I think you're okay….okay."

Marty whispered, kneeling beside C, his hand gently resting on Cord's good shoulder.

"They never do, bleed that bad, I mean. Don't know why; just the way it has always been. They'll heal quick too, no problems, always do, although these….haven't had ones quite like these, not all at once, anyway, not in a long time….*long time*."

C winced a cough, between short labored breaths, remembering the skewer of the spiked fence, at twelve.

Marty asked again, looking down at C.

"How the….why are you way the hell out here? Shit, this is State land; *Beaver Brook Wildlife Management*, maybe….no, we're past that, *way* past that; this is, holy shit, I think were in *Jenny Jump,* the way back-end of the Park! *Fuck;* I've never even been here before, not this part. I didn't think *Jenny Jump* went this far, but it's gotta be, it's huge….gotta be. *Why here?*"

No one answered, and it was quiet in the barn, except for the sound of C's heavy breaths.   Until Earl spoke, nervous.

"Now what? What'll we do C?"

Cord's head was mostly clear, but he still had a bit of a slur, from the swell in his tongue and a lingering cloud in his head. He turned slightly and looked at Martin.

"Well, that's up to the Chief here; I think you know my answer."

"*Interim.*"

Was all Marty said, as his voice trailed off.

He'd been in Town his whole life, a Mayberry cop chasing stray bear cubs out of trees and rowdy kids out of the Park, a drunk and disorderly here, a misdemeanor there, in between marching proud in holiday parades and sleeping during speed traps on Water Street; that's was about as exciting as it ever got in Belvidere. The times he'd pulled his gun he could count on one hand, never firing at anything, or anywhere, except the shooting range, out by the old Town dump. He'd shot Button Pierce plenty of times out there, thousands for sure, ripping up paper targets and talking tough.   And he's *Interim Chief* for less than a fucking week, and Button, his nemesis, the thorn in his side his *whole* life, lay dead, not ten feet from him....*dead*....snapped in two and head twisted like an apple stem by the most gentle man, the best man, he ever knew. Marty never even saw a dead body, a real dead body, outside a funeral. He'd dreamed of this day all his life; he'd killed Button at least a dozen different ways, fantastical kills, some with his bare hands, or he locked him up for life, or beat him senseless in front of Lillian, or, or....

"Marty?"

Earl nudged him in the shoulder.

"What're we gonna do?"

Martin looked over his shoulder at Button, one more time, just to check again, to be sure this whole thing, the deadness, was even real.

It was.

"Well, we gotta, you know, deal with this, you know, the right way; uh, I gotta call it in, I guess, call it, you know, we're gonna hafta, you know, that's probably...."

"We're not calling anything in."

Cord winced as he spoke stern.

"C, come on, I gotta; I'm supposed to do the right thing. I've *always* done the right thing; I'm not *him*."

"I am."

C said, in a low, ominous voice. Then he continued, and his words were crisp.

"It's my fault, bringing you out here; shouldn't have done it. I didn't know who else to call, to trust, ran out of options. I was thinking of calling Smillie, but, that wouldn't have worked; it wouldn't have...."

"*Smillie*? The fucking cab-driver? The *drunk*? Are you kidding me? Why? You were gonna call him before me?!"

"Marty, you either help us, or you gotta go, now! We're running out of night, out of time. I'll take care of it, just leave, don't turn around, and just forget this."

"Forget this! Are you fucking kidding me? I'm never gonna forget *this!*"

"Then I'm gone. Give me till morning to leave, and say I did it; Earl was never here, *never!* He can't be part of this; then you can go chase Cord Brin."

"There *is* no Cord Brin, we both know that."

Marty said, matter-of-fact.

"What'ya mean there's no Cord Brin? He's right there!"

Earl pointed at C, then he turned to C, with a plead.

"What'ya mean you're leaving? For good? Forever? Without me? *Without me?*"

Earl tugged on C's shirt and started to choke up.

"It was self-defense C, right? Come on…."

Marty said, in a whispered plea.

C turned his head and glared at Martin, eye to eye, and it was clear the discussion was over.

"Make a decision….*Chief.*"

CHAPTER 228 - HE GAVE IT A LITTLE SQUEEZE

Twenty seconds of silence passed, Martin looking past C, into the darkness of the barn.

He scanned his life in those seconds, in toto. Button first - all the years of hurt and sadness and anger he caused, to him, to Lilly, to Earl, which melted into his career as a police officer - his promotion, the pride; he was so proud to be a Belvidere officer, it's what he always wanted, always; which gave way to his mom and dad, and the farm, and Sam and Buck and Lilly's mom – and how good she always was to him as a kid; and then to Carol, and Ji-Sue; he smiled at the thought of Ji-Sue – how he never really knew her before yesterday. My God, it was only yesterday at the Fair, when things gelled, and then he was back to Lillian, and Earl.

And more Lillian, and Earl, and Lillian….and Earl; the two looped in his head - his closest friends, for his whole life.

And he remembered what happened to Lillian last night, and wondered if she could ever forget it, forget the fear, the pain, the humiliation, and that he wasn't there for her, not like Cord was. And he looked over at Earl, who was on his knees; Earl's eyes were red, staring at Cord, who's head had fallen forward, eyes closed, in exhaustion.

Earl had the look of having lost his best friend, forever.

Earl quietly leaned forward and kissed Ay on the forehead, then whispered something in C's ear, then Earl started to cry, and Martin saw a single tear make its way down Cord's cheek.

And that was about all he could take.

1869

Fuck Marty whispered to himself, slowly shaking his head, making the most important decision of his life, to do what he knew was wrong, because he knew it was right.

"Okay, okay."

And Earl spun and hugged Marty, squeezing him tight, and Martin hugged him back, in silence. And it was a good hug; the kind true friends share, friends for life, through good and bad, right and wrong, it didn't matter….shoulder-to-shoulder, friends for life, regardless of the circumstances, regardless of the risks.

Real friends.

Shielded by darkness, the first blowfly, a lone, common *green-bottle*, which smelt fresh death a good two miles distant, entered the barn doors and landed on Billy Bones' face, on his left cheek, just beside his lips, on a crust of half-dried blood. She carefully, deftly, deposited the first cache of eggs, little whitish/yellow orbs, like rice balls. And soon, more blowfly followed….many more. Within minutes, Billy's beautiful face, still smiling, was covered by miniscule opaque eggs, barely visible, which, by morning, would erupt into a mass of squirming larvae….maggots engorged.

"What now?"

Martin said to the room, exhausted.

Cord raised his head.

"Where are the girls, at the station?"

"I sent Carol home with Ji – to her apartment; Mae went to Margery's. Earl came to the station, with me, then he left, to go stay at the farm, I thought."

1870

"What happened to Buck?"

"I don't know, guess he went home; I don't think he even ever knew what happened, that Button even came back."

There was a moment of silence, then C asked.

"What about Lillian?"

"Holy shit, can't believe I forgot Lilly; *she* came to the station, with me – I wasn't letting her out of my sight. She didn't talk at all, just fell asleep on a cot we have set up off the locker room. I left her with Lloyd, he's a fucking animal – anybody try *anything*, he would fucking shoot 'em, straight-up, no questions, no hesitation.   She's   good,   safe;   well,   obviously safe….now."

Marty cocked his head toward the dead body, to give it another look.

C had turned his head and looked at Earl, and realized, it just hit him, that he must have been the little dinosaur, then the big dinosaur, hiding in the pickers, and he cracked the faintest of smiles, an uptick on the right side of his mouth.

"You're the dinosaur."

C whispered to Earl, barely loud enough to hear.

And the dinosaur just smiled.

C turned to Martin.

"Marty, you gotta bring me back to the house, And we gotta get his sack out of here, with all the tools, and don't forget his clothes, don't know where they are; give it all to Earl - the clothes, the crossbow, the sack with all the shit back in it….*all of it.*"

"What he's gonna do with it?"

Marty asked.

"Don't worry, I'll take care of that."

"What about the body?"

"Marty, don't worry, I'll take care of it, just get me home. But you gotta throw the bike in your flatbed; I hid it under some leaves just to the left of the doors – you'll find it….I didn't hide it too well, and it's fresh. And try to figure out how he got here; he probably walked, figuring he'd take my bike back, but I don't know, just a guess."

"What about the body?"

Marty asked again, in a more anxious tone. Cord winced, and grabbed Martin's wrist as he spoke.

"Marty, the less you know, trust me ….trust me."

Marty slowly shook his head, in acknowledgment, as he spoke.

"Okay. I got some plastic bags in the truck; I'll pick up the bloody hay – yours and his; the stuff that's the worst, and burn it back at the farm, that should do it."

"Be sure to shut the doors, last one out; they were about three inches, from closed."

Cord said, and stopped talking, because he was exhausted, and in pain. Marty got up and made his way out of the barn, into the darkness, to find the bike. Earl came over and stooped next to C.

1872

"What am I doing with the stuff, with *that*?"

Billy Bones had become a *that*.

"Earl, how'd you know where I was? Did you talk to Carol? Did she tell you I was coming out here? How did she know to send you out so soon? How? I told her to tell you later, *much* later, not until 6:30 or so; way too late, it woulda been way too late by then."

Earl just stared at him, silent.

"Did Carol tell you?"

Earl, almost hesitant, like he wasn't supposed to tell, shook his head in a slow *yes*.

"Which one?"

C said, and when Earl didn't answer, but gave a sad smile. Cord's eyes welled.

"It *was* her, in the dark, who helped me come back, wasn't it? It was your mom, *wasn't it?*"

Without a word, Earl reached down, and gently slid his hand inside Cords, and he gave it a little squeeze.

CHAPTER 229 – SLIP IT INTO THE *BIG CRACK*

Marty was still searching for the bike.

"Earl, you're gonna have to put him over your shoulder, and carry the rest of his shit, and run, as fast as you can.....*fast*! Can you do it?"

He just shook his head an eager yes; C knew he could.

"Where am I going?"

"Earl, haven't we been down this road before?"

"What'ya mean?"

C had to stop and breath a bit; the pain was a constant stab in his chest, legs and brain.

"Fuck, I mean, haven't I been here before, on *this* road….with *you*?"

Earl's eyes lit up, and C knew he got it.

"I knew it; *I knew it!* Is it far?"

"No, not far at all."

Earl whispered.

"Can you make it, while it's *still* dark, carrying him, can you carry him, and all his shit, that far, and through the woods, and under the pickers....all of it? You're gonna have to run, fast, and make sure *nobody* sees you, and you have to get in there, *and back out*, before light?"

"I can do it, I can; I can find it in the dark…easy, and the moon will help me."

"Are you sure you're okay? Not too scared? I don't want you to be scared, all alone out there."

Earl smiled.

"I won't be alone."

And C knew he'd be alright.

"C, where do I put him?"

Cord looked at him, and he knew Earl already knew exactly where to put him, the only safe place to put him, but was afraid to say it, aloud. He was afraid of the puppet.

"You know where, in that long, deep mouth, with the crooked smile. Drop him, and drop his shit; all of it; slip it into the *Big Crack*."

CHAPTER 230 – IT'S SAFE, TRUST ME....LEAVE IT AT THAT

Cord didn't quite know where he was….*somewhere.*

It felt familiar; it had familiar features, but the set was a bit off-kilter. Some of it made sense, a place of belonging, but other parts were foreign, out of place….cold. Overall, it wasn't really any place he'd been before, but parts of it were, kind of. And it was one of those vivid, fucked-up dreams that you're *convinced* is real when you're in deep, your heart beating like a mother, and when you wake, it's the one you swore you'd never forget, but you would anyway; you'd forget all of it, every bit of it, and be pissed about it later….not remembering a shred, not a single detail.

But right now, he was thinking all this as he was immersed - in *deep,* well before the wake, well before the forget, and you usually don't know you're there, you're here, in a fucked-dream, till later. But he did, somehow….know. At least he thought he knew.

And he didn't want to be here; this was one he *wanted* to forget.

It was damp, musty, a basement, like the house where he grew up. Maybe it was *that* basement; parts of it sure looked like it was.

And C was trying, for some reason, to shut the basement door, the one that led outside, to a stairwell, since it was slightly ajar. But a thick, black electric cord snaked through the opening, disappearing outside, up the stairwell, which jammed the process.

Each time he tried to slam the door, and he was determined to do just that, a high voltage hum, the kind that says *back-off,* echoed in the wire. And the more he slammed, the louder the drone, as if it was agitated, ready to bite back.

He scanned the length of the thick wire with his eyes, and it seemed to grow, in girth, like the body of a sinewy snake, an anaconda, as it coiled overhead disappearing into the blackness of the ceiling. In frustration, Ay kicked at the snake, and stomped hard on a kink in the powerful, muscular body. Suddenly, a light flashed and the thick strand of cable somehow severed and came to life, the open end dancing like the mouth of a lamprey near his left arm, full of jagged teeth. And a powerful vacuum sucked his arm into the wire, and his entire body trembled, mildly at first, the beginnings of an electrocution.

Despite the danger, he remembered trying to stay calm, as if doing so would lull the creature into releasing its bite. C called calmly up the basement stairs for help, into the kitchen, the kitchen of his childhood, and that door too, was slightly ajar. And, into the crack of space, his mother emerged, holding a blue checkered dish towel in hand, the one she always used, and calmly stared at him, unalarmed, with an air of indifference. It was the first time he actually saw her in a dream, the first time he'd seen her *actual* face, since she died, so many years ago. She looked younger, and healthy, with no hint of the disease that consumed her. C tried to tell her he was being electrocuted, to please help, to rescue him, but no words left his lips. So he began to exaggerate his shaking, to demonstrate to his mother the trouble he was in, to manifest the fry he was feeling, as his skin burned and his insides boiled, but she simply looked at him, mildly confused as to his antics, and slowly turned away, disappearing from the crack of light in the doorway, dishtowel in hand, never saying a word, nor making a sound.

She was gone, and never returned.

1877

Cord looked up, paralyzed, at the empty crack in the doorway, waiting for help, waiting for his mother to save him. But there was no save on the way. Now he was shaking uncontrollably, violently, and the tremble had turned to jolts, the shock was real, and he knew he was close to the end, he could feel it; the hideous, black snake was latched on tight, and there was no shaking it. A primordial bellow emanated from his lungs, growing in strength and intensity, as he stood there shaking himself to death.

Without warning, he abruptly woke.

But he didn't, not really; it was just a shift of some sort, and he ended up in the place he was now, not awake, not asleep, not dead, just somewhere....purgatory.

And he was sitting quietly at the short end of a long dining table, in the shape of an ell.

Earl was also sitting at the end of the ell, on the opposite side of the table, and they were both waiting for some sort of feast, like Thanksgiving, to start, at a table he'd never seen, in a room with no details he knew.

And Earl, the *other* Earl, was already dead, and C knew that, but Little-Earl wasn't dead in this place. Here, wherever or whatever *here* was, Little-Earl was sitting on the table, seemingly healthy, quietly nibbling on a lemon wedge, which morphed to a lime wedge, as if that somehow mattered. And as Little-Earl ate the pulp, eating around the green skin, his paw holding it in place, C smiled, happy to see his friend and happy he was alive, after all.

But that was not to last.

Without warning, Little-Earl began to heave and vomit a black watery liquid; he fell fetal on the table, arching and convulsing the massive spasms of a stroke. C shot up to help his friend, but Earl somehow jumped off the table and ran toward the front door, the one that led outside, which someone had mistakenly, carelessly, left ajar. Cord desperately tried to follow, but his feet were leaden; he yelled to someone, anyone, to shut the door, so he could save his friend, but it was too late, no one paid attention, no one heard, and Little-Earl got out, disappearing into the darkness....and C couldn't find him, and C couldn't save him. C lost the chance to save his friend.

He hung his head in utter sadness; C wanted *out* of this place.

From nowhere, C felt her hand in his, again, this time gently running her finger on his open palm, and up his forearm, the lightest of touch. And he felt safe, and the sadness faded, because he knew Carol was nearby, and it would be okay; Little-Earl would be okay.

And for the first time, he heard her voice; it was soothing, a light breeze across his ear, no more than a whisper.

"C, you're having a bad dream, come on....come on."

She had called him C; that made him smile.

And his heavy lids must have been closed, because he watched them open, like they were someone else's eyes, and he could see Carol's outline, through an opaque lens....fuzzy. She wore white, and she was simply beautiful, more beautiful than he ever imagined.

"Look at me, it's okay."

Carol said gently, still running her fingers up and down his arm. And slowly, he emerged from the fog, and her image coalesced, and their eyes met.

"You were having a bad one; I was afraid you'd hurt yourself. You okay?"

Carol Crowe gently cupped his cheek with her hand, and the disappointment must have shown in Cord's face.

"What?"

She said tentatively, afraid she'd done something wrong. He shook his head in the negative.

"Nothing, just a bad dream; what time is it?"

The speech was tongue-swollen slurred. Carol tipped her arm and spied her watch.

"Just about twenty after nine; you sure you're okay? Why are you talking like that?"

C tried to raise his head, but it felt glued to the pillow.

"Morning or night? What day is it?"

"Morning, it's Sunday morning; what day do you think it is? Are you okay? What happened? Why are you talking like that?"

"Bit my tongue; is Earl okay?"

"Yeah, Earl's fine; why wouldn't he be?"

C didn't answer quick enough, so Carol continued.

"He's sleeping, but he must have been here before; see what he left you?"

Carol pointed to the box of *Animal Crackers* and a bottle of *Vernors*, on the nightstand beside the bed. C cracked a faint smile, then it faded. Then it hit Carol; Marty said

C was alone….he didn't say anything about Earl being there.

"Wait, I thought you went alone; what the hell happened? Was he *with you?*"

Carol said, alarmed.

It seemed to take great effort, but Cord shook his head, barely, in the negative. Carol let out her held breath, in relief.

"I mean how's *your* Earl, you're *other* Earl….Little-Earl?"

Carol tried to smile; it was a weak attempt.

"He….he can't jump on the counter anymore; I have to help him up, and I can feel his bones, all his bones….he's fragile."

Carol's voice cracked, her lips quivering as she spoke.

"He was always *so strong,* pushing his head into my hand when I pet him; he doesn't do it anymore. He seems to be hungry, but he won't really eat, a bite or two, then he drops it, and walks away, and his nose is running constantly, and…."

She stopped and her head dropped.

"But he's purring, like he always does, right when you touch him, and he seems happy, and the vet thinks he might start gaining some weight if we give him some supplements, and…."

Carol raised her head and looked to Cord for agreement, to share in the cheer that neither really believed.

C cracked the smallest of smiles, for Carol's sake.

And Cord was relieved that Little-Earl wasn't dead, for real. He never told Carol, nor anyone, his horrible dream about Little-Earl. And he hoped to forget it, but somehow, he didn't think he would; you never seem to forget the ones you want.

"Why?"

Carol asked.

"Just worried about him; I love that little guy."

C said, barely spitting the words with his swollen tongue. He still felt drugged. He didn't remember, but when Marty dropped him off, he popped two pain killers into Ay, fucking horse tablets, drugs Marty kept in his glove box for the last five years, from the last time his lower back went out. The meds were long since expired, he didn't remember what they actually were - some generic, or what dose to take, but he kept them anyway, just in case. He figured, since he had two left, what-the-fuck, so he gave C both, since two is always better than one, right? Probably twice as good. Anyway, maybe they'd still work.

Work they did.

Cord gave a bit of a shiver, and his lids began to close. Carol went to reposition the blanket, and as she did, she first noticed the Taser burn on his neck, and then the heavy gauze bandage on Cord's shoulder.

"Oh my God!"

She whispered, as she pulled the blanket and sheet down a bit. Cord was naked, except his boxer-briefs, but she never saw past his mid-section; she never saw his legs.

"What happened last night? C what happened? Is it safe? Is he....?"

He opened his eyes slowly, and stared hard at her; he didn't utter a word, or make any sort of movement with his head.

"Did he do that? Is he dead? Did you kill him? Are you okay? Who put on that bandage?"

C just stared at her, then spoke slowly.

"It's safe; from now on….it's safe."

Carol eyes turned red, and she barely whispered.

"C, did you kill him?"

He didn't answer.

"You're sure? It's safe?"

C slowly shook his head yes, eyes closed.

"Thank you."

She whispered, her lips trembling, the tremendous weight of worry lifted. She lightly kissed his temple.

"I couldn't sleep; I couldn't wait till 6:30 am, it never seemed to come. I'm sorry, but I called Marty at 5:58 am, to tell him to go get you – that you may be in trouble, but he said you had already called him, and he brought you home and put you to bed. He didn't tell me you were hurt; well he said you were hurt a little, but you were okay, but tired. I asked him about what happened, who was there, and he just said you were alone, and to talk to you about it, but to let you sleep for now, because you were tired. He said he was at the station with Lilly; she was still asleep, and he couldn't leave. You didn't tell him what happened, to me, did you?"

C slowly shook his head no.

"Who knows?"

He didn't want to answer anymore questions; he didn't want to say anything that would later come back to implicate Marty, or Earl.

"No more, it's safe, trust me….leave it at that."

CHAPTER 231 – A SHARED EXPERIENCE HOPED TO NEVER SHARE AGAIN

Cord was asleep, as was Carol, her head resting lightly on his chest, until she was jarred awake. She felt someone in the room, a presence, standing beside her, even though she saw no one. The hair on her arms stood at attention as she blinked the sleep from her eyes.

She looked down at C; he was asleep, breathing quietly through his mouth. She perked her ears and heard words at the front door, a floor below; she couldn't tell who, and the door soon shut. A quiet shuffle up the stairs followed. She sat up and instinctively pressed her clothing with open hands, trying to primp in the less than ten seconds she had.

The clock said 9:55 am.

And as she stared at the door, she saw the slight figure enter the bedroom threshold, and their eyes met, and her heart sank.

It was her. Not a word was spoken.

Lillian slowly walked toward Carol, toward the edge of the bed, but not in a confrontational manner, more respectful than anything. She never took her eyes off Carol, nor Carol off her.

And as Lilly approached, the long, reddened gouge on Carol's left cheek seem to grow, and Carol's nose came into focus, still sporting a ring of crusted blood on the inside. Her left ear was red and bruised, remnant from a bad twist and grind during a scuffle on the van floor, as she was first bound and gagged. Lillian had never seen a blemish on Carol's skin, the few times she was ever close enough to actually notice.

And Carol looked at Lillian, and saw the light tinge of a red ring still circling her neck, the remnant flush of a recent chokehold; her right eye and upper lip were still slightly swollen, the signature of more than one backhand to the face.

And as the two stood frontal, closer than they had physically been in years, since they first met at the *Palace*, Lilly did something to Carol she had never done before....she half-nodded and frowned; it was a frown of acknowledgment, a frown that says *I know....I know.*

Carol frowned back and half-nodded, in acknowledgment.

And for the first time, without a word, Carol and Lilly spoke kindly to one another....a shared experience hoped to never share again.

CHAPTER 232 – SHE SPOONED AND QUIETLY FELL ASLEEP

Carol rose in silence and left the bedroom; Lilly stood statue, waiting to hear the front door quietly click shut on the floor below.

She turned her head slightly to the right and saw the *Animal Crackers* and *Vernors* on the nightstand; she didn't smile or acknowledge her feelings in any facial expression, she simply gazed blankly, then, mechanically, looked back at Cord, still asleep.

She softly sat by his side, on the edge of the bed, and stared at his face, a probing stare, one that has too many questions and not nearly enough answers. The same one Lillian had on the first day she met him, as she stood over him, eating a sandwich, as he lay unconscious from the door-jam-to-the-face, wondering who the hell this guy was. She didn't know why, back then, she even took the time to wonder; it was something about him….*something*.

Now she felt like she knew this man forever, like he had been part of her and Earl's life for years, and she knew as much about him now as she did that first day, which was next-to-nothing.

She casually shook her head, left to right, in silence, and stared at the mysterious man sleeping before her. The man she dismissed at the Fair, the man who probably saved her life last night, the man she hated, but not really, the man she'd come to love, but wouldn't admit to, the man she endlessly dismissed, but couldn't imagine living without.

She lightly ran her finger across her swollen lip, and her swollen eye; she donned baggy Police Department-issued red sweatpants and an oversized gray tee-shirt; Marty had thrown away the gold mini-skirt and the fishnet mid-riff. She was still wearing Ji-Sue's flats, which surprisingly fit; she wore no underwear, and no bra. She hadn't showered yet and wasn't happy she still carried the scent from the past evening, at the Fair, which already seemed a lifetime ago.

Marty had told her Cord went to see Button, and Button was gone, and wouldn't be coming back. But that was all Martin knew, and she had to speak to Cord....directly to Cord.

And so she looked down upon him, full of questions, full of emotions, but she sat stoic, with an expression of stone.

She wanted to smile, to feel better, but she just wasn't ready, not yet. She shifted and swung her legs up onto the bed, and gently slipped under the warm covers. Cord was asleep, but feeling a body next to his, he instinctively laid on his side, facing away.

She saddled up next to him, feeling his heat; it felt good. She spooned and quietly fell asleep.

CHAPTER 233 – YOU'LL ALWAYS BE SAFE, NOW AND FOREVER

Cord woke to a light crunch, then a quiet, steady chew, followed by another crunch.

Did a squirrel get in?

He opened his eyes, the lids were still heavy, and turned his head to see Lillian, in rumpled red sweatpants and too-big tee-shirt, sitting beside the bed, in a chair she pulled over from the desk, munching on *Animal Crackers,* his *Animal Crackers*.

He stared at her, as she stared back in silence, with a fresh cookie in her hand, ready for slaughter. She slowly raised the hippo to her mouth, her eyes locked on his, and bit off the head in a clean crack. She munched the skull to bits, dropped the headless hippo back in the box, and hunted for a new victim; an elephant was next in line.

"Having fun?"

C said, groggily.

She nodded once in the affirmative, executed the helpless elephant with a single chomp of her front teeth, and dumped him unceremoniously back into the box, as she mashed and swallowed him, while her fingers fished for the next casualty. In the end, the slaughter would be complete.

"What happened? Marty won't tell me; what happened? Where is he?"

Cord just stared at her, and didn't say a word.

"Why did she have a big scratch on her cheek, and a bloody nose? What happened?"

"When did you see Carol?"

C said, surprised.

"What happened to her? What happened to Button? What happened to you?"

"That's a lot of questions Lilly."

She just stared at him, hard and angry, like a rubber band stretched long and tight, dangerous, ready to snap. Then she suddenly let off on the tension, and the band went limp, a harmless rubber loop. And she asked again, this time in more of the plead of a little girl.

"C, what happened?"

And Cord slowly rolled over on his side to face her, grimacing as he did.

"Hey, it's safe, okay? You don't have to worry about him anymore, promise, never again....promise."

"But what happened? Where is he? What happened to Carol? What happened to you?"

C sighed and just stared at her in silence, and she stared back with kitten eyes, vulnerable. He wanted to hug her, to make her feel safe.

"Lilly, please, just believe me and let it drop....*please*."

"I can't."

She said, in defeat.

"Yes you can, you really can."

C said in a shallow sigh.

1890

She stared at him, and he saw the beginnings of a tear, a culmination of years of stress and fear, well in the bottom of her eyes, but it didn't run, not yet.

C sighed again.

"Okay, you get one question, just one, and then we don't talk about this anymore, ever again….okay?"

She tentatively shook her head yes.

Then Lilly stared at him in silence, and he knew she was searching for the one question to ask, but he already knew what it was going to be. It was the one that really mattered, the only one that truly would mean she, Earl, Cord, everyone, was safe.

"Did you kill him?"

C stared at her, searching her face; she was beautiful, even hurt, she was beautiful. He slowly said the word, as he shook his head.

"No."

She scrunched her face in despair, and the welled tear traced her cheek.

"Then it's *not* safe; it'll never *be* safe."

C knew he had to tell her. He reached over and felt for her hand, and could feel her trembling.

"Hey, hey, look at me."

Lilly raised her head and her sad eyes met his.

"No one knows this, just you and me, and you can't tell anyone, ever, okay? Okay? And we never talk about this, or what happened again; no more questions, no more *anything*, ever again....okay?"

She nodded in agreement.

C let out a long sigh, and shook his head once, up-and-down, in the affirmative, in response to her one question, and followed it in the lightest whisper.

"So it's safe, do you understand *[Lilly nodded slow, once, in the affirmative, and started to quietly cry]*? You, Earl, *you're safe,* I promise; you'll always be safe, now and forever."

1892

CHAPTER 234 - HE LOVED THAT LITTLE GIRL TO DEATH, AND SHE KNEW IT

The sun was overhead, straight-up noon, and the procession continued, like the viewing at a funeral.

"Did you like the crackers?"

Earl whispered as he poked C in the arm, one of the few parts that didn't hurt, as he sat as lightly as he could manage on the edge of the bed. Chicken was sleeping on Earl's broad shoulders, like she always did.

"Earl, who do you think ate the crackers?"

C answered, eyes still closed.

Earl gasped, then gingerly opened the box, and witnessed the carnage. He fingered through them, to see if there were any survivors….not a one.

"She killed 'em all C, *every one!* She's vicious! Poor little animals."

Earl muttered low.

"Yes she is."

C smiled, eyes still closed.

Then Earl leaned in and whispered, foretelling a secret, about to be shared.

"Hey C, I dropped him, but I never heard the water, never heard the splash; wasn't there supposed to be a splash?"

Now C opened wild eyes in a start and spoke in the type of gruff voice he never used with Earl; Earl jumped back a bit, startled at the venom.

"Listen to me, this is too fucking important, okay? You were *never* there, you know *nothing* of what happened, you were asleep all night, and never left the house. You never, ever mention what happened last night again; never admit it, never mention it, never think about it, never, ever again, to *anyone*, Lilly, Carol, Marty, even me….got it?"

Earl nodded yes in silence, still a bit scared.

"Good. Now, what did you say about the water, and the splash?"

Earl just gazed at C, frozen, not sure what to say….so he didn't say anything.

Uncomfortable seconds passed in silence, each staring hard at the other, until C broke it with a gentle whisper.

"Exactly, exactly."

Cord squeezed and patted Earl's leg in acknowledgment; Earl let out a breath of relief and smiled at having passed the test. Then Earl started to fidget; C didn't notice at first, but Earl kept fidgeting till he did.

"Earl, what is it?"

"I gotta say this one thing though, okay? And that'll be it, forever, promise; don't be mad, she told me I had to."

"Who did?"

Earl just looked at him in silence, and C knew to pay attention.

"She said I hafta bring you to the doctor; she's worried about you."

"*No doctor*, no; there's never a doctor, that's not part of the rules. No can do."

C was adamant in his tone, and he could see Earl start to fret again.

"*You wouldn't even be here without her!*"

Earl blurted, out of nowhere, in a tone Earl *never* used with Cord. Then the big man recoiled, sheepish, seemingly as surprised by the words, and tone, as C was.

"And I'm sure that was *you* just talking to me, right Earl?"

C asked, dripping with sarcasm, looking at the ceiling. Earl didn't answer.

"Yeah, *big surprise,* tag-teamed again. Well tell her this, here's the deal; I'll give it twenty-four hours. If I'm not feeling better, I'll go; deal?"

Earl sat staring at Cord, through Cord, past Cord, not making a move or sound; he was having his own conversation. Without warning, he slowly nodded his head yes.

And that was that.

"So, how's the little bitch doing? Tired of doing nothing all day?"

C said, cocking his head in a dismissive nod toward Chicken, perched lazy on Earl's shoulders.

"Don't say that, C; she understands, you know."

"I hope she does! I'm the one whose hurt; aren't cats supposed to sense that, and comfort the ones that feed them?"

"But you don't feed her, *I* feed her."

Earl said.

"Well I *used to.*"

Cord snipped; it was a weak defense.   Then he remembered an ace.

"Hey, and I'm the one that saved your skinny butt, when you were starving and scared under the porch, remember that….huh?"

C pointed accusatory at Chicken, but she couldn't be bothered, eyes closed, ignoring the bluster. Earl gently grabbed his groggy girl and whispered to her *Chicken Teriyaki* and laid her ever-so-gently on the blanket beside C. No sooner did her feet touch the bed when she turned and leaped back onto Earl's shoulders, curled up, and closed her eyes again, generally annoyed at the disturbance.

She was a pretty good judge of character, Cord thought; he would stay on Earl's shoulders too, if he was Chicken.

"You little bitch."

Was all C said, shaking his head, but still smiling.

He loved that little girl to death, and she knew it.

CHAPTER 235 – BLACK IS BLACK AND DEAD IS DEAD

Mae and Margery came by together, later that same day; he was happy to see them both, and happy to see them together. Who would ever believe sleeping with both a mother and daughter would be a bonding tool; he smiled at that fucked-up thought. They bickered a bit bedside, but for the most part, they were having fun with each other, and they were both talking to him, and that meant a lot to C. He liked them both, he really did. A rare bright spot.

The day's contingent ended with Buck, along with Marty. Buck wanted to hear all about how C kicked Button's ass, ran him out of Town, but both Marty and C kept the conversation steered elsewhere, and soon enough they too left, and C was alone; it was getting late.

And he was fine by the end of that first day, in fucking pain, for sure, but nothing over-the-counter couldn't handle. No fever, no more bleeding, no infection, no complications, just as he suspected.

Somehow the holes would quickly close, heal and scar, adding to the litany littering his body, and he would be fine, and survive, like he always did, even though he knew he shouldn't have. No one's luck ran as long and deep as his in matters of life and death. But for some reason, his string did.

Maybe it wasn't luck.

No physician required he whispered aloud, to the empty room, taunting Carol; he figured she was listening, at least he hoped she was. It was amazing how he fully accepted her presence, the reality of her, out there, or inside his head, wherever she hid, likely with the rest of the crew. He wasn't sure the exact day he crossed that line, but he certainly had. Earl had said his mother hoped, someday, that C would believe in her. Well she got her wish....he did. And until he came to this shit-ass backwater, he would have scoffed at the thought; weak-minded people who needed some higher comfort, to protect them from the unknown, from being scared of what may lay in wait on the other side.

But for some reason here, in this strange little place, it seemed to make sense, and it seemed real. Carol Liddell seemed *real;* he was convinced Carol saved him in the barn, or at least convinced for now, inside this little black box in bum-fuck nowhereville.

And he wondered if it would last, if that strange connection stayed once you stepped off the board game called *Belvidere,* and returned to the real world, somewhere past the roadside bus stop at *Luigi's Rancho.* He wondered if he would look back at this time, this stop along the journey, and call himself weak, or naïve....just another schmuck who bought into the carney act.

And he wondered when that day would come, when Jenny arrived; the day he was gonna leave this place. It was coming, sure as shit, it always did, and usually, not in a good way.

Truth was, he was always more than ready to leave *wherever* he was, almost as soon as he got there. But this place, he *didn't* want to leave, not yet, not anytime soon. And he couldn't remember the last time he ever truly gave a shit about where he was, or who was there, or when he was leaving. As he lay there in bed, shot-through with three bolts, he thought about death, and how you couldn't get much closer to next-to-dead, or in much worse God-damn pain, than he was in that barn. And despite it all, he wouldn't trade last night for all the money in the world, not if it meant never meeting Earl he wouldn't....*never.* He'd get shot all over again, and again....and again.

He figured that's what *kindred* must really mean.

Just the gift of knowing Earl for the short time he had, knowing someone so pure, someone who somehow saw the little bits of good in C and ignored the rest, was worth all the pain, was worth dying in that barn, which he most certainly should have.

Why didn't he die, finally just die?

And C drifted around that prospect a bit, the same prospect he thought about, much-more-than-once-before, more so since he stepped off that Greyhound on April 20th :

it's hard to die if you're already dead

he reasoned inside his head.

If you died when you were twelve, skewered on an angry fence, shouldn't you know, somehow really know, that you're dead? Was this place the final destination, the end of his journey, where he finally came to realize that none of the past thirty-one years were even veritable, rather simply the unspooling of a reel of film. Was it just the passing of a minute? Was it still 1:13 am, in 1975? Is that when he died on that fence? And who was the puppet? And was that really a dream, or is *this* the dream? Were Button, Carol, Lilly, Earl, Chicken or anybody or anything else in this strange place, and in every place he'd ever been before this, even real, or was it all just him, all alone, different parts of his brain, firing and flickering last gasps, before it dimmed and died? Was Belvidere just another senseless, imaginary stop, the last station-post at the end of a long fool's journey, one very bad nightmare, on its way to dead?

1899

The thoughts bounced hard and ricocheted inside his skull, and his mind raced a thousand miles a minute, like it always had in the past, but hadn't so much in this little Town, not for months, anyway.   The respite had been nice.

But it was racing mad now, and he shook his head hard and breathed deep, to try and reset, and restore the calm between his ears.

He poked himself in the arm, and felt it; it felt like flesh and bone....it *felt* real.

And soon enough, like it usually did, the crazy talk in his noggin began to fade, and he felt foolish for even thinking it through. Of course it's all real, *he's real,* he reasoned. With eyes closed, he whispered aloud to an empty room, as if to reassure himself as to what he knew to be true, when the lights finally, finally went out:

Black is black and dead is dead.

CHAPTER 236 – BACK TO THE WAY IT WAS, NOT REALLY, NOT EVER

No one ever saw Marty's bandages on his legs that day, or later, his pants or shorts covered them, and his shirt hid the shoulder hole. No discussions, no explanations, the typical routine for Cord.

And the hole-punches all healed just fine in due time, as expected; no infection, no doctor visits required; they simply faded and joined the rest. He smirked smug at Carol for that one.

Next up was waiting for the fallout, the heavy static sure to arrive in Town, and soon, due to the missing kingpin of the *Drin*.

A tense first week crawled by, Marty and C both on edge, waiting for the trouble to find them, trouble that was surely on its way.

Week two came and went, and still no fallout....*nothing* happened. No blacks rising up from the south, no Italians infiltrating from the east, no skinheads cresting the hill from Oxford, looking for Billy Bones....nothing.

The Doctor went back to selling drugs in Camden; Crème King stepped into *No. 2 – Ranking Member,* the eastern syndicate settled back into their same-old and the *Drin* disappeared before it ever really began. A pond ripple that disappears.

And Button Pierce simply vanished, fading away, as if he never existed, and no one seemed to care. No family, no friends, naught; in the end, he was reduced to nothing more than a slow rot, wedged deep in the darkness of the *Big Crack.*

And despite all odds to the contrary, things worked out for the better, the bad guy lost, and the story had a happy ending.

But who really believes that?

Things in Town should have been better, should have been *fantastic*, back to the good-times, before Button Pierce ever showed up, before Billy Bones ever came back.

But even with good news, and good tidings, life changes....it simply moves on, and not always for the better; it just happens that way.

Despite one's wishes, it never really goes back to the way it was, not really, not ever.

CHAPTER 237 – I DON'T WANT EARL TO DIE

September 2, 2006, Saturday, Labor Day weekend; a flip to day one-hundred thirty-six. Jenny was still on vacation, with nary a sign, nor word spoken.

It had been just shy of a month since the barn, and life had moved on….sort of.

Earl sat on the loveseat, staring at C, who was staring out over the Park. A light breeze rustled the leaves in the red maple afront *L'antre du Lion*, anchored along the Hardwick Street curb, and continued through the sentry of stately trees across the street. A blue jay squawked every now and then, and house sparrows sang in-between, all unseen, hidden in the greenery overhead. The sun was heading south in the western sky, above the Presbyterian steeple, but it still hung, barely above the treetops, in open blue, forcing C to squint into it, looking at the dappled shades of green in the carpet of close-cut grass in the Square.

Two pre-teens wheeled lazily by on clunkers, arguing about the coolest of cars, and a pair of forty-something squat women with baggy tee-shirts, half-skirting their wide rumps, circled the Green on a late afternoon power-walk, busily jabbering away about nonsense.

Zeke skipped up the front steps, lithe and muscular, and pulled at a dish of dry food on the porch with his paw, knocked out some nuggets, and crunched them down, dropping crumbs on the porch carpet.

C stretched his leg straight to relieve the pain in his right knee; it still hurt from the morning run, like it did most days he ran recently. He did the Foul Rift loop, solo, the one where Lilly dusted him; it had become his favorite, at five and three-quarter miles. A quick one-loop around the Park at the start of the run made it an even six miles. And, save the knee, it had become pretty easy. Earl didn't go this time….he slept in. As usual, it was a quiet jog, and he looked forward to making his way through the one-lane tunnel, over the railroad trestle and hearing the distant rush of the Foul Rift rapids….it was soothing. And the horses were always out, as was that evil ball, still hanging in the tree along that creepy section of woods. He had found himself looking forward to seeing the ball as well, nodding once as he passed; it had become part of the ritual along the loop.

He gently rubbed his knee, lost in thought, as Zeke jumped on the ottoman, and sniffed C's toes, before he settled down beside him, closing his eyes, ready for yet another afternoon nap. The rough life of being a cat living in the lion's den.

Hunter was at the far end of the porch, beneath the coffee table. She seemed fatter by the day, ready to pop. She lay on her back, legs spread wide, like fat cats do, and fast asleep….a happy cat. Big Banana was snoozing under the loveseat, below Earl; C could see his front paws, but that was about it. The *Three Musketeers*: Zeke, Big Banana and Hunter; when you saw one, the others were always near by….friends for life.

Zeke, Hunter and Big B, the threesome spread across the porch, with Cord and Earl in the middle, all relaxing on a beautiful summer day beside the Park. It was one of the nicest days of the year, so far….life was good.

But Cord wasn't smiling. And from the periphery, Ay eyed Earl twiddling his thumbs; it wasn't a good twiddle.

"Earl, they'll be back soon, then we'll know, okay? Nothing we can do till they get back."

C uttered monotone, never changing his lost gaze over the Park.

1904

"Okay."

Earl said, apprehensive, still twiddling away. Then he added the clarifier that no one wanted to discuss.

"I don't want Earl to die."

C didn't respond.

Little-Earl had slept in the attic the night before; Ji found him in the Game Room after a frantic, house-wide search. It had been going that way lately, thinking the worst if no one had seen him in a bit. When they found him, he had bloody mucous in his left nostril. Ji carried him down to Carol's bedroom, gently cleaned his nose and laid on the bed, quietly petting him. He purred long and loud. Carol brought up some canned salmon, people-salmon, diluted with water, so he could drink the slurry; he didn't eat anything solid anymore, really hadn't in the last two weeks, and once muscular and alpha-strong, he was becoming ever more skeletal. Earl expended enough energy to raise his head and lap the juice, just for a bit.

Ji had been giving Earl oral injections of food concentrate for the last several days, a sticky brown molasses-type goo to get some calories in him.

Two weeks ago, they brought Earl to the vet to try and fatten him up; they kept him there four days, overnight. He stayed, and slept, in a small, wire cage. He had never been away from home overnight before, and here he was, sick, sequestered in a cage in an unfamiliar place, dogs barking through the night, when even the slightest foreign sound at home would send him scurrying, he was always so scared. Carol hated the whole idea, but was convinced by the vet it was best for Earl. She drove out on a Friday, early, and visited him at the vet's office, and was brought to tears, seeing him all alone in that cage. She immediately scooped him up and took him home, and had Ji drive him to the vet daily for the next week to get supplements. But even that was stressful, so Carol finally bought the food, and had Ji do it herself, at the house, kicking herself for not doing that at the outset.

Carol and Ji hated giving Earl the goo injection – an oversized syringe of molasses in the mouth, and Earl hated it too, trying to fight it off. But he was simply too weak to resist, and the girls were too weak to let him starve, and Carol wouldn't put him down, no way. She did that once, when she was eighteen years old, to her very first cat, who was also eighteen….a stray female the family found abandoned in the woods a few months after Carol was born. They were the best of friends, all through Carol's adolescence, all eighteen years. She was as much a part of the family as anyone else. And even though she was sick, and eating next-to-nothing, Carol regretted that decision every day of her life since, taking away whatever days her best friend had left. For the last thirty years, she vowed never to do it, to any animal, ever again. So Earl lived, and suffered, because of it. But she hoped the suffering was outweighed by the purr. Little-Earl was still purring, and he seemed happy, except when the syringe of goo was shot in his mouth, or half-in, half-on his cheek; Ji and Carol were timid, and lousy, shots. And, Carol reasoned, although his eyes and face were sunken, and they could feel his backbone, his belly was round and full, and hung down a bit. He had gained a quarter-pound back since the last vet visit a couple days ago, and was getting updated blood work, so maybe the concentrate was working, just slowly. And slow was okay, as long as it was in the right direction.

So Carol hoped.

Carol laid on the bed with Ji-Sue, both sandwiching Earl, each petting him lightly, as he purred. Carol looked at the pink and white lilies, mixed with red roses, in the vase on the fireplace mantle, beside the bed. She

got up and pulled out the note card and silently read it
again, even though she had read it a dozen times already:

Always remember, Earl will never die.

Love, C

She slowly slid the note back in the envelope and
dropped her head in defeat.

"Ji, it's time....let's go."

"Earl, where are we, on the *List;* where'd we leave off?"

"I don't remember."

C tilted his head and frowned.

"Earl, the thing to help Little-Earl, what he *really* needs,
is for us to be positive, and to be in a good mood when
he gets back, when we get the good news that the vet has
some new medicine for him, and the blood work looks
better, okay? You need to think good things; let's think
about the *List*, okay, because nothing's much better than
the *List of Ten,* right?"

Earl stopped twiddling and smiled; C was right, C was
always right about stuff like that.

"Okay, we were on No. 8 next; we already did the first
seven."

"What were they again? Just go through it, quick."

"I don't want to."

Ay knew why.

1907

"Come on Earl, we don't have to talk about 'em, I just wanna refresh."

"Okay, No. 1 was do something with Carol, No. 2 was…"

"Whoa, whoa, whoa, slow down cowboy, hold on; *do something with Carol*?   That's not what it was; I remember it was more like *Go On A Date With Carol*, and have…."

"Okay, okay, **okay!**"

Earl cut him off, holding his *Stop* hand up.

"….and have some kinky *Kama Sutra* sex!"

C still finished the sentence.

"I never said I'd do that! That wasn't No. 1!"

"Yes it was Earl; I'm not debating it now. No. 1 is No. 1, done deal; move on."

Earl scrunched his face and let out a snort.

"Okay, but I'm not saying I'm doing that!"

"You already went on a date with her."

"I did not! *When?*"

The first part was a defiant bark; but for the second part, for the *when*, Earl changed his tone to a quizzical, child-like chirp. It forced a smile on C's face, for acts like that, for the innocence Earl had, and C wished he could share, he loved his best friend.

"When you went to *Couch Rock*, and…."

1908

"That doesn't count! Marty and Ji and Buck were there too!"

"Okay, you're right, that was a quasi-date; but you did go off alone with Carol at the Fair, arm-in-arm, now didn't you?"

"Yeah, but, she grabbed my arm!"

"Uh huh, didn't look like much of a struggle on your part."

"My mom said never be *rude.*"

Earl huffed indignant.

"Yeah, and how about eating funnel cakes at the Pavilion, with sugar powder all over your face, and Carol trying to hold your hand, and you pretending you didn't know she was trying, and moving your hand, but not *that* much."

Earl gasped in fright.

"How'd you know that? Who told you that, my mom?!"

"No, someone saw you, and ratted you out."

"Spying! I betcha it was Billy! And I didn't hold her hand, and she gave up trying anyway, and just held my pinky. And that doesn't count, holding pinkies!"

"Sure it does! Earl, that was a *real* date! You two alone, at the Fair, one of your favorite places, holding pinkies, eating funnel cakes - powder all over your face, having fun with someone you're crazy about – what the hell do you think a date *is*? What you did, that's what dates are all about, that's the *good stuff* - that was about the best date anyone could ever have, and you did it, all on your own!"

1909

"Really? That's a *date*? That counts?"

"Really! So now you can cross off half of No. 1; now we gotta get that second part taken care of. Maybe we...."

"No. 2 is *Go to Panama*...."

Earl cut him off quick.

"When are we going C; when, when?"

"Didn't we say we'd go at Christmas? Well, around Christmas anyway, right?"

"That's right, that's right, we'll go then! And we'll see Little-Earl, the *other* Little-Earl, I hope he's not sick too, I hope he's swimming around the coral and the lobster are all hiding, and the *Wild Things* are living fat and happy on some little island somewhere near our hut, maybe....right?"

Cord forgot they even talked about the *Wild Things*, and them hiding on a forgotten cay in Panama; but Earl forgot nothing....*ever*.

"Right. And hey, you never know; maybe you can bring Carol, on a *long* date."

"And you can bring Lilly!"

C shook his head negative at the thought.

"Earl, you know she'd never go; she's not even talking to me anymore."

Lilly had moved back to the second floor Palace apartment the day after the Fair, that Sunday, in the afternoon, after she went to see C in bed, after he told her it was safe. She never told anyone - just packed her

1910

bag and left, walked home. No thank-you, no goodbye, no see-you-later, no nothing....not a word to anyone, even Earl.

And the very next day, Monday, August 7th, without a word, with Carol back in the City, Earl quietly packed up and moved in with her, with C in tow, up on the third floor. It took till Wednesday for C to have the courage to call and tell Carol; Earl had stage-fright about the whole matter and Ji wasn't spilling *those* beans....no way.

Surprisingly to C, Carol didn't blow up. She told him she'd see him for breakfast the following Saturday, and moved on to stale, perfunctory topics, till the semi-warm, somewhat formal call ended less than five minutes later and she went back to work, still scouting contaminated sites to populate the new Brownfield Fund.

She pressed back in her burgundy leather chair and stared past the dark-stained, wormy chestnut paneling, to the window beyond, and let out a single, long huff of resignation. She knew that call was coming, it was inevitable, but she had hoped for a bit more boys-time next door. She got none.

But she had already decided not to make a fuss, for Lilly's sake, given what Earl's sister went through. She still disliked Lillian, but not nearly as much; that brief moment of silence between the two, at C's bedside, stuck with her. It meant something, at least to her – she felt it, the smallest hint of a thaw, and she hoped Lilly, in some small way, felt it too. And her letting the boys go, without a fuss, it was her way of acknowledging whatever tiny fiber of bond she felt with Lilly, when their eyes met, their shared bruises, and abuse, at the hands of Button, acknowledged. Maybe this would help it along, just a bit, if not for Lilly, then for Earl. Whatever she could do to make Earl's life easier, happier, she would do it, because Earl was going to be a part of her life, always and forever, if she had any say in the matter.

"Give her time C; she feels....*alone*."

Earl whispered to his best friend.

"I know that! I try to do stuff with her, and she blows me off and is *nasty,* just like the beginning, even worse now. I don't get it, and I don't know what to do."

"Just keep trying, she'll turn around; she likes you, she always has, even if she doesn't always know it. She'll come with us at Christmas, I know she will."

And Earl smiled sad at his friend, and placed his hand gently on C's shoulder.

"You, me, Carol and Lilly in Panama, now that will be *some* Christmas present, wouldn't it Earl?"

They both smiled at the thought.

"Okay, keep going."

C said, and Earl did.

"Okay, No. 3 is *Solve A Mystery,* like Ken and Sandy do all the time – they are the *best* at it, and they do the really hard ones; we still haven't done that one yet – not even an easy one! And No. 4 is *Go To Skeleton Island.*"

"Shit Earl, we gotta start moving on this stuff!"

"I know! How about No. 5, C? How about *Get Real Mail.*"

"Done!"

The two yelled it at the same time, by fluke. That was
Carol's Bacchanalia invite, on October 14th, which was
quickly approaching.

C watched Earl's face glow; he knew he was thinking
about Carol's party, and the sleepover....with sleeping
bags, and *S'mores,* and *everything.*

"Earl, you know that's only *[C looked skyward and did
the math in his head, quick]* forty-two days away, a little
over a month."

Earl started rubbing his hands together, his tongue-tip
sticking out, licking his lips and wiggling his toes – both
feet, all at once, like he did whenever he was too excited
to keep it inside. C smiled at the antics.

"Okay, so we can cross of half of No. 1 and all of No. 5;
what's next?"

"It's you and me being brothers; that's done too, right?"

Earl asked, half-tentative.

"Of course we're brothers! For real! What we have,
together, you and me, that's what real brothers have. In
fact, most real brothers aren't even lucky enough to have
what he have; you're unfortunately kind of stuck with
what you're dealt....but not us!"

"And we'll be *even more* real brothers when you marry
Lilly!"

Earl yelled. And C just looked at him cocked.

"She not even *talking* to me, and now you have us
married? You know something I don't know?"

Earl shook his head no.

1913

"Just hoping."

Earl whispered. C half-smiled at his friend, and let the topic drop. Cord took up the mantle.

"Okay, what's No. 7?"

"Don't you remember?"

Earl asked incredulous, as if *anyone* could ever forget No. 7.

"No, that's why I'm asking you."

"It's *Riding A Knucklehead Motorcycle*! To wherever that levee is you rode on, right when the sun comes up, and we'll put on that song you like, *Sunset Grill*, on the radio. We got that bet you know, two more Ken and Sandy books; you shook hands and *everything*....no getting out Mr. C!"

"Yeah, I know the God-damn cheating bastard bet you made, cheating with your mom. I should renege on that fact alone, but I won't, because you mom is *so* wrong, and you can tell her that too; no way Earl, there is absolutely no way you can beat the dust riding that Harley. You never even rode a bike before, and atop that levee, it's fucking dangerous, and scary as shit! I don't think I can even do it; there's no way you're doing it. The levee is way too long, and you gotta cross the railroad tracks, on that crazy dog-leg curve, no fucking way. You and your mom are going down on this one, for sure."

C pointed at Earl, taunting him.

Earl smiled at C, the kind of condescending smile that pats you lightly on the head, like you're a chump.

"Trust me Earl, you're going down; I ain't buying no more Ken Holt books for you....you're done."

Earl kept smiling.

"I'm sorry C, but I'm gonna beat the dust, and no backing out....*no* take-backs!"

"Stop saying that Earl! I never said I wanted a take-back. I'm in for two more Ken and Sandy books, but I'm not gonna have to pay up, trust me on that one."

"When are we going? When am I gonna see the levee?"

"Soon....maybe, after Panama, maybe. We'll do it in the Spring, before it gets too hot; summer on the levee is hot as balls."

And Cord thought to himself, the Spring, that would be a full year, a year in Belvidere - he rarely stayed anywhere that long; Jenny simply wouldn't allow it. But this place was different, for sure, so it was a possibility. He wondered if he would *really* still be here, if he would really keep that promise to Earl. But he knew he had to, even if he had to come back and get him. But he hoped he would have never left. As always, that decision was not his to make. And, of course, there was that small matter of dodging a bullet to the brain, seventeen percent. But he never worried too much about that....not really.

"Okay, now we gotta finally get to No. 8; what's No. 8 Earl?"

Earl didn't hesitate; he answered in a low, somber tone, which brought them full circle.

"I don't want Earl to die."

CHAPTER 238 – SO BAD, MAYBE EVEN A LITTLE GOOD

C looked at Earl with sad eyes.

"That's not really a To-Do, buddy, it's more of a wish, that really can't hold. How 'bout we make No. 8 *Spend a lot of time with Earl, and make him happy*; who knows, that could be for a long, long time, maybe years, even, because he gets better, right?"

Earl half-smiled, wanting to believe his friend. But before he could answer, he saw Ji-Sue's car slowly pull up to the curb by the front walk, just in front of that beautiful red maple, and roll to a stop. The car engine cranked off, and the vehicle sat silent, with no movement inside.

Earl and C sat quiet, patiently staring at the car like dogs at the front door, waiting what seemed forever for something to happen.

And they waited.

C finally got up and half-jogged down the front walk, finding himself at the door. Carol's head was down, with Ji-Sue lightly touching her shoulder. He could see Ji-Sue had been crying.

Earl was afraid to leave his seat.

"What? What?"

He yelled from the porch, high-pitched and cracked, like the voice of a frightened child.

Cord slowly opened the door, and saw Carol's shoulders heaving a bit, but he didn't hear a sound. He looked in the back seat and saw Earl in the carrier, staring blankly ahead, not at him, not really at anything….just staring.

"Hey buddy."

Cord said; then he quietly opened the back door, grabbed
the carrier and brought Earl up to the porch, opened the
grilled-metal swing door, gently extracted him from the
cage and placed him on the loveseat by Earl, who was
crying.

"Don't cry Earl, just give him a kiss; he's been waiting
for that all day from you....you know it makes him feel
better."

And Earl leaned down and kissed Earl on the head, then
lightly scratched under his chin, which got Earl purring.

"There you go; see, that's all he needed."

C said, his eyes red.

"Hey buddy, how you doing? Okay?"

Cord talked to Little-Earl, as Earl lightly scratched his
chin. The snot in Earl's nose blew a bubble in and out,
as he breathed. Cord went to wipe it with his fingers,
but Little-Earl wouldn't let him, too sore from the
constant run.

Carol and Ji-Sue joined them quietly on the porch.
Neither was crying, but both had been, their faces
speckled red, sniffling.

"What's the deal?"

C said matter-of-fact, as he lightly stroked Earl's fat
belly, which had been shaved by the vet. And Carol
spoke, spitting fragments between light sobs.

"He's got....cancer....in his liver, maybe his bones too;
they said he's not in pain, but there's nothing more they
can do for him. She gave me the name....of a....vet in

Bethlehem that….an oncologist, and an internist; maybe they can do something, but they don't think so. They said he's so weak, she's not sure….that…."

"But he's getting fat, and better; look at his belly!"

Earl pleaded, hoping someone would agree.

"He *wasn't* gaining weight Earl; his belly's full of black liquid, it's full of cancer cells….they checked it, they showed it to me."

Carol put her head down; she was mad at how naïve she, they all, had been about his belly and thinking it was a good thing. How could they have been so stupid?

"Did you call the other vet?"

C said, lightly rubbing Earl's distended belly, while he purred.

"Yeah, on the way back. The vet, our vet, talked to her too, and they said they could see him at eight o'clock tonight, or tomorrow morning, early, at five; they're open twenty-four hours, an emergency center, and they could get him in."

"Nah, not tonight; give him a break, enjoy home for a bit on such a nice day. We'll bring him tomorrow morning; I'll bring him, with Ji."

"No, are you *kidding*? I'm going too."

Carol snapped, a bit angry at the presumed exclusion; but C was just trying to give her a small break from all the stress.

"Me too."

Said Earl.

1918

"They gave him a steroid shot, and an appetite enhancer, and a decongestant; maybe it's helping, a little."

Carol's voice trailed off.

And Little-Earl watched the discussion, with blank, distant eyes, laying on the loveseat, next to Earl, as his friend gently scratched under his chin. He was still purring, and things didn't look so bad, maybe even a little good.

CHAPTER 239 – IT WAS ONE SHE WOULD NEVER FORGET

Everyone had left.

Carol rested her head against the rough-hewn, stone wall in the shower; she had stopped crying, but she couldn't keep her mind from racing, so she jumped in the shower to relax, and thought about Little-Earl. He had spent dinner with all of them, sitting quietly on the kitchen island, each telling their favorite Earl stories, as if he was already gone. It was strange, the beginnings of a death watch, even though there may still be hope, options, with the oncologist tomorrow.

Ji stayed next door, at *Boreas*, as did C; Earl had to go home, to take care of Chick and not rile his sister. She wouldn't care two licks about Little-Earl, so Earl never even discussed the topic with his sister.

Carol was dead-tired, emotionally drained. She crawled into bed by 10:30 pm, curled up with her laptop, ready to watch a movie; this was always Little-Earl's favorite time. Whenever she opened the laptop, no matter where he was in the house, that little click of the plastic, laptop hinge would bring him running, ending in a single leap onto the bed, like a dog. He would utter a single, loud meow as his front paws hit the comforter at the end of the pounce, each time; it was his announcement that he'd *arrived*. Then he'd creep slowly over to the laptop, cautious, like it was something new each time, place his head on the edge of the warm keyboard, purr, and watch the lit-screen right along with her; it was their own, little, secret ritual. It was one of Carol's favorites with Little-Earl….one of the best.

But this time, Earl couldn't jump on the bed….he was too weak. So Carol carefully picked him up and placed him on the end of the bed, and he saw the laptop, open, and walked up toward her pillow, plopping down beside it, on the left side, his head barely touching the *Ctrl* button, same exact spot....like always.

Carol looked at him and creased a weary smile; lately she didn't feel like working out, she wasn't horny, or excited about work, or anything; she was wholly consumed by soaking in every second she could with Little-Earl. And she *never* wanted 5 am to come, she didn't want a tomorrow; this was where she wanted to stay, lying in bed, watching movies with Little-Earl's face inches from her, listening to his steady purr....that deep hum was the best ever.

The movie was *The Secretary,* and they both thought it pretty-much-sucked. But with Earl's head, fast asleep on the keys, purring, his side rising and falling with each breath, it was just about the best movie Carol had ever seen, and it was one she would never forget.

CHAPTER 240 – THE MOOD IMPROVED, TILL THE SECOND CALL CAME

Sunday, way early; September 3rd. Day number one-hundred thirty-seven.

"Hey, wake up."

C whispered to Carol, who was curled fetal, wrapped in blankets. She didn't move.

"Hey, come on, it's 3:45; we gotta leave in a half-hour.

Carol stirred, then startle-jumped upright in bed.

"Okay, okay; where's Earl?"

She said, only half-awake, patting the bed around her and seeing he was nowhere in sight.

"I don't know; you get ready, I'll find him. Where's the carrier?"

"We're not using the carrier. I'll carry him in; he can stay on my lap in the car. Look in the front parlor; he's been lying under the couch lately."

Carol said in a just-woke, gravelly voice.

"Okay."

C said quietly as he squeezed her shoulder; then he disappeared from her bedroom. Carol cleared her throat and wiped the sleep from her eyes, upset that tomorrow had come so fast.

The four of them rode in silence; Ji drove, with C shotgun. Carol sat in the back with Earl on her lap, and Earl by her side. Little-Earl sat still, staring straight ahead, with beautiful green eyes, that were simply blank.

There was no other way to describe them. Carol gently pet Earl with one hand and reached over to hold Earl's hand with the other. And Earl let her, without a fuss, and even squeezed her hand every now and then, because his mom always told him a little hand squeeze, at just the right time, meant more than just about anything. Normally Carol would be ecstatic, and Earl terrified at even the thought of holding hands, but they both just stared at the road unfolding before them in silence, with the day's first blush of light painting the sky before them.

It was 5:30 am as the car rolled to a stop in the Allentown parking lot of the veterinarian clinic; it was empty and eerie quiet. The morning sky had just turned, with more light than not, pushing the prior night's darkness aside.

The check-in process took an hour, including a quick physical of Earl by the nursing staff. Both women commented on how sweet Little-Earl was; *sweet* was the term they both used, independent, and it felt genuine, not a standard moniker they gave to all pets that came through the door.

Truth was, Little-Earl *was* sweet, it was the best word to describe him....you just felt it. And so did both nurses, right from the start.

Little-Earl walked gingerly around the examination room floor, Room No. 4, exploring and purring, while they waited for the nurses to return. Carol followed and pet him gently; even a little pressure on the stroke would jar him off his footing.

Carol looked around; it was antiseptic....these kind of rooms always were, even when they tried not to be. But this one didn't try very hard.

She already hated this room, and she hated this place.

The nurse placed him in the weigh-pan; he registered just under seven pounds. Carol knew when he was healthy, he was a solid, muscular fifteen, or more, no fat. She hung her head; more bad news heaped on.

She was tired of bad news.

By 6:30 am, the four of them kissed Little-Earl and were on their way. They were going to keep Earl for the day, run some tests, and would let them know how things panned as they happened; Carol gave them her cell.

Several hours later, as they all sat on the front porch at Carol's, the first call came. Carol nodded her head, pen in hand, writing notes. She flipped the phone shut.

"The first round of blood work is in; he's got a real low red cell count, anemic, but we knew that. But this is the worst reading yet. Good news was his bilirubin was okay, as were the rest of the results for the first battery of tests."

"Good."

C said, shaking his head.

"What's bilirubin?"

Earl asked.

Silence.

"I don't know, I'll look it up."

Carol finally said.

"But whatever it is, it was okay, as was the rest of it; we'll figure out a way to deal with the anemia."

They all nodded in agreement.

And the mood improved, till the second call came.

1925

CHAPTER 241 – IT'S WAY WORSE

Carol listened intently, but her lips were pursed tight, and her writing was fast, and sloppy. She kept asking them to repeat, repeat, repeat, as she wrote furiously, her pen digging into the paper, her voice automaton. The three watchers saw the drain in her face, the longer the call lasted, the quieter it became, and it was quiet to start.

"NO! Absolutely not! *No, No!*"

Carol erupted, and was still shaking her head negative as she listened, as if they could see her on the other end of the line. Then, without warning, she quietly said *thank you....goodbye* and hung up.

She looked up at them, without emotion, a poker-face.

"The other vet, our vet, was wrong; it's not cancer...."

Earl's face cracked into a big smile, and he was just about to stand up and cheer, when Carol finished the sentence.

"....it's way worse."

CHAPTER 242 – SCREAMING NO, *NO, NO!*

"It's called FIP, *Feline Infectious Peritonitis*; it's a virus. Most of the time it doesn't do anything, just sits there, dormant….maybe for life. But sometimes it mutates, or the immune system screws up, but it only happens, not that much, less than ten percent of the time, but when it does *[Carol exhaled a deep breath of regret, and continued]*, then it's bad….*real bad.*"

Carol's head was down, and she was concentrating, speaking technical terms in a slow, even voice, as she carefully tried to decipher her scribble, parsing it to the group. She looked up from her notes, and they all were staring at her, in silence. Head down, she continued.

"It attaches to, and tricks, Earl's immune system, and makes his own immune system attack itself, so instead of trying to fight the virus, he fights himself, killing himself in the process."

"Why can't we tell him to just *stop*….hurting himself? I'll tell him; he'll listen to me!"

Earl pleaded.

"You should try, Earl, if he'll listen to anybody, it'll be you, for sure."

Carol choked up.

"How'd he get it?"

C asked, mad.

"They didn't know; it's not common, not at all. They hardly ever see it, and they see just about everything. It usually happens to cats under two; he's six; it usually happens to cats with feline leukemia, or weak cats – he didn't have leukemia, and he certainly wasn't weak, or sickly. Bottom line, it doesn't make any sense; he should have *never* gotten this disease, no way. But it doesn't have to make sense, it never *has to;* sometimes, it just happens."

Silence.

"They said he could have gotten it a week ago, or even months, even *years* ago, and it sat dormant, just waiting, for something to somehow trigger it. Then, when it got bad, it got bad *quick;* and the signs are all the stuff Earl had – he had them all: runny nose, losing weight, lethargic, weak and a big belly of fluid, even the belly is bad. And as if getting FIP isn't bad enough, he's got the worst kind of FIP, the absolute worst."

Carol put her finger on her notes, so as not to lose her place, and looked up.

"But what about his belly? I thought he was gaining weight? We kept bringing him to gain weight."

Earl was hoping asking the question again would finally change the answer.

Carol looked into Earl's eyes.

"Sweetie, when Ji and I went to pick up Earl, our vet showed us that vial of liquid they took out of Earl's stomach; it was brown-black yucky stuff. They said it was full of cancer; well, they were wrong, it wasn't cancer. Earl hadn't been gaining any weight – none; that fluid is from the virus, from the FIP. It's called *wet,* versus *dry* FIP. Even in FIP, he's got the worse version, the *wet* version. It's called *effusive,* that's what the vet called it, and a tell-tale sign is the distended belly, full of black/brown liquid; they thought the other vet should have figured this out awhile ago. Anyway, they didn't."

"But…."

Earl said, and he didn't say anything else; he didn't know what to say, or ask, he just wanted Carol to say that Little-Earl was gonna get better.

"The antibodies, in Earl, that are supposed to help him, to protect him when he gets sick, they actually turn around and infect, or help to infect, I think, the red blood cells, and they go all through his body. Then everything gets intense, I mean, *fuck*, I can't follow my God-damn notes, not intense, *inflamed*....inflamed....in his belly, kidneys, or his brain. It just keeps getting worse and worse, until it's over. The vet said there's no other virus like it....it's really bad. One of the worst."

"I don't get it; what's *over*? How can we fix it?"

Earl whispered, looking to Carol for help.

And Carol choked up.

"Earl, Little-Earl is *really* sick; he's got something inside him we can't get out, and we can't stop it from hurting him, and from him hurting himself, and there's no way to shut it off. If I could, I would....I would."

She stopped and locked eyes with Earl, then she turned to C and Ji.

"I got other notes, but...."

"But what?"

C said.

"It's too late...."

Carol said, barely above a whisper.

"He's too far along, his red cell count is twelve, twelve *what* I have no idea, but they said it means his organs are

starving for oxygen. And there's no cure for FIP; there's
some experimental stuff they aren't even sure works, but
they can't do it on Earl anyway, he's too weak."

Carol put her head down.

"They asked me if I wanted to put him to *sleep;* why
don't they just say *kill* him and at least be fucking honest
about it. Anyway, I said no, I can't, I won't....no."

"How long? How much time?"

C said, matter-of-fact.

And Carol's face crinkled, and she started crying.

"He might have a stroke first, or go blind, or both, at the
very end. I don't want him to suffer C, not Little-
Earl....not him."

"How long?"

He said again.

She composed herself.

"A week, ten days at the most, probably less....a lot
less."

Without a word, Earl, who had started quietly crying,
jumped up and simply ran wild....off the porch, down
the walk, and into the Park, his hands over his ears,
screaming:

No, *No,* ***No!***

1930

CHAPTER 243 – NO ONE HEARD, BECAUSE SHE WAS ALONE, ALWAYS ALONE

Lilly was half-heartedly surfing for porn, alone in the apartment, when she heard the door open and slam shut, followed by the bedroom slam.

She frowned, rose from her chair and went to the door to deal with another Earl crisis, the kind she had dealt with all her life. She quick-knocked once, perfunctory, as she turned the knob and opened the door, without delay.

"What? What'd he do now? What?"

Lilly assumed it was Cord, it was either him or Carol, and she wasn't going to even acknowledge her.

Earl was fetal, curled away, giving her his back. All she heard was him whimper, quietly.

"I can't help you if you don't tell me."

Lilly's voice went to soothe, and she sat on the edge of the bed, her hand rested gently on his hip.

"Earl's gonna die."

He whispered into the comforter. Lilly sat upright, confused.

"Earl? *Earl who?*"

"Little-Earl, my friend; he's...."

And it hit Lilly.

"Her cat? Her stupid *cat*? Are you crying over...."

And Lilly never saw it coming; how could she, because she had never seen it before.

Earl sat up in a shot, his face already red from crying, turning crimson with anger. He aggressively leaned forward, so their noses just-about touched, and he screamed, at the top of his lungs, into her face.

"Take it back, Lilly; take it back!"

Lilly didn't speak, she couldn't; she was speechless. She held her breath, not sure if she should be scared.

"I *love* Earl, and he's sick, real, real sick, and he can't help it, and he's hurting himself, on the insides, and he doesn't even know it, and he can't even stop it, and we can't help him, it's too late, and he's too weak, and he's all alone, and scared, just like Fred was, and he's only got a week to live, maybe even less! And how would you like it if Aloysius was dying! Who cares, he's just a ***stupid bird***, right Lilly?! **Right?!**"

Earl's face was trembling red as he spit the words at her. Then he jumped up and ran by her, out the bedroom, slamming the apartment door as he bolted down the steps, onto the street. In mere moments, he was long gone.

And Lilly realized, for once, how big a jerk she really was. She quietly walked into her bedroom, crawled into bed, curling fetal. She apologized to Earl, not once, but twice, but no one heard, because she was alone, always alone.

CHAPTER 244 – COMMOTION ERUPTED ON THE BEDROOM FLOOR

Little-Earl looked happy on the porch, moving between stints of rest on the slate seat afront one of the bronze entry lions, the slate walkway and the porch steps. On his own, he jumped on the loveseat, just barely making it, and curled up.

Except for the shaved belly and shaved right paw, for bloodwork, and a perpetual runny nose, he looked deceivingly fine. And he *was* fine, moving slow and a bit unsteady, but curious, alert….almost normal. Maybe he could sense it; no more trips to the vet, no more carriers, needles, poking, prodding….he was done with all that. The Sunday morning sun warmed his black and white coat; he was surrounded by all sizes and shapes of hands, taking turns, scratching and rubbing, here and there. Life, at this particular moment, given the shit-situation, was about as good as it could get.

Earl had come back; he didn't tell them what Lilly said. He simply apologized for running away, and both Carol and Ji gave him a big hug. He didn't have to apologize for loving Little-Earl, Carol said; C patted him on the back, and smiled, without saying a word.

The four of them spent the rest of the morning and a lazy afternoon on the porch, joined by Marty for a bit, who was on shift and stopped more than once to see Ji and Little-Earl.

It was another beautiful late summer gift; perfect weather. Carol took dozens of pictures of Earl, on the loveseat, lying beside the porch steps, sitting beside the bronze lions, regal, and lying with Big B and Zeke, especially Zeke. The two, like best brothers, hung together most of the afternoon, Zeke licking Earl's head and ears, over and over, as they laid beside one another on the porch deck, looking out over the Park. The two had become friends late in the game, and late was better than never.

At Earl's suggestion, Carol recorded Earl's purr, on an old mini-tape recorder she dug out of a desk drawer. They played it back and let little-Earl hear it, but he wasn't much impressed.

At two-o'clock, Carol and Ji gave Earl a steroid and an appetite enhancer – slipping the little pills in his mouth. At one time, the process was gargantuan; Little-Earl fought like crazy when they tried to pry open his mouth. But now, he didn't seem to mind, putting up token resistance. Earl fed him some mayonnaise and poppy-seed dressing, his favorite, and Little-Earl licked his fingers half-clean, then lost interest.

"He's six years and four days old today."

Carol said aloud to no one, for no particular reason, and Earl clapped at the news, smiling. Carol was happy Earl made it to the six year mark, as if that fact somehow mattered.

By five in the afternoon, Little-Earl finally dozed off, lying beside Ji. He had slept, at most, ten minutes the entire day. The steroid kept him awake, until he crashed.

Alas, the nap didn't last; he was wide awake again, less than five minutes later, eyes the size of globes. He wanted to sleep, but couldn't.

Carol was conflicted; the steroids gave him the little energy he had, but she couldn't stand to see him lie there, wide awake, when it was clear he simply wanted to rest, to sleep. She decided against giving him any more pills; no more….no more.

Earl stayed wide-eyed well into the evening. By nine pm, everyone had left, emotional exhaustion. Carol crawled into bed less than twenty minutes later, her mind numb. Like Earl, she had no appetite; she hadn't eaten a thing all day.

She cradled Earl and placed him on the bed, opened her laptop and slipped in another disk, *East of Eden*. But Earl was distracted, and after a few minutes, he left her side, crawling to the end of the bed, alone. He never left his spot beside the laptop when a movie was on; but this time, he did. It broke Carol's heart to see him walk away from her. He stepped into Carol's black overnight bag, the one she took with her from the City for the weekend, and curled into a small ball. Carol heard him settle, but couldn't see him….black cat, in a black bag, enveloped in the darkness of the bedroom, beyond the glow of the laptop screen.

She couldn't stop thinking that he left her side; he had never done that before, not when the laptop was open. She didn't remember dozing off, but it must have been quick, and the movie prattled on alone.

Carol woke in a start, and sat upright; it must have been early morning, still dark, but with the hint of dawn in the sky. Her eyes adjusted as she sat in silence, and the bag at the end of the bed came into focus….it was empty. And she knew Earl had left to go and die.

She sat statue, staring at the bag, half-asleep, exhausted, for what seemed forever. She wasn't going to look for him, not now; she couldn't bear to find him now. At some point, of which she had no recollection, she laid back down and fell asleep.

She rolled over, the clock registered 5:52 am, and her bladder was about to burst. Carol stumbled to the toilet, like she was punch drunk.

And there was Little-Earl, perfectly still, lying by the wardrobe, in the dark.

1935

Earl was alive, his eyes still the size of saucers; he was breathing heavy, through congestion in his lungs.

Carol fetched him some water, and some mayonnaise, but he had no interest in either. She laid on the floor beside him, curling close to his body, her face near his, and pet him gently, in the dark. She was so happy he was still alive, since she had already let him go.

After a bit, she let him be and climbed back into bed. She laid still, staring at the ceiling, wondering what to do, when she felt a presence, the feeling you get somewhere inside you, it must be in your head, but it feels like the pit of your stomach, when you know something is near, something you can't see.

She sat up and saw that Earl was gone; his spot by the wardrobe vacant. She scooted down to the end of the bed, and there was Earl, staring up at her, with the sweetest, most innocent face. She smiled broadly, full of joy, and scooped him up, planting him at the foot of the bed; he was purring lightly.

She went to grab her pillow, to flip her position, feet-to-head, when a sudden commotion erupted on the bedroom floor.

1936

CHAPTER 245 – SHE CRAWLED INTO BED - THE THIRD AND FINAL TIME

Big Banana had cornered a large moth, a behemoth, almost two inches across, and was swatting at it, ready to pounce.

Earl's ears perked, and he leapt off the bed, taking control. Big B stepped back as Earl batted and swatted the moth against the baseboard, alongside the chest-of-drawers, with energy Carol hadn't seen in days, in weeks. And that small act brought her happiness; a glimpse of the old Earl.

She didn't let him kill the moth; she cupped it and let it go out the dressing room window; it lit and disappeared into the cryptomeria, beside the front porch. On his own, Earl had followed Carol and jumped on the dressing room sill and stared at the crytomeria, stoic, striking a regal pose, a lion in control.

And that's how she remembered him, as she crawled into bed - the third and final time.

1937

CHAPTER 246 – *EXACTLY....SHE SAID; EXACTLY*

Monday, September 4th, Labor Day; one-hundred thirty-eight days inside the rabbit hole.

Little-Earl was gone again, and the day began as the last one ended, a roller-coaster. And, as Carol laid in bed, she wondered who this whole process was truly for, Little-Earl, or her?

A death-watch is exhausting; layers of emotion constantly competing with one another. Carol had always spent time with Little-Earl, during the entirety of his life, but was it *enough*? Was it *ever* enough? And cramming in time now? For who's benefit? And obsessing about his every move, and spending all her waking time attending to him: petting, looking, listening, documenting, daydreaming, reminiscing, bear-hugging every second of every minute, as if it's the last, and when it's not, bear-hugging the next, and the next, prolonging the process, stretching it to breaking; who did it really serve? And how long could it last? At what point does it switch from love, and tender care, to guilt, and hopelessness, and simply pathetic?

But Carol was powerless to stop it; there was no way she could stop, to do so would feel like giving up on Earl, on failure, on giving in to the virus, to death. And she *wouldn't* do it, she *couldn't* do it.

Lying in bed, Carol raised her legs and did some half-hearted leg lifts; it didn't feel like exercising when lying on a mattress, but she did them just the same. Ebi jumped on her chest, wanting to be pet, as Carol strained to keep her legs aloft. Carol whispered to her about how sick her brother was, as she ran her hand down Ebi's back and tail; it was a respite to see how healthy little Eb was, not a care, other than wanting to be forever pet.

Carol found Earl downstairs; he followed her into the kitchen, another ritual he had done his whole life, the past six years. Carol in the kitchen, in the morning, meant food. And it seemed part of Earl wanted to eat, or at least wanted to maintain the morning process, a creature of habit….a cat.

Carol got the food ready for them all; she picked Earl up and placed him on the counter, his usual spot. He lapped two licks of tuna oil, but that was it; then he sat, meatloaf-style, in the open dish-towel drawer, to the right of the sink. Carol found an old shoestring in the kitchen drawer and ran it by Earl, like she always used to do. He got excited, trapping it under his paw once, then twice, staring at it like he did as a kitten. But just as quick, he stopped, too weak to play. He laid his head down and closed his eyes, his tongue-tip sticking from his lips; Carol was relieved – the steroid must have finally worn off. She just wanted him to rest, peaceful.

It was another gorgeous day; sun-soaked, with nary a cloud, just a wisp of white here and there. Earl, C and Ji were all back; the four of them hung with Little-Earl, Zeke, Hunter and Big B on the porch again. Little-Earl made the rounds, chasing ants on the sidewalk, stalking some unknown quarry hiding in the English ivy and staring down a rogue squirrel digging in the front yard. And in those times, it was if Earl wasn't even sick, like the whole episode was a bad dream, easily whisked away.

Carol had decided to give him another appetite enhancer and half a steroid, even though she convinced herself yesterday she would do no such thing. Her decisions were all near-term….right now, and malleable.

It was a little after noon; Earl and Earl were on the loveseat together alone; they had just switched spots. Carol and C were in the kitchen, along with Ji, making lunch. Earl's fur was warm in the sun, curled up, beside his friend, laying on a newspaper trying to sleep.

She walked the Third Street sidewalk, going the long way around, the perimeter, instead of cutting across the center of the Park. It delayed the arrival time, which was fine by her.

Up ahead a group of ten high school girls were making noise, standing in three-line formation, hair in ponytails, or pulled into messy buns atop their heads. It was a kaleidoscope of red, blue and tan short-shorts, mixed with orange, pink, white and red tee-shirts. In the dappled sun of the Park, the young girls shot their hands to the sky, then punched the air before them, clapping hard, before chopping toward the ground in emphatic drill strokes.

Seaters….Hold….That Line!
Seaters….Hold….That Line!

"Hi Lilly!"

The head cheerleader called out, as Lillian slowly strolled past the group; a couple other *hi's* trickled from the formation. She smiled and half-raised her hand to return the greeting, but Lilly didn't say a word.

The girls broke formation and started gabbing and giggling about things Lilly couldn't hear, and didn't give a shit about. One girl did a hand-stand, while another scratched her calf with her shoe; most just stood, hands on hips, waiting for the next practice cheer.

The girls regrouped and got in line, ready for the next shout-out:

Seaters….Score….Six More!
Seaters….Score….Six More!

Earl never saw his sister till she was standing on the sidewalk afront Carol's house, beside the red maple; she was happy no one was on the porch but Earl.

"Is that Earl?"

She said, loud enough for Earl to hear, but no louder.

Earl swung his head and saw Lilly, and he smiled wide, rubbing Earl's belly in the sun.

"Yeah, this is *Little-Earl;* we call him Little-Earl so as not to confuse anyone with me. It can get pretty confusing, you know."

Lilly smiled; she knew her brother would forgive her, but was happy to be sure.

"You wanna say hi?"

Earl asked his sister.

"I don't know, Earl; I don't think I'm wanted, you know, on the property."

And before her brother could answer, Little-Earl put his head up, without warning, and hopped off the loveseat. He walked over to the steps and looked out over the Park. Then, he walked down the steps and into the lawn, right toward Lilly, stopping three feet in front of her, in the shade of the lawn. And he just stared at her.

Earl sat flabbergasted.

"Lilly, he doesn't do that for *anybody*....***ever!*** Pet him, Lilly! He's so sweet, and he likes you!"

Lilly smiled, took a few steps into the lawn, bent down on one knee in the soft lawn and carefully rubbed Earl's chin. He closed his eyes and started to purr.

1941

"I can hear him purring all the way up here! He *really* likes you Lilly!"

Earl shouted.

And Lilly ran her hand down Earl's back, and she could feel every bone in his back; and she felt horrible for the things she said to Earl, about Little-Earl.

"Hi, I'm Lilly....hi."

She whispered to Little-Earl, so low that even her brother couldn't hear her.

The front door bounded open, Ji carrying a plate of lettuce, tomato and onion sandwiches, a six-pack of *Vernors* and bowls of just-washed plump raspberries and crisp bing cherries.

"Wow!"

Earl said, 'cause he was hungry.

Ji caught Lilly's eye, and stopped short; the other two bumped into the back of her. And both C and Carol saw Lilly kneeling in the grass, a mere fifteen feet of yard separated them.

Lilly spoke first, directing caring eyes toward Carol.

"Sorry, I was just passing by; I'm sorry he's so sick."

Those were the first kind words Lilly had said to Carol, ever. *Ever.*

The next practice cheer erupted in the background:

Touchdown....Seaters....Let's Go!
Touchdown....Seaters....Let's Go!

1942

"Whoa, half-time entertainment, just in time!   Very nice, very."

C said, slicing the awkwardness.

"Thanks. Would you like a sandwich, or some fruit?"

Carol said in a soft, kind voice to Lilly, ignoring C. Lilly stood, and smiled, shaking her head no.

"I was just passing, don't want to...."

"Lilly have a sandwich; they're the best!   They're *LTO's*!"

Earl grabbed a sandwich and a bowl of fruit and bolted off the porch, before Lilly could escape.

"Did Little-Earl go down there *on his own*?"

Carol asked aloud, looking at Little-Earl lying content in the thick grass beside Lilly's feet.

Both Ji and C shrugged their shoulders.

"Earl, I shouldn't be here."

Lilly whispered.

"Why not? You're my sister! And Earl likes you!"

Earl and Lilly sat on the lawn, side-by-side, knees pulled up to their chests, with Little-Earl between them, backs to the porch. Little-Earl rested his head against Lillian's ankle, and the top of her shoe, and closed his eyes. She creased a small smile at the gesture, and Earl beamed at his sister and Little-Earl.

"Earl, do you remember when we used to sit on this lawn as kids, when Doc Beaumont was here?

Remember we used to think about all the animals that....”

Lilly stopped herself, sorry she brought up the mortal thought.

“Anyway, I remember this lawn, sitting right about here, you and me, as kids. It's a lot nicer now than it was then. I remember *really* liking just sitting here, looking out over the Park.”

“I remember Lilly; like it was yesterday.”

Earl leaned over and kissed his sister on the cheek.

“See, isn’t Earl sweet? He *really* likes you; he doesn’t do this with anybody - he usually runs away.”

“He would if he knew me better.”

Lilly said, half-sarcastic, half feeling sorry for herself.

“So, you gonna go down and sit with her?”

C whispered, leaning against the rail, his back to Lilly and Earl, chiding Carol.

“No, I’m not going to do anything. She came to see Earl, not me, and I care about Earl, and his sister is important to him, so she’s important to me. I care about Lilly; I can’t stand her, but I care about her.”

Carol was whispering back matter-of-fact.

“Why is Little-Earl down there?”

Carol said, trying to look around C, who was blocking her view.

“I bet Earl brought him down.”

1944

"Earl was on the porch; he didn't bring him down —
Little-Earl went down there all on his own. You know,
maybe Little-Earl likes Lilly, ever think of that?"

Carol shot him a dagger.

"Hey, if Earl's happy, *both* Earl's, then *you* should be
happy, and take a break, and have a sandwich."

Another chorus erupted from the Park.

.

> ***Touchdown....Seaters....Score Six!***
> ***Touchdown....Seaters....Score Six!***

"What the fuck is a *Seater?*"

C said, suddenly annoyed at the cheers.

"It's the High School name, the Seaters, as in the County
Seaters; you know, the Courthouse."

Carol pointed over to the obvious, half a block away.

"*The Seaters?*   I'm sure that strikes fear into the
opposing team!   Watch out, here come the *Seaters!*
What exactly does a *Seater* look like, by the way?   A
politician? Now that *would* be scary."

"A raccoon!"

Earl yelled, behind him.

C turned.

"A raccoon?"

"Yeah, that's the animal to have representing you, a
fucking raccoon!"

C laughed.

"You mean, we're not lions, or tigers, or bears? Instead, we're politicians, represented by a raccoon? Well, a raccoon kind of looks like a criminal, so makes sense. Good God, I wouldn't want to be a cheerleader for a bunch of fucking raccoons."

C looked out over the Park at the ten nubiles. Eight of them were thin, one was a heifer, and one was quasi. I guess these days you had to have some chunky cheerleaders on the team, equal opportunity. The older girls were scolding some of the newbies for not screaming loud enough, making them practice their call-outs alone, over and over. But for the most part, it seemed pretty relaxed; a bunch of young girls giggling and hanging out. And the thin ones had....C's daydream was interrupted.

"Stop drooling."

Carol said condescendingly, seeing C creepy-guy leering at the girl's gyrations in the Park.

"What? I'm not doing anything."

C said.

"It's what you're *thinking,* and I know it's not good; it never is."

The girls moved onto the next cheer:

You Got The Ball, We Want The Ball,
Hey….Defense….Defense!
You Got The Ball, We Want The Ball,
Hey….Defense….Defense!

1946

"You know, not everything's about sex."

C snapped back.

"Uh huh; what were you thinking then? As you were staring out into the Park, with your mouth open?"

C just looked at her, *mokusatsu* - Japanese silence - when you're busted, with nothing much to say.

"Exactly....

she said;

Exactly."

CHAPTER 247 – IN HER HEAD; NOTHING, AND EVERYTHING

Carol didn't know whether to be jealous, or grateful.

Little-Earl was curled up beside Lilly, and Lillian was gently running her long, thin fingers over his back and rear leg; she couldn't see Earl's face, but she figured he was asleep – she hoped so.   Why Little-Earl slept for her, and not Carol, she figured was because he was mad at her, for keeping him alive, making him eat that awful sticky supplement, giving him the steroid that kept him awake....all of it. It really made no sense – Little-Earl wasn't *punishing* her, but that's the way it felt, to Carol. A slight, that really hurt, from a little-boy she loved so much.

The trio stayed that way for a good hour or so, backs to the porch, Lilly and Earl talking quietly, touching each other now and again, with affection; and one or the other, or both, always had a hand on Little-Earl, petting him gently. Lilly at times leaned into her brother, head resting lightly on his shoulder.

And while Carol talked quietly with C and Ji, and their conversation rambled, she kept a constant eye on the three of them on the front lawn. And although emotions were certainly mixed, overall, she was truly happy - she couldn't believe it - but she was happy to have Lilly there, on *her* lawn, her own little safe island, making both Earl's feel better.

And she felt good about herself for feeling that way, by being a better person, an adult. She smiled, a bit proud of herself for being a grownup in a situation where she could have easily been a child.

"What's that cheeser for?"

C asked, seeing Carol smiling at nothing, looking blank
into the distance, beyond the Green.

"Nothing."

She said aloud.

And everything she said in her head; nothing, and
everything.

1949

CHAPTER 248 – WHISPERING WHAT SHE KNEW WAS THE TRUTH. *BUSTED*

Earl eyed it nervously, looking up at Lilly, and back at the plate, and back up at Lilly. She smiled, knowing the game; they had played it since they were kids. She finally killed the suspense, and gave the go-ahead.

"Yes, you can have the rest of the sandwich."

She said flatly, as she ran her fingers through Earl's soft fur on his side, and on the shaved part of his warm pink and white belly. Earl smiled and inhaled the *LTO* before Lilly changed her mind. She had only taken a bite and a half, and a couple raspberries off the second plate.

"You *really* like her?"

Lilly was surprised the words actually left her lips. She wasn't sure what part of her brain gave the go-ahead; those thoughts were usually tightly controlled, and swam endlessly in her head.

"Yeah."

Was all Earl said, drawn out; he smiled mischievously through the response, thinking good thoughts about Carol.

"You would like her too, Bibby, you really would, and she wants to be your friend."

Lilly huffed; it was almost as if that reaction was preprogrammed. Then, after a bit of reflection, she let out a long sigh; she was so tired of the endless fight.

"Someday Earl, maybe, someday; just not yet, okay?"

He rubbed Lilly's back.

"Did you like the sandwich? Ji's a good sandwich maker, especially *LTOs*."

Lilly nodded her head yes, without answering.

"Hey Lilly, how come you're not talking to C? He thinks you don't like him again."

Lilly looked down, then over to Little-Earl, and scratched along his cheek; his nose was full of snot and a little blood. Without a thought, she gently wiped it away, rubbing the crust stuck to her fingers in the grass, and surprisingly, Little-Earl didn't fuss when she did.

"It's complicated."

Was her non-answer.

"*What's complicated?* It's not complicated Lilly, not even to me, and I'm not very smart, especially about stuff like that. You're *way* smarter than me, so it shouldn't be complicated to you, not by a long shot. He likes you, you like him, so why don't you...."

"I don't *like* him Earl."

Lilly snapped, keeping her voice low, cutting him off.

And Earl turned to look at her, put his hand on her cheek, to turn her eyes toward his.

"Say it again; look right at me and say that you don't like him Bibby, and *don't* fib; you know I can always tell when your fibbing."

Earl looked into her eyes, and she into his, and she was silent.

Earl slowly smiled sly at her, and she cracked the faintest of smiles herself; she couldn't help it.

1951

And Earl stole one of C's favorite lines, whispering what she knew was the truth.

"Busted."

1952

CHAPTER 249 – SHE KNEW, FOR SURE, THAT EARL WAS ALREADY DEAD

It was still Monday, Labor Day; the weekend had been an emotional anchor.

Carol got in the car; it was already dark, later than it should have been, to head back into the City. She had multiple meetings with investors, sites to scout and a half-dozen already-late financial reports to run; it was going to be a crazy week.

And she really didn't give a shit about any of it.

She gathered her belongings and called Ji, asking her to come over tonight and sleep at the house, all week, which, of course, she said she would. She'd be there in an hour, or so.

Carol looked at Earl, sitting in the second floor hall, dropped her bags and knelt down, caressing his lower belly. Earl always had a hanging belly – more loose skin than anything else - like an empty, furry bag, and Carol had always loved to pinch it gently between her fingers, and it always made Earl purr. But now, it was a round pouch, a water balloon full of black toxic liquid….disease, and she hated it, knowing what it was.

As she gently caressed his belly, Earl didn't purr. And she frowned, her head dropping in defeat. She moved her hand up to his face, and rubbed gently under his chin. And to her surprise, Earl let out an almost imperceptible purr. It was short, ending almost as soon as it started, and she almost didn't hear it. But she did, and it made her smile.

She didn't know it, but it was the last one Carol would ever hear.

1953

She kept eye contact with him all the way down the steps, saying *Bye Sweetie* over and over, till she couldn't see him anymore.

And the back door closed quietly behind her, and the house was dark, lit only by the second floor hall light, set on a low dim.

She was on the road less than ten minutes; she hadn't made it back to Route 80, she hadn't even made it to the Halloween sycamore, feeling horrible about leaving, half-listening to the radio, which was playing softly, mindlessly flipping stations on scan-mode, one after another.

Then she heard the song, and Carol knew he was talking directly to her:

> *'....that long black cloud is comin' down;*
> *I feel like I'm knocking on heaven's door;*
> *Knock, knock, knocking on heaven's door'*

A rush of dread washed over her. When do you ever hear Bob Dylan on the radio anymore, and how often do you hear *that* song?

And now? *Now?*

It was a sign; Earl was dying, right now, in a dark house.....*all alone.*

She never looked to see if anyone was coming the other way; she simply slammed on the brakes and U-turned the *Spider* in the middle of the dark road, kicking rocks in the shoulder and pointed the car back to Belvidere....back home.

Before she could slam the accelerator to the floor, out of nowhere, a lone bat appeared, and flew alongside the car, windshield level. It kept up with her for thirty-odd yards, fluttering up and down like it was drunk, side-by-side with her driver's door, no more than ten feet from her window, ten feet from her head, traveling about forty miles per hour, till it just as suddenly veered to the left and disappeared into the blackness.

Gone.

The whole weird encounter lasted less than five seconds; as quickly as it happened, it was over. She looked at the empty scene out her window, the darkened woods whizzing by, still processing the strangeness that just happened. Nothing like that had ever happened to her before; she wondered if it had ever happened to *anybody* before.

The hair on her arms rose, and then she knew, for sure, that Earl was already dead.

1955

CHAPTER 250 – SHE HAD BECOME A ZOMBIE

He wasn't.

She sprinted into the house and up the steps in a *tourbillion*, out of breath, already crying, expecting the worse.

Little-Earl was sitting quietly in the same spot she left him, staring blank down the dimmed hall. When he was young, when he was healthy, he would have been hiding under the bed at the first rattle of the door knob; but now, he never moved, nor even acknowledged her presence, as she laid on the hall carpet beside him, emotionally spent.

Carol didn't move for five minutes; she just stared at the ceiling in silence, listening to herself quietly catch her breath, as Earl stared down the hall, in a bun beside her.

Carol unpacked and stayed home, for the entire week. She would work from Belvidere; she had remote access to her files at the office, and any papers she needed, she'd get a courier to deliver. Meetings would be rescheduled, or done via conference call, or not done at all.

Simple.

And Little-Earl and Carol spent the next four days together, not that it was good.

After Labor Day, his occasional bursts of energy, his bright eyes, and, of course, his purr, one by one, faded away. What was left was a shell; comatose eyes staring blankly at nothing, sitting quiet under a couch, under the bed, under something, always in a bun, with the tip of his tongue extended.

Any other time, that picture would be adorable; it was anything but.

He wobbled when he walked, and couldn't keep his front paws clean; they had a tinge of brown, like a feral, and as much as Carol tried to clean them with a moist towel, she just couldn't get them white again. And his beautiful coat of black and white acquired a tinge of mange, a symptom of the virus she simply couldn't brush away, no matter how much she tried. His nose was caked with dried snot, mixed with blood, and a constant dribble of fresh green mucous ran from his always-sore nostrils.

Carol couldn't help feeling Little-Earl was mad at her, unhappy with all her mostly-failed attempts at cleaning him, and feeding him. Getting the goo in, and the appetite enhancer, and the steroid, it was a constant three-prong assault. The fur on his left cheek was coated thick with the dried molasses goop that didn't make it in his mouth; it was like glue in his fur....she couldn't get it off. And she vacillated as to what to do with each hour; but, in the end, she always knew she couldn't stand by and watch him starve.

Organ failure was going to be the issue; what a shit choice - organs or starvation, but that was the hand they had been dealt.

She lined up all his favorites: pistachios, tuna oil, treats, sardine juice, mayonnaise, milk, ice cream, poppy-seed dressing; he ate none of it. The last solid food was a single square chicken-treat; he ate that on Tuesday morning, the same day she got a full syringe of food in his mouth. Two small victories in a war that was already lost.

But that was it, no other food, nothing but partial shots of goo.

1957

Earl spent a part, most actually, of every day and every evening at Carol's that week, along with Ji. He helped her with chores, pet Little-Earl, talked to Little-Earl, laid beside Little-Earl, helped Ji some more, and looped the routine over and over again. In-between, he went down to Sam's, stocking shelves, and spent a bit of time at the farm, helping Marty's dad with late-summer chores. C stopped in periodic, less often as the days passed, and didn't stay long, since Carol was deep in work most of the time, staring at her laptop, near wherever Little-Earl happened to be sitting bun.

Carol had spent just about every waking hour in Earl's view. At night, she set her alarm every one to three hours, she lost track sometimes, and woke to search the house to ensure he was okay.

Over and over and over.

She couldn't bring herself to sleep through the night, obsessed that he would be alone, dead for hours, by the morning.

Carol didn't know what possessed her to act like she was, but she couldn't help herself; if she thought about stopping, about letting go, she would feel as if she wasn't trying hard enough….that she failed, somehow.

And she wouldn't apologize to anyone for it, or her behavior, and fuck anyone who felt different, or didn't approve. She loved Little-Earl, and this felt like the right thing to do.

She had become a zombie.

CHAPTER 251 – IT SIMPLY WASN'T SAFE, AND HIS THOUGHTS WENT DARK

Thursday, September 7, 2006; day one-hundred forty-one. Third floor, above the *Palace Of Sweets.*

C had largely divorced himself from the death-watch, and because of it, hadn't seen Carol nor Ji for much of the last four days, or even Earl, for that matter, since he spent most waking hours at *L'antre du Lion.*

He and Earl hadn't run together in awhile; he went solo for some longer jaunts, five and six miles, watching the fields of corn and soybean grow, along roadside ditches painted a beautiful, dusty blue - wild chickory. He caught up on his pile of unread newspapers, scanning most articles, ripping others out, for what reason he didn't know, because he didn't feel much like sharing them with anyone. He started *1984* again, flipping to a random page to read, but quickly stopped; it wasn't the right book….not now. He was thinking about going back to Sam's to help out, but it largely fleeting – it never got past the *think* stage. Invariably, he found himself alone, in his apartment, playing with Chick, talking to Jonsey - Earl was letting him visit - and debating as to whether he should jerk off again, and if so, to what. Invariably, the answer was no; his head didn't have much interest, and neither did his dick. It was too much work, and he was bored with the same stale stories, rehashed too many times, of fucking Mae, or Carol, or Margery, or Samantha, or Linda, or Selena, or whomever, or watching them get fucked by someone else. He couldn't even bring himself to think about fucking Lilly, it was just depressing, since it was never going to happen, and he certainly wasn't going to think about her getting fucked by someone else, since he knew who that inevitably would be, even though that prick was long post-bloat, and must be pretty well rotted off the bone by now, wedged deep in the *Big Crack.*

But it didn't matter, even as a corpse, Button still *owned* Lilly; he probably always would.

He *never* saw Lillian; she was physically less than twenty feet from him most days, her holed up in her apartment, he in his right above her, but she might as well have been a thousand miles away. And C had a hunch early on that she was purposely avoiding leaving and entering her apartment at times when she might run into him. Sensing the slight, he doubled-down, and modified his schedule to ensure he *never* ran across her either. So here they were, physically close, but never seeing, talking nor interacting in any way, other than practiced avoidance; two middle-aged juveniles, and neither would budge.

They were both stubborn, and miserable.

Cord wondered when he would ever see real pussy again, and got pissed that he threw away that sure bet called Mae with the whole Margery gym fiasco. Then after the Fair, with a second shot within reach, along came the Lilly and Button chaos, and he let it slip again, never calling her, or even trying to further mend the fence. The last time he saw Mae, or even spoke to her, was bedside, the day after the barn. That seemed to go well, with her and Margery, but after that, nothing. Mae never reached out; he was sure it was a test – her putting the onus on him to take the next step. And of course he dropped that ball; Christ, that was *four weeks ago*.

Stupid, stupid, stupid he thought as he knocked his fist against his thigh. Four weeks? That potential open invitation to pussy was long past stale, right? What the hell; maybe he should give it another shot; what the fuck was there to lose? He couldn't be in a worse dog house than he had already been. Maybe he should call Mae *right now*; maybe he'd be deep between her legs within an hour, maybe two hours at most, depending on how patient he was with the negotiations.

1960

But C decided the whole matter was a *no* before he finished the carnal thought. Too much work, too much baggage; not worth the effort. Jerking-off was much easier, and devoid of the drama. But he did miss tagging that little senior pussy.

He just finished smoking his second cigar, blowing the smoke out the front window screen – clearly a violation of Landlord rules. His stomach was sour; it always got sour on the second blunt, even if they were *DeMuths*. He had smoked more cigars the past three days than he had in the past three months, always alone, keeping quiet company with a glass of port, or a cognac, or a bourbon, or an Irish whiskey, or a Scotch, or a shot of vodka, or some combination thereof. All neat, and always in excess.

Somehow, he wasn't sure quite how, he made his way from the window, overlooking the sidewalk afront *Nonpareil,* and now found himself prone in bed, in black boxer briefs and a white tee, with a limp dick, a sour stomach and a haze in his head; he lost count after he downed the sixth shot of chilled *Stoli Elite*. He drank a slew of grain before that, and he might have drank more after, but we wasn't entirely sure if he did, or what it was. He was sure it was lots of something.

And it was then, with that toxic slosh of alcohol and tobacco coursing his veins, that he felt her whisper quietly in his ear; it was a confused mumble that made no sense, but he recognized the voice all-the-same.

He hadn't thought about her in awhile, but over the last day or so, she had started to creep into his conscious thoughts, mornings mostly, but she also appeared at random, like now, and it was occurring more and more. And that was always a harbinger, and a bad one.

And he resigned himself to the fact that his time in this place was coming to a close, he *felt* it. Jenny was coming to visit…..soon; that was the garbled message, that was becoming ever-more crystal clear.

C slowly ran his fingers along the herring gull feather as he laid in bed, staring at the ceiling, trying to focus on beginnings, and endings. And inexplicably, his mind started to race, heart beating wildly in his chest.

C clenched his eyes and tightly clutched the feather, trying to redirect, and slowly, his heart calmed and his thoughts drifted to the herring gull lying on the cold, stony shore, with dead eyes, rocking gently with each lap of waves at the high tide-line. It was a drizzly, gray and ugly New Year's Day, and it seemed as if the gull was waiting patiently for him to pass by, to rescue, or to imprison. Maybe one and the same. To C, that day, that dead gull, was the unfortunate end he knew too well, that visited far too often. But it was also, for the single feather he plucked, for him, a new beginning, that would finally turn out well; it meant both to C, always did, or at least it was always supposed to. But the *finally* never seemed to come.

He didn't remember falling asleep.

Cord opened his eyes, and found himself, alone, in that familiar room, in that immense old house he'd been in so many times before, although he couldn't tell you where it was, or how to get there, or how to leave; he only ever arrived there in manner, and was always just *there*, never on his way to, or from.

And he was always alone.

And as he stood statue, staring at the wall, the water began to drip from the ceiling, and the drip morphed to a steady, hair-thin stream, a barely cracked faucet, like it always did, and the dread sunk in, as the puddle slowly expanded on the wooden floor, beside his shoe.

1962

He found himself atop the attic stairs, although he didn't know how he got there, from where he just was. And he looked to his right, like he always did, always to the right, and the unfinished attic space was immense and old; exposed, century-old wooden rafters from the steeply pitched roof sheltered piles of forgotten unknowns, stacked haphazard, hidden forever under tarps and dusty linens. The air was thick, musty and stale, with just enough filtered light from a small louver at the gable end to illuminate the scene in a dull pallor.

And he was scared to death.

He knew he had to walk to his right, but he didn't want to go. He could hear the water run from some distant, unseen hole in the roof, the patter of the insidious liquid hitting the attic floorboards, before it disappeared, absorbed into the bowels of the house, causing unseen damage and destruction as it traveled south, infecting all it touched.

And as he stood still, the sound of the breach was getting louder, the leak growing ever-larger.

Before he took his first step, he saw the shadow dart across the far wall; it was *big*, scary-big, standing upright, hunched and amorphous. It knew he was there, and it knew he was coming its way. It dodged between the tarps and linens and went quiet - hidden, soundless....lying in wait.

He only ever saw it once; he never, ever saw it more than once. But he knew it was close to the leak, and it was waiting for him.

He walked toward the water, and the attic path between head-high piles of unknowns narrowed. He brushed against the monstrous tarps with his arms, and the chafe made an indescribable sound, one that meant no good was on its way. His heart raced as he passed each blind, black, side-aisle, hidden between the looming piles; he was waiting to be sucked into the blackness by it, whatever *it* was.

He found himself beside the water source, dropping from far overhead, some unseen breach; stray droplets of water splayed his face. He was surrounded by tall sheets, covered in dust and web, and found himself staring at the closest linen, inches from his face, and it seemed to move, just a bit, like it was breathing, but then it wasn't, and he wasn't sure if it ever really did.

He searched for a pan, or a bucket, and always found one, conveniently nearby. He placed it under the leak, and watched the water collect in the vessel, fixated. It would begin to fill, but it would never get very far. Because that was always when he would hear a strange noise; each time it was different.

This noise, *this time*, sounded like a shuffle, and a peck, and a scratch. An agitation of some sort, and it was right behind him, inches away, close enough to almost touch him.

He could feel the flesh-creep, and the spook crept his spine, as he slowly turned to eye whatever it was, standing right behind him. And he knew this was the end.

But behind him was nothing but emptiness, the color of ink....thick with nothingness.

The water had stopped, and silence rang his ears, save his own slow, steady breathing, at least he thought it was just him, or was something breathing in tandem, just beyond the thicket of shadows.

He felt its unseen eyes upon him, breathing low and heavy; it was so dark, *it* could have been inches away, yet still unseen. He never thought to close his eyes, but

1964

he should have. He simply stared into the gloom for whatever was there, hiding in the shadow, just beyond, wondering when it would attack.

He abruptly held his breath, and it was deathly quiet; *it* stopped breathing whenever he did, a perfect mimic. His breath still held, he debated as to when to breathe again, to trick it, but he felt it in his head, and it was thinking the same things he was thinking, at exactly the same time.

He didn't remember ever breathing again, his breath held forever.

And in that state, slowly, from the blackness, emerged the faint outline of something moving steadily toward him; he was frozen, unable to move. It morphed into some sort of box, a rectangle, with a shiny oval in the middle, a single eye, but not. It looked to be the size and shape of a hopper window, like a casement on its side, but he wasn't sure why he thought that, because it wasn't a window at all, as much as it was a solid panel, somehow built into the eaves, which had come right up to his face. He reached for the eye, which was now a handle, to twist it, to drop the panel open, tilting in, towards him, to reveal itself.

But his hand didn't grab the handle, a hooked talon did, where his hand should have been, and an immense vulture materialized beside him, obsidian. And as the panel fell open, the vulture simply stood beside him in silence, haunting him with a single jet-black eye, the side of its hooked beak inches from his face.

And within the box, was revealed a dirty, divided window, compartmentalized somehow, with each pane containing a black crow, squawking loudly, as if they were hungry, and trapped….and wanted out. There must have been a half-dozen, a cacophony of caws filled his

1965

ears. And he couldn't understand what it was they were trying to say.

And he realized the vulture had since disappeared, dissolved into the shadows.

He looked to his right, and saw something squirm, like a white larvae, a large grub, alongside the wall, half in the wall, above a sofa that he hadn't noticed before. He took a step closer, and it morphed into some sort of newborn kitten, small enough to fit in his palm, surrounded by shredded paper and straw, as if in a nest. He looked closer and realized it wasn't a kitten at all, but some sort of mouse, and soon other newborn mice emerged from their hiding places in the shreds, as if they trusted him. They were weak, and blind, and vulnerable, and he worried they would be eaten, all of them....and soon.

It simply wasn't safe, and his thoughts went dark.

1966

CHAPTER 252 – THE CRICKET DISAPPEARED INTO THE NIGHT

It was still Thursday, but late, three minutes shy of midnight, when Earl's phone rang. They were both still up.

That specific ring-tone meant only one thing, only one caller. Normally, Lilly would make some smart-ass comment, which Earl would ignore, but this time, Lilly was worried, and sincere.

"Pick it up Earl!"

She yelled.

"Hello?"

He said, tentatively, even though he knew who it was. And then he listened, and Lillian thought the worst.

"I'll be right over; I'll bring C too, okay….okay."

And he flipped the phone shut.

*"What? **What?**"*

"She can't find Earl; she's crying."

"Well, get over there, and find him! Hurry up! *Run!* And call me!"

And Earl darted out the door, up the steps, and, seconds later, back down, with C in tow, still drunk, half-asleep, in his boxers and tee, with black penny loafers on his feet. Cord didn't remember a lick of his fucked-up dream, which was a good thing.

After a five-block half-sprint, because C simply couldn't run any faster in his shoes, and in his condition, they found themselves at Carol's, with Cord out of breath. Then the three systematically searched the house, high and low, for a good half-hour.

No Little-Earl.

Carol was a mess.

After another half-hour, on the third pass of the third-floor guest bedroom, C noticed a tiny floorboard ajar, along the front wall; a remnant of recent, sloppy air conditioning repair by the contractor. Ay laid on his belly, with a flashlight, his stomach still cigar-sour, and, in the darkness, he saw Little-Earl; twenty feet away, much too far to reach, sandwiched between the joists, facing away, in a bun, not moving, despite repeated calls of his name.

"He's dead...."

Carol said softly.

"I can't tell that; I'm not sure. *Earl!*"

C shouted in frustration, his head still in a fog. But nothing happened, and he didn't move.

"He can't even walk, and he comes to the third floor and crawls in this little fucking hole in the floor; *are you kidding me!*"

C said aloud, spitting mad, to no one in particular.

Two hours later, after ripping up more floorboards with a claw hammers and crowbars, and opening a portion of the floor in the Billiard Room, C ran a metal, retractable tape measure between the joists in the spare bedroom, gently poking Earl in the back.

1968

But he still didn't move, and the tape bent, and fell to the side.

"Fuck! Earl! *Earl!*"

Nothing.

"He's dead; he died all alone."

Carol started to quietly cry. C was sweaty, nauseous and exhausted.

Earl lightly tapped C on the shoulder, and Cord gave way. Earl laid down, and half-stuck his head in the hole, and spoke gently to Little-Earl. And just like that, Earl moved. But it was five feet further away, never turning, never making a noise.

"He's alive! But he ain't coming out; he's going the other way toward the Game Room!"

Earl said exasperated.

"He hates me."

Carol said, rubbing the bags under her eyes. C shook his head at Lilly's brother.

"Why didn't we have *you* talk to him *two fucking hours ago?*"

Earl quietly got up and went to the Billiard Room, laid on the floor and started talking gently to Earl; as C ran out the metal measuring tape again, gently prodding Earl in the backside. Finally, after another twenty minutes of coaxing, Earl simply walked, slowly, the rest of the way, right into Earl's hands, like the whole ordeal was nothing but a bother. Carol kissed him on the ear, and wiped the cobwebs and dust off his whiskers.

1969

Exhausted and sweaty, Earl carried Earl downstairs and placed him on the porch loveseat, then they crashed all around him, Carol kissing him gently on the cheek.   It was three-thirty in the morning, Friday September 8th, and the Town of Belvidere, afront the Park at *L'antre du Lion*, was eerie quiet; nary a sound broke the night silence, except the constant, background din of countless, unseen crickets.

The trio broke out the cognac and port, and proceeded to get drunk, Cord for a second time. And they shared a round of cigars, and then a second. And C didn't remember getting sick again, or much of anything.

"Are you wearing your underwear?"

Carol said, incredulous, looking at C's boxers, seeing them, seemingly, for the first time.

"Yeah, for the last three and a half fucking hours crawling around your house; where have you been? But thanks for noticing."

C said, sarcastic.

Carol eked a tired smile, and looked at Little-Earl with relieved, but sad, eyes; she was exhausted. She gazed at her phone, it was close to three-forty-five in the morning, and there was a message. She held the phone to her ear; even that was tiring.

"Hi Ms. C, it's me, Ji. It ten-forty-seven, sorry so late, Marty and me looking pictures of Earl and it's still so not real that he's so sick; um, just calling to see how you guys are holding up, love you both, very much....bye."

"Who was it?"

C said.

"It was Ji; she called asking how Earl was. I'm not calling her now; I'll tell her the whole thing in the morning. Christ, it's *already* morning. Anyway, I'll tell her later; she's with Marty."

Cord half-smiled and shook his head in disgust at himself; even Marty's getting some, and he isn't....pathetic. He could have had Ji, if he wanted; he should have taken the shot when he had the chance. But despite the sulk, he put on a good face, a game face, to belie the envy.

"Really? That *dirty dog*! Good for him, and for her....cheers."

C held up the glass to the night sky, a beautiful shade of blue-blackness, as did Carol and Earl.

"Oh boy, I forgot to call Lilly! She told me to call; I'm gonna be in *big* trouble."

"For what?"

Carol snipped, alcohol and burnout let the anger slip.

"She wanted to know how Little-Earl was; she talks about him, and asks how he's doing, all the time."

Earl said, tentative, scared by Carol's tone.

Really? She really cares about Little-Earl....*really*?"

Carol was incredulous.

"Yeah; she *loves* Little-Earl, I know it! She's so sad that he's sick; she's the one who yelled at me to run over here so fast when you called, and she made me promise to call once I found out if, that, Earl was okay. She's worried about him; she never says anything bad about Little-Earl....*never*."

Carol was worried about calling Earl so late, figuring he would get nothing but grief from his sister, and now came this little surprise. What a gift; and from Lilly, of all people....Lilly. And to her surprise, Carol slowly raised her glass and tipped it in tribute, into the night sky, to the Park, to the treetops and beyond.

"To Lilly."

Was all Carol said, as she wore a smile of respect, barely keeping her eyes open.

"To Lilly."

The boys parroted as they all downed the balance of their drinks; none added a word. None was needed.

And amidst the revelry, drunkenness and reflection, wholly unnoticed, a small cricket landed on Earl's belly and sat there for a second....silent. Earl never even gave it notice, while Earl quarter-turned his head and simply stared at it, sans expression.

And a moment later, with the process already slowly set in motion, the cricket disappeared into the night.

1972

CHAPTER 253 - ONE LAST THOUGHT ON THAT TOO-SOUR SUBJECT....EW

It was Friday evening, September 8th; day one-hundred forty-two, just shy of five months from that first step off the tired Greyhound, across from a throwback, *Luigi's Rancho*.

Little-Earl had made it through another day, six days from the terminal diagnosis. The veterinarian said Earl would likely last *another week, seven to ten days, at best;* that was the vet's best guess, and it was looking spot on.

She smiled wide at him, and he smiled back; it was the first time they had been alone in a long time....a *long* time.

And she again felt that familiar pang in her chest; it had been coming on and off all during drinks and dinner. He felt no pang. But he *did* want to fuck her, or her, either or. That was behind his smile. No jerking off tonight; that was the goal. And so far, so good; no landmines to dodge, simply polite, conversation, safe, banal topics, shared amongst the trio. And all he could focus on was pussy, one or the other, being taken at the end of *this* tunnel.

"How's Earl doing?"

She asked, sincere.

"Which one?"

He replied offhandish, his mind elsewhere.

"Well both, I guess, but I was asking about the little one, Carol's cat; Margie said he's pretty sick."

And C thought about Little-Earl, and felt guilty about his crude sex mind-wander, as Earl's life was wilting away.

"Yeah, the little guy, he isn't good, not good at all. Had a scare last night, this morning, actually, was over Carol's with Earl for Christ, three plus hours, till three in the fucking morning, trying to get him out of the floorboards, on the third floor; thought for sure he crawled in there to die. The whole thing doesn't really seem real…feels kinda fake. Anyway, it's pretty sad around the house, but in a weird way, cause everyone's trying to smile, trying to make the time left the best they can. But the *happy* is just a veneer, a shitty cover; it's like he's already dead. Carol looks like shit….she's so tired."

"I hope that doesn't happen to me."

Mae said, suddenly despondent, thinking about her own end-of-the-line, under the floorboards.

"Hope *what* doesn't happen?"

Margery said, just returning from the bathroom.

"Just talking about dying, the lead-up."

Mae said.

"Dying? Whose dying?"

"Earl; we're talking about Earl….Carol's cat."

C said, flat.

"Oh, Little-Earl; Lilly can't stop talking about it. She feels so bad for him, for real, too. Never saw her care about an animal like that one, any animal, come to think of it. Actually she doesn't care much about anything, even people, except, of course, for her brother."

1974

Somehow C hoped Carol would mention him in that little care-group, even though he knew he wasn't.

"Well, Earl, Little-Earl that is, kind of took a liking to Lilly; he's good at that, a sweet little boy."

"He did? She didn't tell me that. I was wondering why she cared about Carol's cat, seemed kind of strange — figured it was about Earl; Big-Earl, that is."

"Yeah, well, it is, but it's also about the little guy too, feeling as bad as he feels, still going over to her and rubbing on her, sitting beside her, on Carol's front lawn. And he never did that to anybody, even when he wasn't sick, he was always skittish, so I guess it affected her, in a good way."

"Why was *she* at Carol's? That doesn't seem right, possible, I mean."

Margery said, sideways.

"She came up the sidewalk, looking for her brother for something or other, and Little-Earl saw her, and even as sick as he is, he jumped off the porch and went out her, just like that....made no sense, but he did it. And then the three of them, the two Earls and her, just sat together, on Carol's front lawn, with Carol on the porch, just fifteen feet away, at most. Pretty amazing, actually. Good for them."

C said, and raised and drained the last of his red wine. He really didn't like red wine, but was too lazy to get up and snag anything else from Mae's cabinet, so he begrudgingly drank what they were drinking, and was annoyed about it to boot.

Margery and Mae silently shook their heads in agreement.

1975

The call to get together for dinner came from Mae, but it was Margery's idea, and it was a good one. It was a break C needed, away from *himself*; and since the bedside visit by the duo after the barn, he hadn't seen either of them.

And C's mind wandered back to the subject of sex, and it started to once again race circles in his brain. All he could seem to focus upon were the two of them, both already tagged, sitting idle, waiting in the chairs to either side of him, literally inches away. He started to obsess, wondering which one he would end up with before the night was over.

"How's Joe, mom?"

Margery launched a bucket of cold water. Mae threw her daughter a wicked look, huffed in annoyance, and answered curt.

"He's fine."

Cord looked at her, then at Margery, confused.

"*Joe who?*"

"Joe, next door."

Margery said, tilting her head toward the other side of the cul-de-sac. And then it registered to Ay.

"*Tool-box guy!?*"

He said in utter surprise.

"Mom's been seeing him a lot lately; *right mom?*"

C cracked his knuckles and looked at Mae, waiting to hear her response. Her mouth got pasty.

1976

"I'm not *seeing* him, just trying to be a bit nicer, is all. Just trying to be nice."

Mae took a defensive posture, and made eye contact with no one. She needed a glass of water.

"*Come on mom*; you have breakfast just about every day together, doing crosswords, and long trips to the garden center, picking out flowers that you plant together; what are you embarrassed about?"

"I'm not *embarrassed*; I'm not. Do you want coffee, espresso, cord....I mean, *port*....anything?"

Mae awkwardly changed the subject, furious with Margery, while maintaining a polite smile. She was hoping the answer to coffee was yes, at least hoping *his* answer was; Margery could leave, and five minutes ago wouldn't be fast enough. She didn't want this night to end, not yet, not now, and *certainly* not on a *tool-box* note. She already laid the groundwork for Joe not to call or show up tonight, saying she had a special dinner planned with her daughter, and wanted to try and mend fences. She was a bit proud of the ruse, since the lie was true, partially, on several fronts – classic politician cum-lobbyist talk. She as indeed having dinner with her daughter, and mending fences was also on the menu – true all around. She just failed to mention the third wheel invited to dinner, and that *he* happened to be the subject of planned mended fences. And to her delight, *Tool-Box* bought it hook, line and sinker. And now, from left field, Margery was seemingly in sabotage mode.

"Well, I'm happy you're being nice to him; he seems like a nice guy."

Cord said, barely getting the words out without curling his lips. *No way* that sounded sincere, he thought to himself. That guy was an annoying, fucking, pipsqueak asshole. Ay tried to crack his knuckles again, but they were all spent. Was Mae fucking *him* now, that little shit? *Seriously?* Now he was pissed, and wanted to bang her even more, and *hard,* but he also didn't want any part of her, and to punish her infidelity, by leaving, *right now.* But the bang impulse was winning out, his dick muscling aside his pride.

Margery saw the pot beginning to boil, and was first to act.

"Not for me mom, thanks, I'm stuffed, and beat, gonna head home. C, come on; you wanna hitch a ride back home?"

Now C, his dick firmly in control of the situation, was trolling for an invite to stay; for Mae to make some gesture, however small, asking him to hang, to *redeem* herself for the audacity of entertaining that little shit. Her *ask* was as good as an apology, and a for-sure all-nighter, and he'd bang her hard against the headboard. But he for-sure wasn't going to ante first, as much as he wanted to, not after that exchange....*no way.* If she wanted to roll with that little, wrinkly Jew, so be it. He was disgusted and outraged, and horned-up but good, all rolled in an angry ball. And that little fuck better not be doing her in the ass; that ass was *his*.

Mae saw the whole evening beginning to quickly unravel, and she was pissed at Margie; she *knew* her daughter brought up Joe on purpose. And yet she knew Margery was right to do it, to protect her from making the same mistake, knowing that Mae would be weak, and it was not good to be weak about this, because nothing good would come out of it, not in the end…not with Cord. So she resolved herself to wait for him to accept her offer, if he wanted to stay for coffee, she would love the company, and she'd do her best to hold her ground, even though she thought about his cock all night, and was thinking about it right now. But she

wasn't going to ante first, as much as she wanted to….no way; she had been good for so long – to beg now would undo all the dignity she regained at the Fair.
She wasn't asking, but God, she wanted to, and hoped he would stay.

Ten seconds of silence amongst the duo felt like ten minutes.

"Trains leaving."

Margery said, gathering her keys off the counter and giving them a quick shake, like she was calling the dog.

"Yeah, I better go too."

C said, not offering a reason why, because there wasn't one. He wasn't really sure what part of his brain decided to say those words, because it didn't ask *him*, or his dick. But they were out there, and there was no putting that bullet back in the gun. He could feel his prick shrink, in defeat.   He wondered what story he'd be jerking off to tonight. And both of them were pissed, hiding behind pursed good-bye smiles.

"Say hi to Joe."

C said, in a too-cheerful tone, fake as shit. It was hurtful, but it came out before he thought about it. And after he thought about it, he was glad he said it.

"I will."

As she leaned over and gave him a light cheek-on-cheek touch, while she closed her eyes and pursed her lips, although they touched nothing but air. It was the kind of cheek-touch that friends, not even good friends, just so-so fake friends give. It was cold, polite and shitty, just as she meant it to be. And as she withdrew, he could see the sting in her face, in her eyes. It was the last thing he

1979

saw, as he turned and headed out the door, following Margie, like the little dog he was.

The first quarter-mile was silent, winding through the sameness that was Brookfield. C was simply staring blank through the windshield at nothing as they passed identical townhouses and crooked mailboxes, one after another after another….sulking. Margery extended her hand and grabbed him gently by the chin, turning his face toward her.

"Let me see."

She said, like a doctor examining a forlorn patient.

"Yep, she's right."

And she let go, and put her eyes back on the road.

After a second or two, he took the bait.

"Okay, what?"

"My mom always said you were cute when you pouted; she's right."

And Margery smiled, and it was hard to stay mad, staring at a shine like that. And then the frustration unloaded.

"But *Toolbox,* come on! Are you kidding me?"

C pleaded.

"What's so bad?"

Margery responded, like a responsible adult would.

"Seriously?"

C looked at her, incredulous; how could anyone not be an outraged as he was? Then he continued in earnest.

"Let me ask you something, and I don't even want to know; is she *fucking* him?"

C winced, not wanting to really hear the answer, unless it was a no, which he was sure it wasn't. Margery chuckled a bit before she answered.

"Come on, roughly my whole life, I couldn't talk to my mother about the weather without it degrading into a shouting match. We couldn't go five sentences, I'm serious, never! The best bet was to avoid each other. So, to answer your question, which you don't even want to know the answer to, I have no idea."

And Margery simply shrugged her shoulders. But then she continued.

"But I'll tell you this; this past month, because of you, we've actually got to know each other, and have had real conversations, without shouting or insults or sarcasm, well, at least *less* sarcasm. That dinner thing just now, you have no idea; *no way* something like that could have *ever* happened. So, for that, thanks for having sex with my mom....and me."

C just looked at her, smirked, and shook his head. Margery was grounded, and she *got it,* she really did.

"Well, I was planning on extending the favor tonight, as if you didn't know."

"Come on C, like it wasn't obvious? I knew what you were up to in two minutes, and why you were even there to begin with. Listen, seriously, my mom, she's spent most of her whole life with guys eating out her hands, she loves it, she expects it, and she can't come to grips with letting it go, getting old. And she's hung on longer than most; good genes. But it's getting to the end of the line, for her. And *you*, you're a *real* problem for her, because she loves you, she truly does, and she's not used to not getting what she wants. She could always rely, *always*, on a smile, a wink, a gesture, to get anything she was after, and that was when she didn't even care about someone, just trying to get a favor, or a deal, or something. Love? Forget it, if she wanted someone, she got them, *always*. It killed my dad, and killed me, for what she did to him all those years, but that's her…it just is. Thankfully, I got my dad's genes, most of them, and not too many of hers, and for that I'm grateful; I can't imagine going through life like she has *[C just stared at her - Margery had no idea her father wasn't really her father, gene-wise anyway; he wished he didn't know that fact]*. Anyway, that gift she always had, at some point, it slipped away, and then you came along, to knock the nail in. I should be gloating, because she's getting what she finally deserves, but I feel bad for her. I love my mom, and I'm even starting to like her."

"Then why'd you even set this dinner up? Just to knock her down?"

C said exasperated.

"Because *you* need to stop what you're doing, and just be her friend. You can't sleep with her, or egg her on, give her false hope….it'll kill her. And this Joe-guy, I don't even know the man, but I know he's enamored with her, he treats her like a goddess, and she needs that, someone who puts her back on the pedestal she's used to. And that's not you C, it's not, and you gotta stop hurting her….please."

"Wow, thanks for the talk; that feels great."

C said, pouting some more. And she smiled at him.

"Do you think she's fucked him yet?"

C couldn't let it go, like watching a horror movie through your fingers, just waiting for the train wreck to happen.

"Listen, the subject of who's fucking whom isn't high on the list of what my mom and I talk about okay, it's not even near the list. And even if we *did* talk about that kind of stuff, we wouldn't, thanks to that little share-issue, called *you*. But if I had to *guess* about sex with Joe, yeah, maybe, probably. She talks about him a lot lately, and she smiles when she does, and, I'm pretty sure he might have stayed over her place last...."

"Okay, *okay!* **Enough!**"

C said, covering his face with one hand and holding up the other, to stop the pain. He scrunched his face in utter disgust, looked at her through his fingers, and followed with one last thought on that too-sour subject....ew.

1983

CHAPTER 254 – THAT WAS *SOME* SQUAT; SWEET DREAMS, BAGGAGE-BOY

"You know, you can still lift at the gym, if you want; it's not off-limits, or anything."

C just looked at her, with no particular expression, as she turned onto Oxford Street, down the hill, past the High School, and the Cemetery. And C wondered if Carol knew what Margery was thinking; he always thought about her, and what she was up to, every time he passed by the graveyard. Carol always had an agenda, and failed to share it with C.

"I promise, no squatting."

She added, smiling at him wry.

And C studied her face, looking for clues, since he wasn't sure what kind of squat she was talking about. But his dick figured it knew, or at least hoped, and came out of hiding, starting to stretch.

"Then what's the point? Squatting is the best part, isn't it?"

C said, trolling for the flirt he was hoping to get in return. Maybe he'd get fucked yet, and this would be a pleasant surprise, since he never really expected seconds from Margery.

She didn't answer.

"How's Walter?"

Cord said, exploring.

"Ah, Walter. We'll, I finally ended it with Walter; he admitted to his little pierced plaything, and I told him I'd had enough. Funny, once I cut him loose, he's more clingy than ever, like that toy you don't play with, till someone takes it away, then all of a sudden it's your favorite toy ever."

"Does he still get to play with the toy?"

C said.

And Margery laughed.

"Good one; he stops by at least once a week, usually late, sniffing around, wanting to get laid. He's usually drunk, but not always; it's pretty funny, now he's trying to cheat on *her* with *me*. For the most part, he's harmless."

"You don't give in, do you?"

C had his *please-say-no* face square-on.

Margery looked at him, cocked.

"And what if I did? Weak little girl?"

That's *exactly* what C was thinking.

"No, but...."

C said, and she cut him off.

"Well, the answer's no, except once; once I let him in. We practically ripped each others clothes off, like animals, and we fucked hard and fast on the cold slate foyer floor, less than five feet from the front door. It was quick and raw and dirty, and as soon as it was done, I literally shoved him right back out the door, locked it, and shut out the light. He was half-dressed and half-dazed at what just happened *[Margery smirked at the memory]*. I was horny and couldn't help it; let his new girlfriend stress about it."

1985

And C smiled and shook his head; Margery was pretty cool, and a real guy.

"So you're done?"

C said, confirming.

"We're still kinda friends, kinda; I don't totally hate the guy. Mom's happy, but yeah....done."

C kept a straight face, but inside he yelled *score* in a big way, and wanted to smile in the worst way.

"Well, that was the right choice; that guy was a dog."

C said, scholarly.

"Yeah, you know those dogs."

Margery said, staring at C, and then smiling.

And before he knew it, the car had stopped moving; they were idling in front of his apartment door, at the *Palace*. Shit.

"Well, you know, we could...."

"Goodnight Mr. Brin."

She cut him off.

He gave a frustrated half-huff. She answered the huff.

"Listen, I like you, I really do; you're interesting, and good-looking, and smart, and funny....and you have *way too much* baggage."

"Baggage? What...."

She cut him off again.

1986

"Come on, seriously? For starters, my mom, Lilly...."

"Lilly?! She hates me! *Hates me!* And your mom? She ended it at the Fair, a month ago, and she's fucking *Tool-Box,* and I said I'd stay away from her; come on!"

Margery chuckled at the little-boy-pleading.

"You never actually said you'd stay away from my mom, but I trust you will, since I asked you too. I want you to be her friend, just don't lead her on."

"Okay, okay....deal."

C said, eagerly extending his hand to shake on it, doing his best to be agreeable to anything Margery said. Then he looked at his crotch, and waited for her eyes to follow. He pointed at his dick with a nodding head.

"A month ago....more!"

He said weakly, as in, he hadn't got any, from mom, Lilly, or anyone else for that matter, except his left hand. The sympathy angle didn't play; Margery simply raised her eyebrows, in mock....something. Then she looked at him, and the smile left her face, and she got serious, the tone of her voice said so.

"Listen, my mom doesn't like you, she *loves* you. And Lilly? Lilly doesn't like you either; Lilly's in love with you, for real, even if she hasn't come to grips with that herself....yet. And neither one of those is a joke, and it's not something to be played with, not if you're a decent person, right C?"

Cord settled into resignation. He certainly wasn't decent, but he had to be, or pretend to be, for this conversation, lest he lose the respect of one of the few women who had any for him to begin with. And Margery's respect....he wanted that.

1987

He let out a long sigh.

"Okay, okay, but if there wasn't the mom issue, *and* the Lilly issue, and you weren't with Walt, or anyone else...."

"That's lot of *ifs*."

She said, monotone.

"Okay, but what *if?*"

"Then we'd squat, sure, lots and lots of sets. I like squatting with you; you're a good spotter. Good night."

"Shit!"

C yelled, and his dick got hard; it didn't have the brains to know for naught.

"Come on Margery, you're killing me! Let's go have a drink, and just talk some more!   Come on...."

"Alcohol, now *that's* a good idea."

She said sarcastic, and a mischievous smile framed her face. She kissed him lightly on the tip of the nose, like he was ten years old....a big girl teasing a little boy.

"You know what, when you think about it, that squat of ours....that was *some* squat; sweet dreams, baggage-boy."

1988

CHAPTER 255 – HIDEY HO….DEAD ON *SHADES OF DEATH*

She sat alone on her bed, neatly folding the last of his just-washed clothes, placing them in separate piles: guinea tees, jeans, underwear and socks; that was mainly it, four small piles. They laid silent, next to her, still warm and perfumed from the tiny dryer freshener sheets; *Renew Rain* was the scent. *Renew Rain?* What idiot came up with that one? And what the fuck is *that* supposed to smell like, she thought; they all smelled the same anyway. Stupid.

There were no shoes; the only boots he wore were on his feet when he left, along with his watch, his wallet and his rucksack. They were with him, wherever *that* was.

She glimpsed over at the large brown paper grocery bag set alongside the wall, by the nightstand, the stuff that he never unpacked. That was the extent of his worldly possessions, at least the ones that came north for the visit; what he had elsewhere she could only guess. The top of the bag was loosely rolled shut, concealing the contents.

She'd never dared look into that bag, not that she was told she couldn't; but it was clear it was off-limits, and no way was it worth the risk of a grab, a twist, or a choke, if she was lucky, or a punch in the chest, or the face, if she wasn't. She had avoided it since the day he placed it on the floor; she rarely even acknowledged it.

Until now.

She gingerly grabbed the loot and placed it gently on the bed, like an heirloom, and did nothing more than eye the crinkled brown paper. Her heart was racing, and she was scared to open it; she thought about putting it back on the floor and forgetting the whole thing, making sure it was replaced in the exact same spot, at the exact same angle, it previously sat. She noticed and remembered such things before she even grabbed it, an important habit….you had to, to avoid unnecessary trouble.

But she didn't do anything, just yet, she simply stared at it, looking over warily at the bedroom door once or twice in-between.

Nervous.

After a minute or so, she let out a heavy, extended sigh, reached over, pulled the sack toward her, and unrolled the top. Lillian slowly stuck her hand in, tentative, like trying to gingerly grab something in that dark corner of the basement, maneuvering around the cobwebs and spiders and whatever else you couldn't see, and didn't want to anyway.

She groped around and fingered what felt like a small paperback, and pulled it into the light of the bedroom.

The first item out of the bag.

Her heart was still pounding in her chest, and she kept looking over at the door, waiting for trouble to arrive, being caught in the act. That was the worst.

It was nothing but a trashy pulp; soft-porn, dog-eared and worn, like he got it used, or read it too many times, likely the former:

The Canadian Mounted

She quickly fanned through the rag, front to back, looking for anything incriminating scribbled in the margins, or stuck between the pages - a scrap of paper, a card, a phone number, a name, a note….anything.

Nothing.

She sighed at the lack of drama, and placed it gently on the bed, and went back for more.

She pulled out a three-pack of abridged, graphic novels, soft-cover; essentially fancy comic books:

- *The Red Badge Of Courage*;
- *Classics of Mark Twain*; and
- *The Wizard Of Oz*.

They were all brand new, and looked as if they had never been opened. The first was still sealed, prophylactic, in a cellophane sleeve.

She figured why Button had them, and why he never read them in front of her, or even acknowledged their existence. He was intimidated by C; everyone had told him Cord was smart, and he didn't want to look dumb….she knew that was the real reason. Button had never read a real book on his own, by his own choice, in his life. Button didn't care what anyone thought of him; but she guessed, sometimes, at least this one time, he did. And she knew if he found out she saw those three graphics, there would have been *big* trouble….*punch-in-the-face* trouble.

There were some more clean, rolled-up clothes he hadn't unpacked; she refolded them neatly and placed them in the appropriate piles.

Next she felt a small scrap of paper, like a receipt. She pulled it out; it was CJ's obituary, cut out, quick, careless and crooked, from the newspaper. It was yellow with age. There was no date, but Lilly didn't need one; she knew it was September, 1985. God, twenty one years ago….*twenty one years he'd been dead.* She shook her head at the thought.

1991

Her mom was already dead four years by then. She had that habit; whenever a date came up, Lilly quickly assessed it, assigned it a place, as pre- or post-1981; that was ground zero, and all other dates were measured against that date - *April 7, 1981.* It was reflexive; she did it in her head every time, instinctively, whether she wanted to, or not.

She held up the scrap and read the first line, or two, then her eyes glazed and she stared at the nothingness before her.

CJ Hammer, Button's best friend, all the way back to when they were little kids. She missed him; she always liked CJ - he had such a great smile. A tall, skinny farm boy, sinewy, from years of working, dawn to dusk, on the family dairy farm. He was a strawberry blonde, with the faintest of freckles, and the cutest little butt, and he always wore his favorite *John Deere* baseball cap, the one his dad gave him as a kid. She was sure he wore that thing to bed. She remembered his blonde wavy hair, sticking out, just below the edge of his cap.

CJ was quiet, and sweet, when he wasn't glued to Button, which was next-to-never. With Button, he was a parrot, a follower, always was. *The Hammer,* everyone called him that, especially Button. It made him sound tough, and mean; but he was neither, not really. And Lilly knew, deep-down, CJ always liked her, really liked her, *a lot,* just by the way he talked to her when they were alone, looked at her a bit too long, his eyes a bit too bright; it was as if he was, at any moment, ready to just jump up, grab her hand and run away, and keep running, *forever.* The two of them together, forever.

But the clues were always carefully veiled; if CJ ever made an obvious play for Lilly, one that Button saw, Button would have snapped his best friend's neck. No question, no hesitation, and no regret. That was Button.

1992

She let her hand drop to her lap, still holding the scrap of flaxen paper. She wasn't there, but Button told her what had happened.

They were out driving, Labor Day weekend, end of the summer, and it was just after midnight; one of their famous midnight runs. Both of them were a bit ripped, Button behind the wheel; Button always drove. CJ was shotgun, just the two of them. Button didn't see CJ down anything, but he must have, pills or powder or juice, *something*, because he was jacked, acting spacey and weird, not like anything Button had seen before. They were driving over seventy in a thirty-five zone, radio cranked to rock, banking blind curves and kicking up rocks on *Shades Of Death Road*, in Great Meadows.

It was their favorite road to gun, fifteen minutes east of Belvidere. Button stole the street sign years ago, when he was a kid, and kept it in his room, hung on the wall: *Shades Of Death.*

He thought it was the coolest sign ever.

The route to get there was always the same, hook a left off Route 46 onto Hope Road, at Saints Peter & Paul Church, and cruise up to *The Shades* on the right. That's what they called it, *The Shades*. They would cross themselves and feign pious when they passed the church, and then laugh, since neither of them believed in God, or Jesus, or anything like that; church was just a place for ass-bangers to hide, the whole thing was a bunch of bullshit.

And how fucking cool was it to take a left onto a road called *Hope*, and then a right onto a road called *Death;* the two of them talked about that all the time. CJ always said he wanted *that* job, to be the guy who gets to name roads; how do you get that job?

What a cool fucking job.

1993

Shades Of Death was a hair under seven miles long, a serpentine road, double-yellow the whole way, with no pass, *no way*; there were countless telephone poles, massive trees and jagged rock outcrops jutting ominously toward the cartway, mere inches off the white line.

Way too close for comfort.

Every sharp turn had danger arrows, yellow and black omens to *slow-the-fuck-down*; but the sight of them just made Button go faster, a green light to gun it, gripping the wheel and fighting gravity to keep the car on the pavement.

Neither wore a seat belt, ever. The thought never crossed their minds; only pussies wear seat belts.

Both had always said it would be cool-as-shit to die on that road someday….*Shades Of Death*. And they talked incessantly about how and where. The coolest would be at midnight, with *Stairway To Heaven* playing on the radio.

Too cool.

During the day, the road was dotted with long tractor trailers, moving slow, piled high with rolled grass, grown on the sod farms out in the flats. There was one grass farm after another, hundreds of acres of table-flat loam, called the *Muck Flats* by the locals. Thick carpets of grass grown in the *Muck Flats* were trucked all over the State to make new, instant lawns; it was some famous-ass grass.

Past the *Flats* came the deep woods and the boulder fields; the road ribboned through huge rock outcrops at the edge of Jenny Jump State Park, known simply as *Jenny Jump* by the locals. Two large swamps settled between the rocks, off the left shoulder of the road. The swamps were huge, extending far out of sight, covered by a glaze of algal scum, the swath broken by thick, scattered patches of reeds. The trunks of dead trees, scores of them, emerged from the green water, like the arms and hands of corpses, lurking, unseen, just beneath the murky surface, right out of *Deliverance*.

Picture perfect for a spook show.

Button and Hammer often joked about getting a friend good and ripped, then tying them up, throwing them in a canoe and floating them out in the swamp in the middle of the night – leaving them there, and laughing as they shit their pants, waiting to be pulled under by whatever goblin lurked beneath the ooze; those swamps were made for that. One of them always mentioned it each time they raced passed, another buddy ritual.

Beyond the swamps and the boulders and *Jenny Jump*, the road crept under Route 80 and opened wide, the only straightaway in the seven mile *Shades* jaunt. For a good half-mile, up to Bear Creek Road, you could really crank it, before you hit the dairy farms at the other end, where *The Shades* died into Long Bridge Road; CJ thought whoever named that road should be canned.

That night, in ’85, just past midnight, the two of them were rocketing; it was desolate, headlights cutting a thin slice of white in the black before them; streetlights on *The Shades* were non-existent. And Button was driving faster than usual, which was already too fast.

They had cruised the *Flats*, the rocks, the swamps and crossed under Route 80 without a hitch, like greeting the checkered flag. And they hadn't passed a soul, just endless ink.

Then, without a word, without warning, Button cut the headlights and gunned it blind on the half-mile straightaway, heading to Bear Creek, quickly climbing close to ninety, the engine whining.

They were all alone, careening down an asphalt drag they couldn't see, ninety-plus in a thirty-five. CJ was scared as shit in the pitch black, adrenaline pumping; the seconds felt way longer than seconds, as the car, somehow, stayed on the pavement, blind.

CJ grabbed the dashboard tight; he wanted to yell, to tell Button to turn on the fucking headlights 'cause he was gonna shit his pants. But he knew Button wouldn't listen; the lights would go back on when Button was ready, and not a second before…and any plea to the contrary would keep them enveloped in black that much longer.

And just then, just like that, with no warning, *Stairway To Heaven* came on the radio.

The green from the receiver dimly lit the cab, highlighting their profiles, and nothing more.

Freaky.

And Button looked at his best friend and whooped in excitement at the serendipity, punching his fist into the air while they barreled down the road, engulfed in the murk.

But CJ didn't join in.

Almost in slow motion, he let free his death-grip of the dashboard, turned to Button and simply smiled; it was a weird, fucking smile – creepy - his features basked in a glow of diode green, and calmly said two words that he'd never said before in his life, and would never say again:

1996

The speedometer ticked past ninety-nine as CJ hooked the handle, cracked the car door and simply rolled out into the night. He was gone in an instant; the gloom swallowed him whole, as *Stairway* played.

Hidey Ho….dead on *Shades of Death*.

CHAPTER 256 – *BUTTON WAS BACK!*

Button never rode *The Shades* again after that night….never.

The last time Lilly ever set eyes on CJ, he was in his coffin; he was the second real dead person she ever saw.

It was at Brockman Services, the funeral home in Belvidere, in their smallest room, way down at the end of the hall, farthest from the entranceway. Like the littlest, shittiest theater in the multiplex that the crap movie moves to at the very end of its short run, when next-to-nobody is still paying for a ticket to watch, right before the movie goes away, forever, *that* was the room CJ was laid out in. It was the cheapest, for-shit, *he-doesn't-really-matter-to-anybody-dead-person* viewing room.

The room was fake wood-paneled, the carpet was wall-to-wall gold pile, worn and stained; the whole set-up was barely a half-step above cheese.

Even though there were some flowers, the only smell Lilly remembered was the slight whiff of mold and must, like an old-person's home, and she remembered thinking that was wrong, she shouldn't be smelling that, not here, not now. She couldn't shake the musty smell from her nostrils.

CJ was wearing his *John Deere* hat. It was right for him to wear it, to wear it forever; she was glad about that. She remembered smiling seeing it.

And as she inched to the edge of the coffin, and wrapped her fingers gently around the edge, fingering the cloth liner he would feel forever, she could clearly see the line of cheap, thick makeup, ending just below his jawbone; the ashen color of the cold, dead skin on his neck didn't come close to matching the yellowish-orange tint they made his face – what a shit job. Worse yet, he wasn't smiling; his lips were pencil-straight, like he was mad, or worse yet, indifferent. To have that face on, *forever*, was wrong; CJ spent his whole life smiling, always smiling…he had one of the best smiles.

He should have been smiling, for forever.

She lightly touched his face with the very tip of her pointer; his skin was cube-ice cold and hard. He felt fake, like a piece of cheap plastic. A bit of the thick makeup came off on her skin; she smeared the smudge back and forth between her fingers, till it wiped away. She wished she had never touched him, because that's all she could recall, that ugly feel. That was the last thing she remembered; she turned around and never looked at him again.

And whenever she smelled mold, something musty, to this day, she thought of CJ. And that was sad.

Lilly wondered why Button put CJ's obituary in the bag; did he carry that thing with him everywhere he went? Why? Maybe it was a reminder to visit CJ's grave when he was back in Town; but did he really need an old newspaper scrap to remember that? And did he visit CJ? He never said anything to her about it. Or was he going to talk to her about it, about him, for some reason, and that was his reminder? What did CJ have to do with *anything*, at least now?

She wondered.

And the wonder drifted to the really big question left unanswered, that swam constant in her brain; where *was* Button? Specifically where was he, **right, exactly, now.** He must be *somewhere,* physically; he had to be….right? He didn't just disappear into thin air. And was he thinking about her, wherever he was? She couldn't get her mind around the possibility of him being gone, really gone, for good....forever. *Button* and *dead* didn't go together; she felt that Button simply wouldn't allow it. He was still out there, somewhere, she was sure of it, and Cord was simply lying to protect her, to make her feel safe. But she was convinced, half-convinced anyway, that he'd be coming back, for her; of that, she was sure.

Pretty sure. Kinda sure.

And then she simply stopped wondering, for now, and silently placed CJ's yellow newspaper clipping on the bed, in its own neat little pile of one.

She stuck her hand back in the pumpkin, and pulled out the next prize.

An envelope, on noticeably thick, brilliant-white paper, which screamed *special, important*. It was post-marked March 2, 1981, addressed to Button at his Barracks Post, and it was still sealed....never opened.

When Lily she saw the date, *1981*, she *knew* it must be special, because *anything* that happened in that sacred three-hundred-sixty-five day span, de facto, was special to her, because it was *that* close. She immediately thought of her mom; not just the date – 1981 – in abstract, and the resultant math, days or months before or after April 7th that always followed, but of her mom herself.

And it all happened in less than an instant.

It was one of those memories that pops *tout de suite*; triggered by that special smell, sight or sound, that immediately reels you back somewhere in time. Everyone has them, and so did Lillian; hers was CJ and musty-mold....but it was also her mom, and an ugly year.

1981.

Button's never-opened letter was post-marked March 2nd; her mom was *still alive* on March 2nd when this so-special letter traveled through the mail, carried by postmen, and would be for....she clumsily did the math in her head, counting the days of March and April....for thirty-five more days.

No, thirty-six days....*thirty-six*. It had an *extra* day, and to Lilly, that fact was important to calculate, to know; an extra day was priceless.

And this letter was *never opened;* that fact was crucial....a wholly unexpected, stumbled-upon, beyond-rare gemstone. It had that special quality, exactly like the one she carried in her pocketbook for the last twenty-five years. It was a trip back, time-travel back. Whatever it said, was *never* said, because it was *never* opened. It was **still** March 2, 1981 *inside* that envelope; the air in there, the paper, the ink, the thoughts, it was all still *then*. Inside that sealed envelope, her mom was *still* alive, and would be, forever.

Lilly's hands inexplicably started to tremble, shaking the letter like a leaf. She placed the envelope on the bed, face-up, pushing down with her hands into the softness of the comforter, to stop the shake, and stared at the white rectangle, intensely.

Her mind started to race.

She wondered what her mom was doing on March 2nd; had the two of them talked that morning? Surely they did, they always did, but about what? Boys, Button, Earl, school, homework, chores, what-to-wear, fussing over the red scarf and who got to wear it? Probably all the above, and then some. And she wondered what was going through her mother's mind that 2nd day of March, what was so important, that wouldn't be, in just thirty-six days, when *nothing* would be important anymore.

Every day you wake, every day of the fucking week, you're one day closer to dead. Just this morning, Lilly was one day closer herself. But who thinks that when they open their eyes and bat last night's sleep away? It's just a fresh, new day, just one more of an unlimited number on their way, to bitch and complain about whatever is fresh to bitch and complain about.

One day closer to dead, and Lilly didn't even care, at least right now she didn't.

Her mom was thirty-six short mornings away, the day the post-office marked that letter to Button. Thirty six, and counting.

She wondered if she knew, if her mom had planned it all along. What was so special about April 7th? Why was *that* the day?

She wished she had kept a diary, maybe a clue would surface, hidden somewhere between the lines, amongst the words from those days, so long ago.

Maybe.

Lilly stared at the return address; the letter to Button was from the *SOI*, the *School Of Infantry*, Quantico, Virginia. It was from the *Scout Sniper School,* the Marines; they had a base there.

Lilly knew all about the Marines and the *SOI*; she knew it well - all the acronyms, all the steps, all the glory. It was all Button ever talked about on the phone while he was away, how he was gonna be an *MOS 8541*, a *Scout Sniper*, his Holy Grail. *MOS - Military Occupational Specialty*; she smiled at remembering the jargon.

Button talked non-stop about being an elite sniper, before he even enlisted. A license to kill people, the ultimate hunter, working solo. Snipers take out whoever is *key*, he used to tell her, *whoever* was important, be it enemy leaders, equipment operators, messengers, observers, radio operators….whoever was a vital link for the enemy. Taking down *the man,* whoever *the man* happened to be for that mission, wherever *that man* was. Even if the *wherever* was five football fields away, that's what a sniper did; and if you were good, it ended in a casualty. *One shot - one kill,* that was the sniper's motto. And Button knew he'd be damn good.

How cool was that he used to tell Lilly; it was his dream.

And beyond that, Button wanted to be a specialty sniper, to get his *Urban Sniper* tag, to hunt in the urban jungle. Then, if he was lucky, he'd get to kill monkeys, with a free pass no less….that was beyond golden.

The *Urban Sniper* part, he never mentioned that one to Lillian.

Lilly remembered all the steps; Button used to rehearse them in detail, like memorizing vocabulary words for a test, saying and spelling them over and over and over again.

Demand the impossible to get the maximum possible; that was from Peter the Great he told her; Button loved that line. To him, that was the Marines; that was *him* in the Marines.

But the process was a bitch, for sure.

First he had to get through *Marine Boot Camp,* then *SOI,* at Camp Geiger, North Carolina, which made *Boot Camp* seem like pussy-school. Lilly remembered him telling her that people died in *SOI,* suicides mainly; guys just couldn't hack it.

But Billy Bones did.

And out he came, a *MOS 0311 - a Rifleman,* a true grunt. He qualified with an *M16A2 service rifle,* an *M203 grenade launcher* and a *SAW - Squat Automatic Weapon.* He spoke about the weapons as if they were a part of his body, part of him. To a *Rifleman,* his *M-16* is his most cherished possession; it never left Button's side. He slept with it in his hooch.

After *SOI,* you had to get assigned to an *Infantry Battalion,* which Button did, and then you had to get assigned to a *Scout Sniper Platoon,* and that wasn't a given, not by any stretch.

But Button got in; he was most proud of that.

But even being in the *Platoon* didn't guarantee an invite to *Sniper School;* in the *Platoon,* you were kinda in purgatory, waiting for a coveted slot to open. Invites only pinched twice a year. And there were no second chances at *Sniper School,* one shot and done, in or out, make it, or don't. And six out of ten didn't.

But those were *other* guys.

While Button waited in *Platoon,* he was just a *PIG - Primarily Instructed Gunmen.* If you got into *School,* and made it through, ten grueling weeks, and another four on top to make *Team Leader,* you graduated as a big fucking *HOG - Hunter of Gunmen,* a hunter of *PIGs.* And that was top alpha dog; there was no higher to go. She couldn't imagine Button being anything but.

He was born a *HOG.*

The *Sniper School* invites were like gold, dished to senior platoon members first. Hardly anyone got invited unless you were a year-old *PIG;* by year three, if you were gonna make it, you had better have gotten the letter.   Button enlisted in 1979; the letter Lilly was holding was postmarked March, 1981....two years in.

That's it! This must have been his *Sniper School* invite! She was holding the *actual* invite!

Then she cocked her head a bit, when the thought had time to settle.

Button told her he never applied to *Sniper School;* in the end, he decided against it, even though he said his *Platoon Leader* begged him too, since he was a shoe-in. But he held firm, and declined, despite the pleas by his superiors, because *School* would have taken him away from coming home to see her. Button Pierce didn't apply to *Sniper School*, to what mattered to him most in the world, all because of his unconditional love for Lilly; it was one of the most selfless sacrifices Button ever made for her, to show how much he loved her, how much he cared.

And she *loved* Button for it. It was major glue for her, always had been.....*major.*

So then what was this letter? A letter urging him to apply, that he never opened, because he couldn't be convinced to change his mind, because of Lilly? Did he bring it to Belvidere all these years later, to finally tell her so? To fess?

She smiled, remembering all the training he did, waiting for the Invite, to improve his chances. He passed courses in land navigation and patrolling, surveillance, reconnaissance, stalking and concealment, field sketching and a bunch more she couldn't recall, or with names and acronyms she didn't understand. The physical fitness part was a joke – running three miles under eighteen minutes, the five hundred meter swim, and all sorts of endurance tests; he passed those aces.

Perfect eyesight, no color blindness.

And the intangibles, the ones that mattered most: maturity, patience, independence – both mental and physical, common sense and no sense of panic. All those, he had cold.

He was a *School* shoe-in.

Stealth....Silence....Precision....Violence

Button used to repeat that to Lilly on the phone, at least once during each phone call. It was the sniper's motto - what made a sniper a sniper. And it was what made Button a sniper, that's what he would always tell her.

And through all that reminiscing, all through the trip back in time, Lillian had never flipped over the sacred envelope, until now.

And that was the first time she saw the scribble of pen on the back, a mash of crooked writing, fragments of thought, hurried....bitter, written with a heavy hand, angry underlines, haphazard:

Failed mental test? Fucked!

What to do??

<u>Call Jake!</u> *Fix it!*

NJP???? It fucking counts? Did my time!

Done? No recourse!

RK said **no chance, no school - <u>it's over!</u>**

2006

Fucked!!

Lilly stared at the haphazard writing, as it all began to process. For some reason, she pictured Button with a phone cradled, pinched on his shoulder, furiously writing as words fell into his ear. That's how the words felt, that's how they looked.

Failed mental test, no chance, no school, it's over, done, no recourse, fucked. What did that all mean?

All of a sudden, like a fillip to the head, she realized: she'd been had. Button never gave up *Sniper School* for her; he was rejected! He applied, and got *rejected!* **Is that what all this fucking scribble meant?**

From nowhere, Lilly went ballistic, tearing open the envelope like an animal, forgetting her mother, the sacred air, the time travel, the gemstone that it was. Now, it was simply a fraud, a fraud of the most cherished sacrifice that Button never really made.

She unfolded the single page of thick white stationary, crinkled and creased by her attack, and scanned the words with wild eyes, quickly passing the entry accolades, the perfunctory preface of the good soldier, before the hammer dropped in paragraph three.

And there it was….the only lines she really had to read:

While you have never been subject to court martial, your multiple NJP infractions, with their requisite restrictions and reprimands, mar your otherwise exemplary service record. That alone gives us cause for concern. However, the serious nature of your repeated infractions suggests a troubling pattern, which caused your Commanding Officer to order a full mental evaluation, before a slot in Scout Sniper School could be proffered. Unfortunately, the results of your recent evaluation has caused your Commanding Officer and the Scout School to withdraw any slot invitation to Scout School now, or at any time in the future. You are encouraged to contact Dr. Diane Brukardt if you have any questions. You will retain your current MOS 0311 designation. This matter is considered closed.

Liar!

The word bounced in her head. *Fucking liar*, soon joined by another - *betrayal*, and a third....*fool*. All three circled her head, a chaotic merry-go-round.

She slowly folded the letter and placed it back in the envelope.

Lillian sat silent for awhile, trying to figure out how she was wrong, trying to envision the brilliant excuse Button would quickly counter with, that she would quickly believe. She was good at that.

She didn't even realize she stuck her hand back in the bag, shaking her head in the negative the whole time. She grabbed another loose paper, ripped from a notebook, the eyelet scraps still hanging on the left edge, making for a ragged look.

Lilly half paid attention, as the words came into focus.

Drin To-Do – Vito Aug Meet

- *Safe house – Oxford?*
- *Circuit – A.C., Philly, New York....where else?? Lilly - talk about – high end shit....6K-10K++/night. She'll do it, no prob.*
- *Other end - sex slaves - any interest? South covered; North? Untapped out here! 14-16 prime, trash and immigrants – anchor babies*

and beaners – easy local finds, bed-times, biscuit-heads, chonkys, clickers (Togo), Cossacks. Double dip - crossing money + hourly. Need pharmacist....ideas?

- *Take Easton, P'burg - tag it....first stop local. Crips, Bloods, Latin Kings, MS-13, Pagans - input on sets and chapters? Contacts? Fight now? Oxford boys to scout/hold. When? 240 towns to take!*
- *Expand/consolidate shore - need safe house – ideas? Not often – quick in/out....backup.*
- *Shrooms Interest? Fresh, or dried? Both?*
- *Loans - to wangsters - interest?*
- *Meow – distribution – piece?*
- *Counterfeit software – MicroSoft, Adobe - easy targets, low-risk, <u>huge</u> profit! Mexican operation connection, corrupt software – backdoor access to internal accounts – huge!*
- *Counterfeit – big; Dr. wants in!*
- *Meet? Or distance with Dr. - nig issue*

She scanned the bullets quickly, as her mouth dropped.

This was what the *Drin* was? What Button was doing with that black guy, from the Marines? This was why he was really here, why he was really back? It was never her, but this? This was the octopus with all the arms she didn't need to know about? But she was smack in the middle of it, bullet number two, as a primo fuck-whore, and didn't even know it. She didn't understand half of the words, the codes, the shorthand, but she really didn't need to.

She understood the big picture; she had *no idea* who Button Pierce really was.

As she slowly shook her head in the negative, Lilly dropped the note back in the bag, and looked in, to see what other trash she would find. And at the bottom, below the note she just tossed, were about a half-dozen small, zip-lock, plastic pill bags.

She took them out, and placed them on the bed. Each was filled with a handful of green plastic capsules, like headache-pills, unlabeled, holding what appeared to be some sort of white powder, the residue which dusted the inside of the zip-lock cocoons.

Each baggie was labeled with a black marker, some numbering system, hieroglyphics, that meant something to somebody.   There were also words scribbled on the bags:

Meow Meow
Spice
NRG-1
Bubble Love
Plant Food
Bath Salts
Pond Cleaner

And Lilly got scared.

She didn't know what to do. She didn't want that stuff in the apartment – she had no idea what it actually was, but knew it had to be bad – illegal drugs of some sort. But she was afraid to get rid of it, just in case Button was on his way back, someday….just in case.

But the scare washed over her, and with that, she quickly swooped up the bags and rushed out of the bedroom, dropping and picking up zip-locks as she scampered down the hall, to the bathroom. Her heart was racing as she emptied the baggies, one at a time, into the toilet, and flushed. She kept flushing as she dumped; some of the green capsules opened, and white powder dissolved into the toilet water, as it whirlpooled and disappeared down the drain.

She was dumping the last packet when the apartment door slowly creaked open; she let out a little yelp: *Fuck! **Button was back!***

CHAPTER 257 - A FLICK OF THE WRIST AND A TOSS IN THE TRASH CAN

Lillian froze.

She was unable to move; the only sound was the water returning to the bowl. She wanted it to end, but the toilet seemed to fill forever.

"Earl? You okay? The door wasn't closed."

C called out. And Lilly let go a breath of relief.

"He's not here."

Lilly yelled, checking the bowl to be sure no remnants remained.

"Where are you?"

"I'm in the bathroom."

Then she felt the pang in the pit of her stomach, but it was too late. She left her bedroom door open wide, affording him a full view of her bed, and its contents.

She came around the corner to see him standing in her bedroom doorway, with a confused look, eyeing the piles of neat laundry, the books, the underwear - *his* folded underwear. All neat as a pin.

Cord turned and spoke; he wasn't happy.

"Are you fucking kidding me?"

Lilly didn't answer.

"What the fuck are you doing? You did his *laundry*?"

Still no answer. No smart answer, no polite answer….nothing.

"Get rid of it, all of it….now! Don't you trust me? Underwear? Laundry? Jesus! I told you it was safe; safe, *Safe, **SAFE** [C smacked his hand against the door jam, harder with each word]*! For Christ's sake, let it go, already! He was a bad fucking guy and now it's SAFE! Do you want me to draw you a fucking picture?!"

"I don't even know what safe feels like!"

Lilly screamed at him.

"The only place I feel safe is here, and all the bad things that have ever happened to me, all my life, have been **here**; how is that safe?! It's the only safe place I know, and I'm not safe. I've never been safe….*never!* You saved me, but *you* don't feel safe. He was bad to me, at times, and at the end, but at least I knew what I got. With you, I know nothing! ***NOTHING!*** How can I trust you when I don't even know your *fucking name*?!"

"Earl thinks I'm safe; your mom thinks I'm safe! And they know I care about you, and will protect you."

"Really, like with the dog, who was going to attack me, at the boat ramp? How did you protect me there? He was gonna rip my fucking throat out, and you stood there, frozen; Button wouldn't have done that! He would have killed that dog, ripped ***its*** fucking throat out, and *you* just stood there. And by the way, I don't talk to my mom, and she doesn't talk to me! *She* thinks you're safe? And *she* thinks you care? And *she* thinks you're gonna protect me? Really? I'd like to hear that for myself! Why don't you pass that little fucking tidbit on to her! Tell her I'm waiting; I've been waiting *my whole fucking life!* **I can't hear you! *Speak up!*** *[Lilly screamed at the ceiling, the veins bulging in her neck].*"

2013

C just stood and stared at her; he couldn't think of a thing to say. All that ran through his head was Margery telling him, not five minutes ago, that Lilly loved him. What a big, fucking joke; the whole thing was a big….fucking….joke.

He was lost in thought, when he heard her say, calmly, as if she just screwed on the head of a different person, a sane person, like switching out a burnt bulb.

"How's Little-Earl?"

He looked at her, incredulous at the quicksilver change; and yet, not, since that was Lilly, and he knew, she simply made no sense. Cord let out a huff, one that signaled confusion and frustration and general disbelief, standard fare when dealing with Lillian. He answered calmly, more defeat and fatigue than anything else.

"I don't know, I wasn't there; why don't you go over and see him? He likes you; why, I have no fucking clue, probably the same reason I like you - *stupidity*. We both just don't know any better….gluttons."

Lillian just stared at him shaking his head, as if she was truly surprised at the assessment. But that was classic Lilly, no other response would have felt right. That *was* the response you get from her, and C should have long-learned that by now.

"You know what Margery just said to me, not five minutes ago? She said you were in love with me; it was *obvious [C chuckled aloud at his own words]*. I told her she was crazy, just like I tell everyone else that tells me that. I told her you hated me, it's just in different degrees, depending on the day. You're in love with the guy whose underwear, washed and folded, *[C shook his head]* is on your bed, you always will be, even though he didn't love you, not one bit - sorry, but he didn't….his words, not mine. And there's nothing I can do about that, I guess, and I'm not sure if I even want to anymore. Lilly, it's either zero or sixty with you, there's no middle ground....at least with me. You don't care about me? Fine, I accept it, and I'm tired of trying, I really am. I'm done, with you. Just one favor, I plan to be friends with your brother, hopefully for a long time, and that will invariably involve interacting with you, in some limited capacity, anyway, it's inevitable. I'll try to minimize it, but I doubt I can avoid it, totally. So at least be cordial to me, try anyway, and I'll do the same to you; okay, deal? For Earl's sake? No caring, we don't need caring, just cordial; it'll just make it....easier."

And in his face, she saw hurt, defeat, and surrender.

But I do care about you! I care about you more than anything! I thought we were best friends! Lilly yelled, but C never heard her, because the words never left her lips, as she watched the apartment door quietly close behind him. She cocked her head, her ear tracing the fade of his footsteps up the stairs, to his apartment; she was waiting for him to turn and return, to swing open the door, smile wide, and tell her everything would be alright.

But he didn't.

In silence, Lilly gathered and carefully packed all Button's belongings back into the paper bag, including the freshly laundered clothes, securely taped it shut and placed it on the floor, along the wall of her bedroom, adjacent to her night stand.

She stared at it for awhile, sitting upright, back straight, on the edge of the bed. There was an explanation about the *SOI* letter, there had to be; that's why Button brought it back, to explain....to set the record straight. And the *Drin?* Well, she just wouldn't think about that right now; maybe she'd think about that tomorrow. And invariably, like they always did in times of stress, in times of uncertainty, her thoughts ran back to happy times with Button, when they were kids, and all the fun they'd had, the secrets they shared, the ones that no one else would ever know, the traipses they made in the corn fields, in the woods, down by the river, on the farm, and how much in love she was with him, and he with her. C was just talking sour; Button loved her, he always did, and always would.

She returned and found herself fixated on the bag, her eyes coming back into focus. She decided she'd leave it there, it wasn't hurting anything, and figure what to do with it later, maybe in the morning; no need to rush.

She undressed, turned off the light and laid in bed, staring through the darkness at the ceiling....all alone. C was right above her, less than ten feet and a whole world away, sitting on the edge of the bed, head in his hands, staring at the floorboards....all alone. *Why he was here, and when he was leaving? And why did he ever have to meet a girl named Lilly?* Lilly's weren't supposed to happen, not to him. His heart hurt, and he wasn't familiar with the feeling. And he wanted it to just go away....forever.

She laid in bed awhile, rigid, digesting and re-digesting all the words C said, mixing and matching them in her head, knowing they were true, and realizing what she was losing, what she was throwing away – a best friend - more even, although she still couldn't bring herself to say, to herself, that she loved him, even though she knew she did....for sure....probably.

And then she did something she rarely did, she asked her mom, for help, for what to do. And Lilly cried, because her mom gave her the same answer she always gave Lilly....no answer at all.

Somewhere along the way, the tears dried, and she fell asleep.

Later, well after midnight, Lillian Liddell awoke to nothing in particular; the apartment was silent. Half-dazed, half-asleep, she quietly grabbed and walked Button Pierce's paper bag, groggy and barefoot, automaton, wearing nothing more than an over-sized tee-shirt and sleep-shorts, out to the street, around to the rear of the *Palace*.

And just like that, the bag was gone; a flick of the wrist and a toss in the trash can.

CHAPTER 258 – AN UNEXPECTED FINISH
DRIBBLED FROM THE LIPS....STAY

"It's getting late Earl, you sure you'll be okay? Tired?"

"I'm okay; you okay Ji-Sue?"

Earl asked, passing the question on.

"I'm okay."

She said, smiling at Earl.

The trio were lying on the carpet in the rear parlor, surrounding Little-Earl, who was in a typical bun, tongue out, eyes wide open, with no hint he was going to sleep anytime soon.

Ji grabbed a handful of popcorn from the stainless steel bowl, and dropped some in Earl's hand. She gestured to Carol, but she shook off the offer. Carol kissed Little-Earl lightly on the forehead, and extended her finger to Earl's nose, and lightly rubbed it, like she always did, like she had tried to do for the past four days, with no response.

But this time, Little-Earl finally pushed back, into her finger, like he used to, before he got sick. It was the faintest of pushes, not like when he was healthy, and strong, and would bull his head into her hand, but it was a push, all-the-same.

Unmistakable.

"He pushed back! Did you see that?!"

Carol exclaimed; both Earl and Ji missed it, eating popcorn. But they both hopped up, excited nonetheless. Carol tried again, but it was a one-shot deal.

She sighed.

"I don't want to do this *stupid Victorian Days* stuff tomorrow, Ji; I wish we could just cancel."

"Me too."

Ji said, and it wasn't simply a parrot - she meant it.

For the past nineteen years, *Victorian Days* was *the* annual event in Belvidere, always in the beginning of September - the second weekend of the month. It was the one weekend where the curtain pulled back on the sleepy hamlet, and outsiders were invited in to enjoy the Town's nostalgic charm.

And each year, over ten thousand people would partake, locals and outsiders alike. The outsiders filtered in from other parts of Jersey, as well as New York, Pennsylvania, and a smattering of outlier areas. Although there was some modest advertising, most of the influx seemed to stumble in by word of mouth, surprised that such a place even existed.

Most who came once, came back again.

It was a two-day affair; the weekend events included a smorgasbord of themed afternoon teas on Victorian porches, historic house tours, horse-and-carriage rides around the Square, antique vendors plying in the Park, classic car venues, old-time baseball reenactments, spooky Cemetery ghost tours, and, for the past thirteen years, an elegant *Victorian Fashion Show*, staged on Carol's front porch, Saturday morning, starting at 10:45 am, every year. Like clockwork. And for two hours, *L'antre du Lion* was center stage for a runway cotillion, spanning a century of fashion.

Carol volunteered use of the house to the *Fashion Show* contingent; about two dozen models - a mix of professional and amateur - women, men and children - would descend upon *L'antre du Lion*, like a Broadway production, draped in handfuls of antique hats, dresses, umbrellas, swimsuits and shawls. Along with it came clothes racks, mirrors, sound systems and the like, hastily erected and engulfing the entire first floor of the house in a cacophony of couture, with each model changing ensembles four to five times during the Show.

They would waltz through the large double-doors, down the front porch steps and slate walkway, spinning at the street, and ascending the steps once again, before disappearing into the house, to change and do it over again, all the while, their wardrobe explained in workmanlike detail by the emcee: button-types, collar-styles, fabrics, feathers, hemlines and the like. The garb was not limited to Victorian times, but rather ranged from the late 1800's through the 1980's....an eclectic mix of fashion, frivolity and fun.

Carol even commissioned a real, red carpet for the event, spanning a full fifty feet, from the front porch to the Hardwick Street curb, which Ji dutifully rolled out, swept, and rolled up, each year.

The *Fashion Show* attracted several hundred people, sitting on lawn chairs and spilling out into Hardwick Street – closed to traffic for the weekend – who would watch and applaud as the models, young and old, strutted and preened down the red carpet, to period music.

It was free to all, and always a favorite. And Carol enjoyed the spectacle, happy to offer the house – a small giveback to a Town she had grown to love - a Town which felt, more now than ever, like her real home.

In addition to the *Fashion Show*, there was the annual *House Tours;* a half-dozen historic homes scattered about Town were selected each year and the owners asked to open their doors for tours to the curious. Given its architecture and prominent spot on the Park, every second or third year, the organizers would invariably come, hat in hand, and request that Carol, once again, allow *L'antre du Lion* to be on tour.

Carol always obliged, and for two days, close to a thousand people would hoof through the house, asking questions on architecture, history, furnishings and finishes - wallpaper, ceramic tiles, woodwork and the like. For this part, Carol always made herself available, standing in the kitchen, fielding questions and providing all the answers she could. And although there was always the small contingent of Belvidere busy-bodies, trying to worm their way into Carol's house, to spread bad gossip about her, for the most part, the ticket-holders were a polite and interested group, caring not about Carol, but the bones of the house. It was for them she opened her doors.

The *Fashion Show*, the *House Tours,* it was all good, clean fun, and Carol had always looked forward, every year, to the beginning of September in Belvidere, even before Cord and Earl entered her life.

But not this year.

Thank God, the house itself wasn't on tour; it was an off-year.

But the *Fashion Show*, as always, was on, and Carol wanted no part of it.

"We can't let anyone upstairs, like normal Ji, and we have to be extra careful this time. You stay upstairs with Little-Earl, okay? They got me in the stupid show this year, modeling dresses. Every year I say *no;* figures I say *yes* this year, and Earl gets sick. I wish I could get out of it."

Carol frowned, looking at Little-Earl.

"I'll be here; I'll help."

Earl said.

And Carol smiled at him and mouthed *thanks*. Then Earl continued, in almost a whisper.

"You know what? I watched the *Fashion Show every year* since I knew you lived here, which is *every* year you lived here. I would hide in the back, so you couldn't see me; I never sat in the seats, *no way*, 'cause I stick up too high, but I used to watch you go in and out of the house sometimes, before it started. I always wanted to help roll the red carpet - that looked like fun, and after, when everyone was cleaning up and getting ready to go, I used to say *hi* to you, but you never heard me, you know, not 'cause you were being mean or anything, but 'cause I was just kinda whispering, quiet, you know, and no way you heard me, but you smiled at everybody, so maybe you were smiling at me too. That's what I thought, anyway. It made me feel *real* special, and I never got to thank you for that....so thanks."

Earl put his head down, embarrassed he said all that, out loud anyway.

Carol shined.

"Why'd you hide Earl? I woulda said hi back; you know I would have! I wish I knew you, really knew you, then; I wish you would've just come talk to me."

"No way! I was way too afraid!"

Earl yelped, then said it again.

"I was *way* too afraid!"

"Of what?"

"Of you!"

He yelped a third time.

"Well, thanks to C, you got over that….mostly."

And she touched his nose with her finger, and he blushed.

"Thanks C."

Earl said aloud, just above a whisper.

Carol never did remember seeing Earl out in the crowd, and that made her sad. All those missed years, what a waste.

"It's after midnight, Ji; the house is as good as it's gonna get. They show up at the door *way early,* at eight or so, remember? Sometimes earlier even; we need to get to bed."

"Okay."

Ji responded.

Just then, Carol noticed a bunch of the cats had congregated around the three of them; she went through the count, and saw Maguro sitting between the pocket doors, Tobiko lying on the crest of the front parlor couch; Zeke, Hunter and Big B were all under the same couch, lined up in buns like the Three Stooges they were. She turned around and little Ebi was on the rear parlor couch behind her, and there, sitting quietly, just a foot behind and to the right, was Edamame.

All seven cats, and Little-Earl, number eight, were sitting together; she couldn't remember when, or even if, that had ever happened before. Ji and Earl saw her doing a mental count as she turned her head, and they noticed it too.

"Everybody's here!"

Earl said, happy.

"See Earl, everybody's keeping you company, all of us!"

And Earl bent down and gave the gentlest of kisses to the top of Little-Earl's head.

"Earl, you're welcome to stay, if you want; I know I ask you every night, and every night you say no, but figured I'd ask again, hoping you'll change your mind. I know Little-Earl wants you to stay."

Carol whispered, as Earl put his head down. Carol knew the same answer as always was on its way.

"Um, I don't know, if, you know....Lilly, um."

Carol smiled tired, and let Earl off the hook.

"I know, I know. But please do me a big favor and tell Lilly Little-Earl is still hanging in there, and that he misses her....a lot. Okay?"

"Okay, I will...."

And Earl's sentence should have ended there, that would have been expected by all. But strangely, it didn't. Like the final drip from the faucet, the straggler that falls last into the sink, once you turn the handle tight to close, Earl lent one last word, a critical one at that, to the sentence; it was an unexpected finish dribbled from the lips.

"....stay."

CHAPTER 259 – HE HUNG HIS HEAD TO HIDE THE BLUSH

There was no chance, whatsoever, to retract that cast of the line.

"What?!"

Carol yelled in utter surprise.

"Really?!"

Ji screamed at the same time.

The two screeches ricocheted around the room, bouncing off the walls, scaring Earl and scattering half the cats from the room, all before Earl could change his mind, before Earl could even figure out why he said that fateful last word.

And scared he was. No way Earl was ready for a sleep-over, not yet, that wasn't supposed to happen till October, the *Bacchanalia.* He thought he had time, *lots* of time.

But time was up, and his heart was racing.

Oh boy, oh boy, oh boy was all he kept saying in his head; I gotta take it back, I need a take-back! I need C to help me with a quick take-back!

Oh boy was all he could think about, and *oh boy* wasn't helping.

Before he could blink, Ji was on her way, bounding up the stairs, gathering the linens for his bed, and Carol was smiling at him, smiling like she hadn't in a long time.

"Thanks Earl, thank you *so much,* really. It means a lot to me, and to Little-Earl; he loves you so much."

And Earl knew right then, there was no backing out, no take-back, not even a good one from C was gonna work him out of this fix. And then he looked at Little-Earl, and realized he really didn't want to be anywhere else.

He struggled to think of something smart to say to Carol, something right, something that would make her feel good, and keep her smiling, 'cause he liked when she smiled. He liked seeing her pretty teeth, with that beautiful space, and the dimple on her chin, and she hadn't smiled like that in a long time, not since Little-Earl got sick. So he smiled back at her, and said the first thing that came to mind.

And it was the best thing he could have ever thought to say.

"You're welcome."

And he hung his head to hide the blush.

CHAPTER 260 – THANK GOD SHE GOT OFF AN EXIT CALLED HOPE

Carol gently rubbed Edamame's soft, white belly, lying on the rear parlor floor, while pushing around the burnt, half-popped kernels of corn at the bottom of the bowl. She hadn't eaten a one.

The last several days she had been conscious about trying to spend time with the others – who were starved for attention, and Edamame, invariably, seemed to get the short end. She was always such a good girl to Carol, affectionate, with a steady purr, but she wasn't a good mom, never was.

From the get-go, when they were just kittens, she would hiss or swat at all her kids if they got too close, or lingered too long beside her. Maguro, Ebi, Tobiko and Little-Earl – all four of them. And despite it all, the constant indignation, for the past six years, they always came back to her, all four, rubbing on her, looking for the affection they never got.

And Little-Earl took the most abuse. And no matter how much Edamame swatted and hissed at him, despite how much bigger and stronger than her he was, he would just put his head down, and absorb the injustice from his mother, and never retaliate, never.

He just wanted to be near her.

Except for now. Now, he didn't want to be near her, or anyone.

And Carol had hoped that Edamame would try and comfort her only son; she was healthy and vital and strong, and he wasn't, he was dying, and that wasn't right. He needed comfort, from her, but she didn't; she simply ignored him. That's just what some cats do.

And that made Carol sad, looking down at her. But she still rubbed Edamame's belly, and Eda still purred in response to the attention.

"Whatcha listening to?"

Carol whispered, but Earl put his finger up a second, trying to catch the end of the voicemail. Then he smiled.

"It's my friend Mac! Remember him? My motorcycle friend?"

Carol looked at him, with mock annoyance.

"Earl, of course I remember him; you only talk about him *all* the time, and how you're going for a ride on his *Knucklehead,* some day, and maybe it's even your *dad's Knucklehead,* maybe."

Earl sat up, excited.

"You *do* remember! You're a *real good* listener, not like C; he's *not* a good listener, especially when he's reading his newspaper, then he just gets annoyed when you even *try* and talk to him....geez! Anyway, Mac's coming tomorrow, to *Victorian Days*! Can you believe it! To see all the old cars, and to see me! He likes me, a lot; he said he doesn't have many friends – he's too picky and cranky, he says, but I don't think he's cranky at all! Well, maybe sometimes. Anyway, he said I'm his *good* friend, maybe the best good friend he has *ever* had! And that's pretty special, don't ya think? And we talk on the phone, and he doesn't talk to anyone on the phone, hardly ever, just me! And we talk on the phone a lot, even when he is with Lucien, which is, like, all the time! Just saying. And I'm not a-scared of him either, 'cause he's my friend! Did I ever tell you how I met him?"

Now Carol had heard this particular story at least a dozen times; she knew it, and Earl knew it too. But she pretended not to remember, and he pretended to believe her. It had become one of their own little secret, special rituals - those quirks between two people that only they get - and that only means something to them. And to them, it means *everything*.

"No, I don't think you ever told me that story Earl."

Carol said, with a wry smile.

And with that, Earl launched the whole backstory, as if it was first-time new, from the hundreds of motorcycles coming into Town, *Rolling Thunder,* to that special Harley, the police cruiser, all black, with a red leather seat, that he was sure his mom had ridden on with his dad when she was young - he was just *sure* of it - even though his mom would never say, either way.

And then Earl gulped a huge chest full of air, and recited, non-stop, fast, without a breath, the rest of the familiar yarn:

Earl rubbing the seat, and knocking the bike over, and Mac running over and being all mad, and Mac was big and fat and scary - his face beet red, and Lilly yelling at Mac for being not-nice to Earl, and Lilly's ears getting red, and Mac making fun of her, and *Oh Boy* how C and Earl knew Mac was in *big* trouble, and Lilly kicking Mac in the groin, and Mac falling down, and C and Marty coming to the rescue, and Earl helping Mac up, and Mac saying he needs to lose weight, and Earl saying he was sorry, and Mac saying he was sorry too, and Mac saying he really liked Earl, and Mac doesn't like many people, and Earl was the *real deal – what you see is what you get,* and then Lilly saying she was sorry, and how Earl and C laughed about that, because Lilly *never ever* says sorry, to anybody, and Mac saying Earl could ride the *Knucklehead* anytime he wanted, and C saying we'd have to set a date, and Lilly asking Mac who he bought the *Knucklehead* from, and was he black, and

Mac saying no way, and Lilly telling Earl it still could be his dad's bike, maybe, and how that made Earl happy, 'cause maybe isn't a *no*, you know, maybe is still a *maybe*, which is still pretty good.

And as Earl rattled off the Mac-story, he assumed his ritual tics and body language, scrunching his shoulders to his ears, then letting them down, just to do it again a few moments later, all while quickly rubbing his hands together and sticking the tip of his tongue in and out, licking his lips every now and then, like he did when he got over-excited. And never once, taking a second breath.

Carol watched the spectacle, provided a: *and what happened next?* every now and then, to help the charade along, and never lost her smirk as she watched Earl weave the same-old tale, yet again, exactly the same every time he told it, to the word; it was one of her favorite quirks.

Just another reason to love Earl, and this place.

And the whole time, as the fable unwound, she found herself thinking again, again, and again: thank God she got off an exit called Hope.

CHAPTERE 261 – HIS BIG PLANS SHRUNK IN HIS PANTS

Saturday, September 9, 2006.

It was day one-hundred forty-three since his first step off the bus; it was day one of *Victorian Days*.

Jessie pulled to the curb and idled; the heavy rumble and hiccup of the tired diesel lightly shook the cab, rattling the door hardware. Marty quickly drummed his fingers back and forth on her dash, like he did whenever he was excited, waiting for the big black doors to swing wide.

He and Jessie had been together twenty-two long years; she was loyal and rarely complained, although, lately, she had become a bit high-maintenance. But the thought of putting her down never crossed his mind, not a gal from down on the farm.

It was the longest relationship Marty ever had; in fact, it was the only real relationship he ever had.

And she was a truck.

And a pretty ugly one at that; beat up, patched and bandaged with baling wire, named after a long-dead mule Marty's dad once had on the farm.

Jessie, and pining for Lilly; that was about all Marty ever had for female companionship.

Until Ji.

And just like that, in a whirlwind, Marty's world opened wide. He hardly ever thought of Lilly anymore, not in *that way*, anyway, and had given up the habit of jerking off - didn't need to anymore. And he thought to himself: *how cool was that?* A wide smile creased his face.

And now he bought condoms at the pharmacy, and actually *used* them; he was the guy who strode to the counter, puffed-chest, to splay an armful of prophylactics, like laying down a straight-flush: fancy colored – *Cherry Cola* and *Blue Steel*, ribbed, dotted, sensual-studded and lubed....even glow in the dark; a cacophony of latex filled the counter, in the eighty-four pack econo-box, for all to see.

He was in his glory.

And as he fidgeted on the cab seat, still drumming his fingers nervous, he thought about tonight, watching the big black doors, like a dog.

And he thought about that dick of his, that big, beautiful, white cock, which sat wasted, asleep in his underwear, most of his adult life. He knew he was bigger than most, bigger than XL; he was in magnum-size condom territory, a shade under nine inches, but he rounded-up to an even nine - one of the few blessings Martin was bestowed at birth. Yet he was cursed to never use it, the big-gun that stayed locked in the cabinet. He knew he was *way* bigger than Button, for sure, because if that jerk-off had any size to his cock, the whole Town would have known about it, with Button leading the parade. And Marty had waited his whole life to let that puppy out in front of Lilly, to see the expression on her face, when she finally eyed his monster, ogling a real cock, after playing with that toy called Button all those years. He had hoped the *Officer's Ball* was the ticket, but it wasn't to be, not even close....Lilly barely looked at him the entire night.

But now, it didn't even matter; Lilly didn't know, never knew, what she was missing.

But Ji-Sue knew.

He'd never forget the first time she saw his *package,* as he flipped the elastic on his white *JC Penney* briefs and let that bad boy out. She didn't screech or yelp or anything; what she did was way better. Her eyes simply grew to saucers, she smiled and looked up at him and said one word:

Wow.

Then she looked down at his pecker again and smiling even wider, said it with that beautiful Korean accent a second time, extended, emphasizing, the word, for good measure.

Wow.

And that's all it took.

That's all it took to make it one of the best days, maybe *the* best day, in Marty's life....ever.

L'antre du Lion's right black door creaked and moaned as it swung wide, and out trotted Ji toward Jessie, with a big grin, the kind she always wore when she saw him. God, he loved her, hiding right under his nose all those years. That's how it happens sometimes.

And as she trotted down the slate walk, Martin's dick responded in kind, stretching against his jeans. It had a whole lifetime of catching up to do.

He reached over and pushed the cab door wide, for her to hop in. Then he thought he should have gotten out to open it proper, like a gentleman; but it was too late, she was already door-side.

Where was her overnight bag?

She hopped up on the cab seat, right on her knees like a school kid, and kissed him on the lips, a dry, goofy kiss.

"Hi!"

She was always so chipper.

"Hi; where's your bag?"

"I can't; Earl's sleeping over! Can you believe? I gotta stay; *no way* he stay if I leave; Ms. C asked me – stay."

"*What?!* But I had plans, big plans for...."

Ji kissed him again, to stop-up his lips, to stop-up the whine.

And his big plans shrunk in his pants.

CHAPTER 262 – NAKED HADN'T LEFT WHEN HE HEARD A WICKED WAIL

It was a cold steel gray.

Carol stared blankly at the solid curtain of leaden billows in the sky as she turned her head in bed, looking to the south, out the Third Street window. The kind of ugly, battleship clouds that put you in a bad mood, the kind that say today is gonna be a suck-ass day.

It was about 6:30 am; she should have already been out of bed. The crows finally woke her, like they did most mornings, congregating and cackling, staccato caws, scattered amongst the maples and oaks lining the southern sidewalk of the Park, across from the Episcopal Church. She laid quiet, and could hear muffled voices, mixing with a cacophony of sound: car doors, trunk latches, the snap of plastic storage container tops, crumpled newspaper, stretches of duct tape and the endless unfold of display-table legs.

Fuck she thought to herself; *Victorian Days,* the vendors in the Park were already well into the routine: setting up kiosks and chatting amongst themselves, complaining about parking, hoping for record crowds and banking on banner first-day sales, and it was still only 6:30 am.

She wished the day was already over.

She was in a strange mood; it was the first day Earl had spent the night, and for that alone, she should have been dancing. But he was in the rear parlor, downstairs, and seemed a world away.

And the melancholy of the day was soon joined by a sick unease, that feeling in her gut, when she remembered, like she did every morning, only seconds after waking, that Earl was still dying. It was still real; the bad dream hadn't gone away.

She had hoped to see Little-Earl walking up the bed sheets, to greet her when she woke, like old times, but she knew that was nothing but wishful thinking. She hadn't gotten up last night to check on him, knowing Earl was keeping an eye on him downstairs, but she felt guilty nonetheless. The last three to four days, Earl had been almost comatose, a true death watch. And Carol was still convinced Little-Earl was mad at her for not letting him go, but she also thought he was holding on because he wanted to live. It was that constant mental struggle, the doubt as to what to do, that tired her; it was debilitating, constantly reworking what to do in her head. And she couldn't share the struggle with her friends, friends outside Belvidere anyway; *it's a fucking cat!* They wouldn't say it to her face, of course – too polite, refined, but she knew they would think it, and they would serve her a plate of sympathy, and give her a pathetic, plasticine smile, all the while thinking she was some unmarried, childless charity case, wed to a bunch of feral strays. Nevermind she was both unmarried and childless by choice; somehow, she was to be pitied, for caring too much about a dying cat. No normal people do that; normal people just *put it to sleep*, and go get another one, or not. What's the big fucking deal?

And Carol wouldn't subject herself, or Little-Earl, to the unspoken indignity in that.

Why couldn't she just be like Edamame, and accept the situation for what is was, and move on? Maybe she should just do that, accept it, as out of her hands.

But she knew she couldn't; it wasn't in her genes, and there was no changing that.

Ji slept in the third floor guest-room – but Carol was pretty sure she was already awake. Still prone, she propped herself on an elbow and cocked an ear to listen. Sure enough, she heard her distinctive shuffle around the second floor, doing laundry, folding clothes, picking up and generally fussing-about with something or another. The pace was quickened, since she had much to do in the quiet period before the *Fashion Show* cavalcade rapped on the back door, and the tidal wave of commotion began. Carol knew Ji shooed Martin away last night, and felt bad about it, but was grateful; she didn't need another distraction on the plate.

Not today.

Carol rose, sighed long, then grabbed a robe and headed to the master bath. She stopped in the dressing room on her way, stood in the window and looked out over the Park, watching the shifts and shuffle of a half-dozen vendors below, across the street from her house. The kiosks stretched the Park perimeter, and along the crossed paths through the middle; at least a hundred vendors, selling a myriad of antiques, food, crafts and tchotchke. But she could only see a handful, from her vantage.

It was then she noticed the road was wet from the lightest of drizzles - fine drops, more like a misting than anything else.

What a shit day.

She recognized the fat, disheveled, antique-postcard vendor, with his dowdy wife, setting up shop directly across the street from her front porch. It was the same vendor, in the same spot, year after year. She didn't remember a time when they weren't there, so it must have been at least fourteen years that he scouted that space. That was common practice in the weekend vendor circuit, like taking the same seat on the bus, day after day.

His distended belly was enormous, stretched tight and ready to pop with the next bite, protruding well beyond his pants, which were scrunched and pinched at the beltline from the barrel of fat. He wore the same black pants and white ruffled shirt – already wrinkled and half-pulled from his pants, from the constant bend-over. It was the exact same faux-Victorian garb he wore every year, along with fake vintage suspenders, and a thick black belt. Always a belt and suspenders, every year; double duty to keep his pants up, and it was still a useless endeavor.

The ensemble was finished with black scuffed, economy-store sneakers; he never sprang for the boots to match the suspenders and shirt. She figured he went for comfort over style. *What a dolt*, Carol thought to herself, shaking her head at the spectacle.

And the profile never seemed to change: he always appeared to be the same barrel-belly weight, with pencil-legs, a stooped back and sloppy posture, paired with the same sour demeanor on his face, as if he was forced to set-up shop on the Park as punishment….detention for some unknown deed. The only variable over the turn of time was his oily, black hair, which thinned and receded in a scraggle toward the back of his head with each passing year, like the outgoing tide.

His wife was short and squat, with oversized glasses, pink sneakers and a too-tight, too-short sundress that accentuated her cankles and the pinches of fat gathered and bunched along her midsection. The dress changed a trifle year to year, either a faded pink or blue, with little flowers and a sloppy ruffle on the hem; but she never seemed to change a bit.

And in the fourteen years Carol had been watching, she never heard the woman utter a *single* word. As her husband played in-charge, barking orders, huffing and sighing, she simply operated automaton, helping set up boxes containing thousands of dingy, antique post-cards, sitting quietly for hours as customers ambled by, fingering the cards and telling boring, long-winded stories about their own postcard tales that no one cared to hear, and helping put the thousands of cardboard mementos back away again in plastic bins at day's end, shoved haphazard in their tired white van, dirty and dented.

And throughout the annual ordeal, the woman sported neither a smile, nor a frown, just a thin line of lips.

She was invisible.

The only steady change were the two children, boy and girl, indentured servants forced to kill a weekend once a year in this stupid, bum-fuck Town, responding to barks from their father to set up *this*, move *that* or put away *the other thing*. They oozed boredom and rarely listened; and when they did, all movement was at half-speed, deliberate or otherwise, which only led to more barking and screaming. Carol had watched them grow, from preschoolers to young adults, and always felt bad for them, for each of the past fourteen years, they seemed nothing but miserable, at least the one weekend a year they tooled around in front of her window. And she was sure they would invariably grow into clones of their miserable parents.

A wretched lot.

Her eyes slowly rose from the postcard family to the crows above, roosting in their two favorite trees. She was always happy to see them, no matter what the day. She wanted to smile at them, but she couldn't bring herself to do it.

Ji stuck her head in.

"Morning; okay for Earl to feed the cats? Little-Earl's sitting in the kitchen; maybe he's hungry."

They both knew he wouldn't eat, but Carol was happy he was okay, which simply meant he somehow made it through another night. Maybe he was happy that Earl spent the night; Little-Earl always loved Earl. He was scared of most people, but not him….never him.

"Sure, I'm gonna take a shower."

Ji didn't answer, turned, and was on her way.

"Did he sleep okay? Big-Earl, I mean?"

Carol belatedly called to her, into the hall. She figured Little-Earl didn't sleep well, if at all, so she didn't ask. Besides, Ji wouldn't know anyway; she'd ask Earl when she saw him.

Ji stopped, turned and simply shrugged.

"I think so; he was smiling when he was cleaning the litterbox."

And that made Carol smile too, a small one, but a smile nonetheless.

She disrobed and stepped into the oversized, stone-walled shower. There was no door on the shower, just a large opening, so as she stood under the rainhead, she watched the vendors through the arched, double-wide window across from the shower, peering between the open Venetian slats. The scalding hot water danced off her head; it felt good.

She slowly closed her eyes, stood still and lost herself in random thought, as the water cascaded down her body, warming her skin, before circling the drain and disappearing forever.

Earl was on his way back downstairs - to the kitchen to feed the cats - having just finished the litter box ritual on the third floor. He loved cleaning the litterbox, both of them, scooping the perfumed clay and shaking the shovel, left to right, left to right, till all tiny grains fell back in the box, then carefully placing the lumps of poop and pee into the black plastic bag, inside the blue plastic garbage can. It was a *very* important job, and Carol and Ji entrusted him to do it alone; and the cats depended on him too. He always felt best when all the lumps were gone, and he got to run the back of the scooper across the cleaned litter, making it flat as a table, with little grooves in it, like the grooves he scratched in the soil under the briar bushes in the woods, on the way to the *Big Crack*.

When Earl was done, Big B, who would always run up the steps with Earl, would sit quietly beside him and patiently watch the process, would look up at him with his yellow doe eyes, give him a single meow, more like a tiny yelp of approval, then step in to christen the freshly raked clay. Every day Earl cleaned the box, Big B was there. He never did it for Ji, just Earl. Earl would just watch him and smile, happy that Big B approved, then clean it once again, after Big B was finished with his business, and both of them, Earl and Big B together, side by side, would walk down the third floor steps….best friends forever.

Ji was switching a load of laundry on the second floor, just outside the library. Earl heard the shower water running, and hustled a bit past the dressing room door, to get away from the master bath, just in case Carol was still walking around, and not dressed all the way, or worse yet, naked.

He wasn't ready for naked.

And the idea of naked hadn't left when he heard a wicked wail.

CHAPTER 263 – ON THE BED, IN A FETAL SPOON, SHAKING SCARED

Earl caromed down the steps and ran into the kitchen, just as Little-Earl bellowed a second time, eyes half-closed, wobbling on shaky legs. He scooped him up just before he fell over outside the kitchen, beside the powder room, and ran, full-sprint upstairs, with Earl convulsing in his arms, shock waves of stiffness, the horrid spasms that come with paralysis, and stroke. His eyes were blank, the pupils rapidly rocking back and forth in the whites of his eyes, like unbalanced eggs.

He was blind.

Earl ran right into the master bath, by this time he was crying uncontrollable and pleading with Little-Earl:

Shh, Shh, no, no, no.

Over and over again, trying to calm Little-Earl as he continued to spasm uncontrollably.

Earl ran to the shower stall, a lavish, open stone cavern, with a ten foot ceiling and no door – with stain glass angels peering down from a reclaimed church panel and an immense seated lion statue, mounted on the wall. Earl was face-to-face with Carol, caught off-guard, a full-frontal nude.

But Earl never saw a thing, his eyes were squeezed tight, head down.

"He's, he's…."

Earl whispered, between sobs; but he didn't say what, or anything else.

Carol could see the spasms, and hear the moans, the first sounds Little-Earl uttered in a week plus. Although what she heard, she had never heard before; deep guttural carps, excruciating....cries no animal, no living thing, should make.

And neither knew what to do.

As quick as Earl ran into the shower, he ran out, dashing into Carol's bedroom and gently falling upon the bed, still cupping Little-Earl in his massive arms.

It was seven in the morning, straight-up.

And there Earl laid, on the bed, in a fetal spoon, shaking scared.

CHAPTER 264 – SLOWLY FLOATING AWAY

It was seven in the morning, straight-up.

He was in a large, cold building, one-story, with low ceilings, in amorphous shades of gray, like an old abandoned school, or an office building, or maybe some sort of institution. It wasn't clear what it was used for.

But one thing *was* clear, for-certain; the space was sterile, and felt dead.

This place, it was flooded, and he was treading water; without checking, he somehow knew it was much too deep to stand – he could sense it, like an ocean....*that* kind of deep.

So he kept his grip tight on the floating debris beside him; he couldn't see or make out, by feel, what exactly he was holding, to help him stay afloat, but he remembered it had the feel of a log, some sort of log....bumpy, but smooth.

He certainly didn't know how it, or he, got there, but he didn't question being in this place, this predicament - he just accepted his lot, as he accepted the log, or whatever it was in his grip, which was submerged, hiding just below the surface of the water beside him.

He ran his fingers back and forth, back and forth, feeling his way up and down the submerged *thing*.

It sure felt like a log.

All was deathly quiet; he didn't remember hearing a thing, not even the water lapping around his body. And as the periphery came into focus, like the slow lifting of a fog, he noticed others half-submerged in the water around him. He didn't recognize a soul, although they were hard to really see, engulfed in an opaque shroud.

The others simply floated in the water in silence, suspended like bobbers on a line, waiting for a fish to hit the bait. Although he didn't notice it at first, one by one they began to vanish around him, to where he did not know, for he actually never saw one disappear. Maybe they slipped under the surface, but maybe not; maybe they just dissolved, like the fog.

Soon, he found himself alone, writing with some sort of marker, on a packet he desperately clung to. He couldn't read what he wrote, it too was opaque, like a view through milk-glass. But what he wrote had a strange feeling, and it *felt* like he wrote:

This is my log

Like some sort of diary, but maybe it wasn't; maybe it wasn't that type of log at all. And maybe he didn't write anything, and it didn't mean anything, at all.

Although he didn't see it happen, nor knew how it happened, just like that, the water was gone.

The room was dry, crisp white and clean, with an endless concrete floor, smooth and monolith, not a blemish. And it shouldn't have been clean, not with the water and detritus and floating bodies, but it was.

It surely was.

And it was dim, dimmer than you'd expect for such a clean, sterile space. Too dim to really see.

And the log, it wasn't a log at all, not anymore, but rather a crate of some sort, which he pushed quite easily along the concrete, as if it was set upon thousands of tiny metal ball bearings, the kind they throw under the

2045

casket, in a mausoleum vault, to move it around, with ease….with the simple push of a single finger.

And he noticed several other *things* shared the space in this dim room; they were there, with him, but he couldn't see, couldn't discern, what they actually were, so he resigned himself to simply call them *things*. They seemed, always, to be just on the peripheral edge of his ken, just a hair beyond what his eyes could focus upon; they were a darkened blur, but they were surely there, off to the side, and there were more than one, whatever it was they were. Many more than one.

Again, nothing made a sound, not even the ball bearings. At least he didn't remember any sounds; if there were, he had forgotten them.

The rest of the space was emptiness, endless, endless emptiness, and plenty of it. There was no other way to describe it.

And in an instant, like the wave that grows from nothing and suddenly engulfs you, a sickening feeling drowned him; he knew, he somehow realized, that he was *utterly alone*, and that no one else was there, or here, or could be, or ever would be….*ever*. He felt as if he was on another planet, not here, where he knew – a place from which he drew comfort, but somewhere else, somewhere lonely, and scary….and far, far away from anything he truly knew. And he sensed there was no way home; no way to ever get back to what felt right, to everything that felt the opposite of this horrid place.

And as he looked around this emptiness, helpless, for some reason, he wondered, and worried, right at that moment, as to where he would sleep.

And with that thought, and for no reason, he began to run, wild, like a dog, up what was now a long, narrow corridor of that dim, clean, horrible space….a full sprint.

He turned the corner, to the left, and yet another endless corridor faced him, which he sprinted frantically through yet again, his head darting left and right, looking around in a panic, for what, he did not know. All he seemed to know was that he was going to be here, in this ugly place, forever….alone.

Halfway down that limitless, white corridor, he noticed another hallway, an offshoot, which suddenly appeared, out of nowhere, to his left.

And it stopped him cold.

Just inside that hallway, he saw her, the back of her head, and she was walking away. And he knew, even after so many years, decades, he just knew, it was *really* her.

It was Kristine, slowly floating away.

CHAPTER 265 - THE COLOR OF DEATH….AND HE KNEW HER

He watched his hand reach for her shoulder, her left shoulder, in slow motion. He had been waiting for this day forever, to gently touch what he'd missed all those years; to finally be happy, safe, to not be alone anymore.

But the instant his fingers first felt the black fabric lying on her bony shoulder, he knew it wasn't her.

She wore a top the color of an abyss, an endless void, and ice-white pants, with hair the consistency of straw, which had no color at all, not even white described it, it was beyond white….simply *blankness*.

And as she slowly turned, a decrepit woman confronted him, with opaque orbs in the sockets where her eyes should set, and transparent, wrinkled skin, its pallor the color of death....and he knew her.

CHAPTER 266 – AN EVIL DEAD SMILE PARTING PARCHED LIPS

The succubus seized his forearms, one in each bony hand, and cinched him tight, much too tight for such a frail corpse; it was a grip he couldn't wrest, as much as he struggled to break free.

He was paralyzed with fear, unable to speak, unable to move his eyes from the horrid orbs.

It was exactly *1:17 am*, in this place, even though this place really didn't have time. But somehow he knew it was 1:17 am, and he was scared to death. He felt it should have been 1:13 am, but it wasn't.

It clearly wasn't.

Not a sound was made, nor a word was spoken, as she began to spin him, counter-clockwise, faster and faster, spiraling ever faster, and his skin began to crawl, as he watched it slowly form on the ghastly face before him; an evil dead smile parting parched lips.

CHAPTER 267 – SHIT-SCARED OF A DEAD HAG SHE NEVER MET

"Wake up! C, C….*let go! **Let go!***"

She was screaming hysterically at him, aghast, as Cord moaned in a voice she didn't recognize, several octaves too deep, as if someone, or *something* was hiding inside his head.

His eyes and mouth suddenly sprung open, unnatural, and that scared her even more. He saw her before him, his heart still racing, his mind still spinning with the hag, unsure where he was, or how he got here, or who this woman was, standing before him. His hands cuffed both her wrists in a vice, the hair on his arms upright in fright. He could feel the gorgon breathing, heavy, just inside his head, hiding in the folds of his brain, waiting for him to close his eyes again, and slip back to her. He was more afraid of that smile than anything else, that evil smile, lifeless, formed from cracked and cratered blue lips.

"Let go! *Let go! **Let go!***"

Her eyes were wide open, scared shitless, as she pulled hard against his iron grip, trying in vain to break free.

Like a time-lock, he set her free, and she was flew fast away from him, like a gunshot, falling hard against the wall. He was drenched in sweat, breathing heavy.

"What the fuck? *What the fuck?* **What the fuck was that?!**"

Was all he said, over and again, as he slowly came back to Belvidere, and the reality of this strange place settled back in.

And as his head cleared of the dread, he found himself back in his bed, and he recognized the woman in the room with him, laying against the wall in a slump; it was Lilly, he told himself, *it's just Lilly,* it's not the incubus, it's safe....you're safe. And with it, a feeling of calm settled over him.

But with that respite, the memories of Lillian rushed back, like the tide, and Cord remembered last night, and Button's freshly laundered belongings, laid neatly on her bed. And his brief calm morphed to utter disdain.

C looked at Lillian with bad intent.

"What are you doing here?!"

....in my apartment, talking to me? Get the fuck out; leave me the fuck alone; get lost; all the above. The mix of bitter thoughts jumbled through C's head, as he watched Lillian slowly reset on her feet from the fall to the floor. He didn't apologize, nor say another word about the incident, nor did she. The spill was simply ignored.

All Lillian heard were the five accusatory words that left Cord's lips, and found herself frightened of the man lying in the bed; she felt as if she was staring into the eyes of someone she didn't know. Instinctively, she stepped back, further away from him, closer to the bedroom door.

She spoke hesitant, apologetic, ready in an instant for flight-mode, should things turn south.

"Sorry to wake you, sorry....but Ji called; you gotta get up to the house – now! Something bad happened, with Earl, Little-Earl."

"Fuck, that scared the *shit* out of me!"

"Sorry, didn't mean to scare you; I knocked, hard, but you didn't answer."

But C didn't hear what Lilly just said, he was looking down, talking to himself - not her, as he watched, and felt, the hair on his arms slowly retreat.

"That was a bad one, the worst one yet....*fucking bad! What the hell was that? Fuck!*"

He whispered, again, talking only to himself, trying to figure what that *thing* was in his head.

Then almost as an afterthought, he slowly raised his head to belatedly answer her, in a nasty, dismissive air. He didn't even want to look at her face.

"Not *you*, the fucking dream *[C said, looking at Lillian, annoyed that he was even having a conversation with her]*! Shit, I just got a chill down my spine, thinking about it. Jesus, I can't shake that old lady, scared the fucking crap out of me. *That felt way too real;* I haven't been scared like that in....years. Maybe ever."

C was again speaking to himself. He briefly closed his eyes, to soothe the awful memory, and just as his lids shut, the hag appeared from nowhere, her hideous face enormous, filling his head....a cavernous open mouth and dead-blue lips swallowing him whole.

"*Ah!*"

C yelled, as he jumped a bit and the hair again rose vertical on his arms.

"What?! *What?!*"

Lilly screeched, as scared as he was, but of him.

"**Holy shit!**"

C breathed out with a forced puff of air, as he jumped out of bed and shook his head left to right, trying to shake her out.

"Bad dream, I *think*."

And now Cord *was* talking to Lillian; as much as he didn't want to, she at least felt safe, as long as his eyes stayed open.

"What is it? Was it?"

Lilly asked, hesitant.

C looked at her, really looked at her, and suddenly realized how glad he was that she was there….that someone *real* was with him. Not that Lilly could do anything, but having her there, in the room, was better than being alone with the gorgon. God, that lifeless hag felt so real, like she was going to pull him back into his head, into that awful building, and if she did, he knew, or at least felt, there was no coming back. He focused on keeping his eyes open, trying not to blink, and if he did so, to make it fast, knowing she was waiting for him, inside his head.

"I don't wanna talk about it; fuck, that really creeped me out, still is. Man, how did that feel *so real?* Some old hag, a dead lady, blue lips, black hole for a mouth; I don't know if she even had teeth, she had me by the arms and was spinning me, smiling at me, but a really bad smile, and she wasn't letting go, and she was bringing me, dragging me, someplace you don't *ever* wanna be."

Then Lilly like the flick of a light, suddenly recalled her own nightmare.

"Holy shit, I just remembered, I had a bad dream too, right when Ji called – she woke me up, didn't remember it till just now, when you said about yours….strange. I don't really remember what happened, just bits, but I was lying down, it was real dark, pitch black, and someone, or something, was standing behind me, right by my headboard, looking down at me, but there was no headboard, and I was scared; then the phone rang. That's it, that's all I remember."

"This dream shit's gotta stop; I haven't dreamed for years, and now that's all I do, and they're getting more and more *fucked up* each time."

C shook his head again, to shake the nightmare away, wipe it clean.

But it didn't work; he knew that thing, that horrible hag, was still there, waiting for him. And he knew one thing; he wasn't fucking sleeping again, not anytime soon.

"Cord, did you hear me before, about Ji's call? Little-Earl's not good – something bad happened – they didn't tell me what. You better go; it doesn't sound good."

Ay set the succubus aside.

"What time is it?"

"A little before eight, 'bout quarter of, I think."

Lilly said.

In less than five minutes, C was dressed and gone, and Lillian was all alone, shit-scared of a dead hag she never met.

CHAPTER 268 – SHE SHOOK HER HEAD NO, AND THE NIGHTMARE CONTINUED

Lilly leaned against her counter, staring blankly at the kettle, taking forever to come to a boil. A packet of jasmine waited patiently in the teacup, to comfort her. Although she always kept a box on hand, she rarely drank it. It was her favorite as a little girl, because it was her mom's favorite, and they both drank it, together, at the kitchen table, with her feet dangling, nowhere near long enough to touch the floor. The flavor, the aroma, was a respite; it brought her back….way back, to a time she could smile about, and take comfort in.

The television droned, muffled, in the living room at the far end of the hall; she had no idea what was on, didn't matter, it simply served as background noise, human voices to sweep away the lingering creep.

The whole run over, C couldn't shake the thought of the hag. He did nothing more than quick blinks, ever conscious of the act. He didn't want to meet her, ever again, and closing his eyes gave her a window.

His eyes stayed open.

He dodged the vendors, the early-birds and the bustle in the Park, and walked straight-in. He didn't remember the exact time, but at some point, obsession with the gorgon finally dissolved into the shadows, for now, and he focused on Little-Earl.

It was about quarter past eight, and Little-Earl was calm; Earl had gently cleaned his nose of crusted snot, and wiped as best he could, with little success, the thick, dried remnants of molasses goo, still there from when Carol was trying to feed him. That futility had ended, but the goo remained….a cruel reminder.

Usually Earl would pull his head, duck and fuss whenever Earl, Carol or Ji tried to clean his face; even weak, he had enough energy to dodge that unpleasant task….he hated it.   But now, he was completely compliant, not from resignation, but from lack of awareness – due to the blindness, and the stroke. He lacked the ability to stop them, even if he wanted.

They really weren't sure where Little-Earl was now; he wasn't here, that was for sure.

As Cord entered the bedroom, he was greeted by Earl's back, still cradling Earl. Carol was kneeling beside the bed, eyes swollen and bloodshot, from an on/off cry. It had been raining steady the whole run over, and C was soaked, but no one noticed, or cared, including him. No one said a word upon his arrival, Carol looked at him briefly and gave a half-smile, a thanks-for-coming, then turned back to Earl, and didn't look at him again.

Carol prayed the *Fashion Show* would be canceled, the rain would surely put an end to that….the only good to come out of a shit day. A call to the *Show* director, as Carol kneeled on the floor, confirmed, in fact, that it was not.

The stupid fucking *Fashion Show* was on.

She cursed and shook her head, as the phone flipped shut.

Just then, Earl licked his dirty left paw, just once, a feeble attempt to clean what he likely couldn't see; it was the last thing he ever did on his own.

And in a warped way, Carol saw it, the lick, as a positive sign; positive in what sense, to what end, she didn't think about - it was simply a minuscule positive in a sea of negative, and that little tic, something you normally wouldn't even notice, was good enough, at least for right now, kneeling beside the bed.

It was silly, really, the whole notion, but at the time, in the moment, it was anything but silly. To Carol, it mattered.

And that's how they stayed for the next forty-five minutes - Earl, Carol and C in the bedroom, with all eyes trained on Little-Earl. Ji shuttled around the house, continuing preparations for the *Show*….a train-wreck on its way.

Cord leaned against the bedroom wall, not too close to Carol's bed; he didn't want to intrude into their space, and he felt like an intruder. No one spoke; each was watching and waiting for something to happen next.

By 9:00 am Earl was still fetal, laying on the foot of Carol's bed, forming a protective cocoon around Little-Earl. Another wave of tics and spasms irrupted, his back arching stiff, unnatural, each spasm certainly signaling the end had come, till it didn't, and he went limp once again, quietly breathing, his lifeless pupils rocking back and forth, like an unbalanced egg.

C saw the first convulsion at 9:00 am, and shook his head; he felt so bad for the little guy. He walked over to Carol and whispered in her ear, asking gently is she wanted him to end it, to smother Little-Earl under a pillow. He had offered it before, in fact as fresh as April, right before that long bus ride to this strange place. But that was different, it wasn't an animal, and it would have been easier. However, even if Carol said yes, he wasn't sure he could do it, to Little-Earl; animals were different than people. And to C, that mattered. Given that, he would have still likely done it, for Little-Earl….and for her. But Carol just started crying again; slowly, she shook her head no, and the nightmare continued.

CHAPTER 269 – SHE KISSED HIS WARM BELLY, ONE MORE TIME

For five hours, sans break, Earl cradled Little-Earl on the bed, through countless spasms, his legs kicking involuntary, his pupils rocking back and forth in a steady, sickening motion, and with each episode, Earl gently whispered to his friend that it would be okay, and that he loved him….all through a quiet cry. He placed his hands and legs on Little-Earls limbs, to pin them down and calm the quiver, his tiny head rested in the crotch of Earl's armpit.

He was so skinny, so frail….just bones.

And that's how they stayed, the two of them, in the quiet of the second floor, while Ji and C tried their best to control and herd the hurricane on the floor below, a chaos of two dozen women and children frantically dressing and undressing in scores of outfits, strewn over tables, chairs and sofas. And in the middle of it all was Carol, trying her best to endure the spectacle with a faint plastic smile, parading around the porch automaton, wearing beautiful vintage dresses she would just assume rip off in anger, in frustration, amidst a steady piss of rain, dropping from a leaden sky.

By 2:30 pm, the *Fashion Show* had come and gone, and the house was, thankfully, quiet again. Mac had canceled his trip to Belvidere; the *Knucklehead* had never felt rain. The decision was just as well; Earl wasn't leaving Carol's bed, no way, no how. Mac and Lucien sent their sympathies to Little-Earl, after Ji had answered Earl's phone, and gave them the sad news.

C left to shower, Ji managed the aftermath and Earl stayed fetal, with Carol also lying on her bed, sandwiching Little-Earl between them. The damp, muffled din of Victorian Days streamed for hours in the street below, seeping through the second floor screen, a

jumble of waterlogged sounds – the same year after year:
the auctioneers bark from the picnic basket charity
auction – to fund high school sholarships, the clog of
horse hooves – buggy rides endlessly circling the Park,
music from street grinders, and the steady sidewalk
shuffle of people passing and perusing the vendor
booths, picking up, eyeing in half-interest, and then
putting down, one tchotchke after another, including the
dingy old postcards, piled on folding tables afront
L'antre du Lion.

Zeke, Big B, Hunter, Tobiko and Maguro were all
asleep, spread in various form across the bed, in and
amongst Carol and the two Earls. Edamame was asleep
on the dresser nearby.   Only Ebi was absent; where, no
one knew.

Carol gently washed Earl's paws, the best she could, and
brushed his fur, rubbing his nose with hers, kissing his
face and belly; he had been calm for the last hour or so -
hopefully the spasms had ended.   His warmth felt good
against Carol's cheek.

"I eat too fast."

Carol said, from nowhere.

"I eat too fast, and I get sick to my stomach. I feel guilty
about eating, since Earl isn't, or can't, so I eat too fast,
wolf it down, can't help myself, like I want to get it
done, quick, before anyone sees me, before Earl sees me,
even though he can't see, not now, anyway. I feel so
guilty, it's…."

And she just stopped, shook her head and frowned.

Earl didn't answer, he just looked at her with mournful
eyes, and gently put his hand on her shoulder.   He
wasn't afraid to, at least not this time. And his hand felt
warm, and safe. Carol tilted her head toward his hand,

pinching it lightly between her cheek and the round of her shoulder. He was a comfort she desperately needed.

"Why's he staying?"

She asked, defeated.

And Earl just shrugged; he wished he had an answer, the right answer, so he could make Carol feel better, but he didn't.

"Maybe he's not ready, not yet; maybe he still likes when you kiss his belly."

And Carol quietly leaned forward and kissed Little-Earl's warm belly, long and hard, breathing him in. And she kissed his belly again, and again and again.

And finally, Little-Earl closed his eyes and went to sleep, as she kissed his warm belly, one more time.

Somehow, Earl made it through the night.

On Sunday morning, at 7:15 am, the 10th of September, the second, God-awful *Victorian Day,* he meowed, once, long, and loud. But it wasn't good; it was more of a guttural wail, a plead.

He was mostly cold by now, to the touch, his legs, his tail, even his belly. Carol had covered him with a green terry hand towel, to keep him warm. Earl always hated to be covered by anything, a blanket, a sheet, anything, for more than a second or two. Even holding him too long created a wig and a mad-dash….a run-away. But he was paralyzed, and couldn't get away from Carol's hand towel; just another reason for him to hate her, forever, Carol thought.

She touched his front paw – the center of the pad, and he closed it around her finger, like he always used to do, a handshake.

"Just a reflex."

She said aloud, mostly to herself, hoping she was wrong, but knowing she wasn't….probably, anyway. Earl shook his head a defiant *no*; the kind of shake that says you're wrong….the kind that says it meant more. Much more.

And for that, she smiled.

Only Earl could make her smile at a time like this, a real smile; she loved them both, so much.

The sun broke through yesterday's gray, and the second *Victorian Day* was dry, and more upbeat. But, like every *Victorian* Sunday, it was subdued - not as many events around the Park, no classic cars, no buggy rides, less vendors, less visitors circling the Square. A warm-down from yesterday's frenetic, main event. But the postcard-monger remained, family in tow, in his same old spot before the *Lion's Den*.

Most importantly, Sunday meant no Fashion Show, so *L'antre du Lion* sat quiet beside the Park.

The locals typically came out of the woodwork on Sunday, after church, of course, to circle the Green, check out the kiosks....to see and be seen. The Sunday *Victorian Days* stroll for the *insiders*.

Carol gave Ji the day off, but she came over anyway, support for Little-Earl. Marty spent the day with her – a ten-hour marathon date – eating funnel cakes, sausage sandwiches and roasted peanuts from the Park vendors, listening to the *Hackettstown Big Band* play a free concert in the center of the Square, sipping iced tea and drinking *Southsides* on Carol's porch, holding hands and smiling at each other like goofy teenagers. Carol actually enjoyed the spectacle; it was a welcome respite.

Earl ran over quick in the morning, before Lilly woke, just to kiss Little-Earl on the nose. But he spent the remainder of the day away, catching up on chores around the house, helping Sam at the store and putting in the requisite Lilly time. Although she felt bad for Little-Earl, she was becoming more and more ornery at Earl's extended absence, and her brother paid in grouchiness the longer he stayed away; him spending Friday night at Carol's was particularly painful - only the excuse of Little-Earl being sick, and Lilly's love of the little guy, saved Earl from even larger helpings of insult and indignation.

Carol spent the day in her favorite porch chair, legs up on the ottoman, reading a pile of newspapers she hadn't gotten to, drinking coffee and simply relaxing. Trying to keep her mind on other things, between thinking about Little-Earl, and the death-watch.

And she missed Earl; just not having him around, not seeing his face, or knowing he was in the next room, for even one day, made her sad.

Buck stopped by to say hi; he was hanging with Linda from the *Palace,* just *friends* he said - he must have felt the need to qualify. The body language, spacing and facial tics between the two spoke otherwise, and Carol wondered whose benefit that statement served. They looked cute together; a nice young couple.

Margery and Mae waved and chatted from the near Hardwick Street sidewalk; Joe was in tow, weighed down carrying a handful of white plastic bags, each filled with knick-knacks and mementos of Margery and Mae's first *Victorian Days* together, no doubt making a handful of vendors happy on a slow Sunday in September. Joe was their own little valet, she thought; but he was smiling, and that was all that mattered. Mrs. Ackerman and Mrs. Klein, from Brookfield, followed close behind, chatting away, both threw a perfunctory wave and a smile Carol's way.

Ryan and Tommy, the priest and his partner, shuffled up the steps, grinning as always, and leaned against the porch rail, earnestly asking about plans for Earl's surprise party and how Little-Earl was doing. They were always so thoughtful, so nice to Carol. She always imagined asking Ryan to marry her, if she ever did such a thing. She never had the inclination, not really, until Earl; Earl Liddell, she would marry. The thought of that made her happy. It was crazy, actually. Thank God for Cord; if it wasn't for him, Earl would still be handing her a hand-written rent envelope and running off the porch once a month, and she would never have known the best present she could ever wish for came and went, unnoticed, unappreciated, every thirty days. She'd thought about spending the rest of her life with Earl, marrying him, half-joking, half-not, more the latter as each day passed, wondering exactly how she would go about asking Earl, without him having a coronary on the spot.

Actually, she knew exactly how she'd ask him....*exactly*. And the thought of it made her cry, every time.

Jim-Bob, the penguin, waddled by the side of the house, down Third Street, but Carol didn't know him, so she missed the walk-by. Nor did she notice Smillie, the drunk cab-driver, sitting on a bench across the way, since she never met him either. He looked sober, his hands folded quietly across his striped shirt, stretched tight over a cartoon beer-belly. At some point, his eyes glazed over, and he fell asleep in the dappled sun.

But she did notice Greg, the State Trooper. She never knew his last name, he was always just *Greg - the State Trooper*. He was a huge, muscular guy, good-looking too. He was a pleasure to look at. His wife and kids were at his sides; they looked like a nice family. But again, she really didn't know him, or them. She really didn't know most of the locals, not really.

But he was a nice-looking guy, which made her, involuntarily, think of Button. She quickly put him, and the County Fair, and the van, out of her mind.

Stinky-Steve walked down Third, on the opposite side of the street, in a certain hurry to nowhere. No one talked to him, nor him to anyone, and eye contact was never made. He was a ghost, like the homeless sleeping on the city sidewalk that people brush by, walking within inches of, but never tread upon, navigated like one seems to avoid bumping into a lamppost, or a street sign, and given as much thought.

Tommy and Vinny passed by on the small clunker bikes the clique of troublemakers all rode around Town, each with a date riding on the back, sporting Goth makeup and barely-enough clothes. The foursome were here and past in less than ten seconds. Carol never even saw them, her head turned to grab a tepid mug of coffee on the side table, in need of a reheat.

Sue, the cod-fish from Sam's checkout counter, and her twin sister, walked up Hardwick side-by-side; Carol recognized Sue from the market, smiled and waved. Sue returned the gesture, as did her twin, even though she didn't know Carol. Sue leaned over and told her sister about Earl's surprise party and *that's the lady doing it.* The sister nodded, and soon, they too were out of sight. Carol remembered Sue being a bit odd-looking – a funny mouth and skinny, with a nice body, but an odd bit of a rounded belly, as if she was early-pregnant, but she wasn't. But today, she didn't look half-bad, nor did her sister. They actually looked kind of cute as a two-some.

Carol's phone vibrated on the glass table beside her chair; she looked at the ID - it was Bud Wiseman, no doubt asking about the *Brownfield Fund.* She was sure it was one or likely more questions as to where the first portfolio properties stood in the acquisition pipeline, the status of end-users, who else bought in – since he was such a gossip about such things - and had she closed the fund yet, with the last question being the only one he truly cared about. She ignored the call, and didn't bother to listen to his voicemail; she would return it later, after dark.

Sam, Woody and Moe waved from across the street; the threesome was circling the Park, each with a hot-dog-on-a-stick in hand. She wondered why the three didn't come over to chat; all three had crushes on her, for years, and once she caught their eye, she figured she was trapped on the porch for an hour, if not more, listening to their silly jokes and sexual innuendo. It was all in fun, and she enjoyed it, but in small doses. With all three, if would surely be a testosterone-fueled old-man feeding frenzy. But instead, nothing happened - they just politely smiled and kept walking....strange. Then she spied the backsides of Moe and Woody's wives, ten steps behind, flipping through plastic bins of postcards; there was her answer. As they shuffled by, neither of the women proffered even a passing glance her way – she smirked at the slight.

She figured Frank was tending the store; either that, or home drunk. No way she'd see Frank enjoying *Victorian Days;* he didn't enjoy anything but a thirty-pack of swill, a couch and being arms-length from the remote.

Up next in the parade, twenty yards back, was that fat-ass gossip Jane, yammering non-stop to some old guy Carol didn't know; he looked simply exhausted from her rant. Carol wondered if his ears were bleeding.

It was actually kind of fun, all the people-watching. Was *everyone* she knew going to walk by today?

Everyone, it seemed, except Lillian and Cord.

She never saw either one of them. Of course Lilly was no surprise, but lately, neither was Cord. He was increasingly absent from her circle, with no one knowing to where he would slip away. And she missed him. When he was around, Earl was much more talkative, and relaxed, and she got the best of both worlds in him and Earl. If she could braid them together into one, that would be *some* package, she thought. Maybe seventy-five percent Earl, twenty-five percent Cord. No, maybe ninety percent Earl, no ninety-five percent; how about ninety-nine?

She smiled at the game.

Then, like a wave, the sick realization that Little-Earl was lying under the hand towel at the foot of her bed returned. And she felt guilty about feeling good, and leaving him up there, all alone.

On and off throughout the day, between chats with neighbors, cups of coffee and sections of news read, Carol would lay the paper down, creep quietly upstairs, through the dressing room and stand in the wardrobe, to watch the tiny green hand towel laying at the end of the bed. Earl was so slight, it was hard to tell that he was even there, under the terry. But his head stuck from the right side, and the tip of his tail from the left. She would focus on the middle of the towel; she had to stare at it for several seconds, to see the tell-tale movement, since his breathing was light and long between inhales. She didn't want to disturb him, so when she saw movement, she sometimes went closer, to kiss him once on the head, but other times she simply let him be. His eyes were always three-quarters-closed; it wasn't sleep, but maybe it was, if he was blind....she didn't really know what to call it. But the quarter-sliver she saw of his eyes were the same brilliant green; Earl always had the most beautiful, most stunning green eyes.

After the fat-ass Jane passed, Carol folded the paper to go check on Little-Earl, for at least the sixth time in the last six hours. It was around 4 pm. She crept quietly upstairs, through the dressing room, through the wardrobe, and into the bedroom, as was the ritual, and silently spied the towel.

And as she stared, she saw no movement. She moved closer, and saw that a single fly had lit on the green terry, on Earl's belly. In anger she swatted the air and it disappeared. She stared in silence at the clock; it was 4:10 pm. She slowly moved her face right down to his belly, looking for any sign of breath....but there was no movement.

It was then, her nose an inch from the towel, that she knew, for sure, as she inhaled the slight scent of death.

2068

CHAPTER 271 – SHE KISSED HIS WARM BELLY, ONE MORE TIME

Saturday, September 23, 2006. It had been one-hundred fifty-seven long nights since Cord stepped off the Greyhound and thirteen days since Little-Earl died at the foot of Carol's bed.

Carol sat at the dining room table, laptop open; the *Brownfield Fund Prospectus* and spreadsheets were strewn haphazard across the table, figures, tables and maps were open in links on her screen.

Big B was asleep on the dining room table beside her, laying fat and happy on his side, splayed across her papers, as usual. His striped back was snug up against the heat of the computer keyboard. Carol looked at him and ran her fingers through the thick, healthy orange and white fur on his warm, too-round belly. She quarter-turned her left hand and looked at the tip of her pointer; she could barely see a shadow of the scab, the puncture where Little-Earl had inadvertently bit her, when she was trying to give him a steroid pill. She wished it would scar permanently, never heal, to always remind her of him.   But it didn't; it had healed beautifully; in fact, she pretended she could see a shadow, turning her finger in the chandelier light to detect the tell-tale shadow. But she actually saw nothing at all; it had faded away to nothing.

She missed Earl terribly.

It had been two weeks since the *Victorian Days* weekend and it felt like forever.   The emotional drain, the cumulative toll, of tending to him became apparent when it ended – a tremendous burden was lifted, and a tremendous grief of a different kind settled in, a feeling of emptiness….loneliness.   To her, Earl was always so much more than a cat, more than a pet; he wasn't a *pet,* he was always so much more….a best friend.

To go through this grief seven more times? That thought
was unbearable.

She looked down at Big; he had always been her pal, but
now, since Earl was gone, he was inseparable from her
side, following her wherever she went.

Carol looked down at Big; he was purring. He was fat,
happy and healthy. She smiled, looking forward to
kissing that belly for years to come. How could she
know, ever know, that he too would be dead in less than
a year.

She bent down and kissed his belly, once, twice, thrice,
breathing him in. Then she kissed his warm belly, one
more time.

CHAPTER 272 – WHATEVER

Thursday, October 5th; day one-hundred sixty-nine had finally arrived.

"Only two days to go, ready?"

Carol said, excited.

"Yeah, think so, better be."

C said nonchalant, standing in Carol's kitchen, leaning against the counter.

"I'm so excited! Does he suspect?"

"I don't know; doubt he has a clue, with Little-Earl, and now with his sister, he's been….preoccupied."

Cord said, distant, barely feigning interest.

"Actually, come to think, how would you know anyway? He says he hasn't seen you much lately. No one has."

Carol stared at Cord, who didn't respond.

"What about you, and his sister?"

C just huffed, a mock laugh, to himself more than her, and didn't say anything more.

"That good huh?"

"It's never been *good;* its just been times of *not-as-bad,* mixed in with *worse-than-usual.* I'd like to say I've moved on, but there's nothing to move off to begin with."

C frowned through the statement, then quickly continued.

"And don't add *but she really likes you;* please….save it."

C beat her to the punch; that was *exactly* what Carol was about to say, although she pretended otherwise, and gave him an indignant look to boot.

"What about Margie then?"

"You worried about me? I'm fine, trust me….big boy."

"Sam and Woodie said they saw you two at the *Palace,* Wednesday night; it was apparently a rare public Cord siting. The word about Town is…."

And Carol stopped, to let him fill in.

But C just looked at her, sans expression, and she at him, and he at her. She raised her eyebrows, waiting for him to break, but he kept clammed.

Truth was, he was lifting again at her gym; she gave him a key, and he usually came in off-hours, to be alone, and she was rarely ever there when he showed up, which was his plan. And when she was, by fluke, they didn't interact beyond a polite hello as he passed her office on his way down the hall, the same kind you share with strangers. And she didn't push it, and he liked it that way. On the odd occasion where he happened to stop by and lift midday, he timed it so she was in the middle of a class – so she wasn't available to talk. He wasn't in the mood to talk to her, or anybody else.

But one time, for some unexplained reason, she snagged him, in the middle of squatting, no less, and asked him if he wanted to get a cup of coffee. He answered a reluctant yes, just as much a surprise to him as it was to her, and for no other reason than to say yes, because she expected a no.

Margery Bastet was the only person he could tolerate lately, and even that was barely. There was nothing between the two, actually less than nothing, just casual friends, a small half-step above acquaintances, sharing a cup of coffee. He could hardly believe he even fucked her; that that even happened seemed surreal….it felt so detached, so remote, like it happened more than a lifetime ago, and it wasn't even really him. That's how it felt, anyway. Over coffee at *Nonpareil,* she made small talk about her mother, but quickly changed the subject when it was clear Cord had no interest in the topic, then the gym, and finally the banality of the current weather. It was awkward. The whole unpleasant ordeal lasted less than twenty minutes – he never took a sip of his coffee, just twirled the cup around on its saucer as she tried to engage him. In the end, he never did find out why she wanted to see him, and frankly, he didn't care.

Truth be told, Cord was simply in a holding pattern, waiting for Jenny to call, and getting more annoyed by the day that she was apparently out of town, on a one-hundred sixty-nine day vacation, and counting. Where the fuck was she? He just wanted this sorry chapter to end, feeling the intruder at someone else's party; he was uncomfortable, and it was time to move on.

This feeling had seeped in before, many times, whenever a stint began to feel stale. And with that feeling, he became antsy; his anger rose, his fuse shortened and that was generally when dangerous situations would arise, trouble would occur and people would get hurt. And he didn't want to see that happen here, because there was no one here he wanted to see hurt, except for one, and he was gone for good, taking a forever *Crack*-nap in a forgotten quarry.

And at that last thought, unbeknownst to C, the puppet smiled wide and chuckled quietly to himself, hiding behind the curtain.

Carol saw Cord staring blankly past her, at the kitchen wall behind her – he was clearly somewhere else. She got tired of waiting, watching his blank stare.

"Hello? Cord?"

She said sarcastically; and he shook his head a bit, came back and reconnected with her face. But he still didn't speak.

"I already know the story anyway *[which she really didn't]* - heard it from Sam, who heard it from Ms. Klein, who heard it from Mae. When's the last time you saw Mae?"

C just stared at her. He hadn't seen Mae, at all, in God knows how long. Nor did he want to, ever again. That door was closed, locked and the key tossed for good.

Carol continued.

"Yeah, well, you know she went public with the Joe thing; I even saw them together during *Victorian Days*....cute. He was carrying her bags, but I'm sure Margie told you all about that."

C curled his lips. No, Margie didn't mention *anything* about that, but he figured she would have, if he hadn't cut off the Mae-talk so quickly. Maybe that was the reason for the coffee, to put the final nail in the Mae coffin, to head off at the pass any lingering idea he had about trolling back into her mother's bed....nice. Just more icing on the shit-burger cake called Belvidere.

"No, hadn't heard that one, thanks. Happy for them."

"Oh, sorry."

Carol said, but didn't mean it; she was actually a bit happy to get a dig in at Cord, since he was generally being a jerk.

"Whatever. Anything else you wanted to share with me?"

C said, annoyed, sarcastic and slightly bored.

"Do you ever worry about the *other thing,* you know coming up, causing trouble?"

"What other thing?"

C said, deadpan.

"You know what *other thing.*"

She said, a bit more desperate, with a tone that clearly suggested *she* worried about it....a lot.

"What other thing?"

C said, deadpan a second time, exactly the same as the first.

Carol took that as he knew exactly what that thing was, and that thing was a no, and the subject of Button was dropped.

"So I guess Margery told you Lilly feels bad you're not talking to her; she says you plan your day to avoid even seeing her. She's only seen your face, what, twice, since Earl died....in the last month? I don't even know how that is possible, living in the same building, above one another. And Earl has to go looking for you in your apartment or around Town, and he can never find you half the time, and you don't even talk with him like you used to, and I know you're not running together anymore, and you're certainly not coming over here for

2075

weekend buffets, like the old days. Earl's worried about you."

C's arms were folded across his chest during the oratory, fidgeting, letting a noisy huff or two through his nostrils, clearly annoyed at the lecture.

He cracked his knuckles as he spoke.

"I thought we got together, I mean you asked me over here tonight, to talk about, help you button up, the *Brownfield Fund;* that was the point right? The pro forma? That's why you asked Earl to ask me over tonight, alone, right? To run ideas by me about the *Fund*?"

"Right, we did that, check it off as done; Georgia-Pacific still tops, got it. Now where off that, and onto...."

"I gotta go."

C said, interrupting her as he pushed himself off his lean against the kitchen counter. Just at that moment, Zeke came trotting into the kitchen, jumped on the island, across to the counter and onto C's shoulders, and plopped around his neck, like a scarf, in a steady purr. All in one motion, like an entry onto the stage. He rubbed his face against the week-old stubble on Cord's right cheek.

Carol huffed, angry at Zeke.

"Why doesn't he ever...!"

C just half-smiled, his uptick, and to tweak her, and for no other reason, because he didn't want to be there anymore, settled back against the counter again, so as not to disturb Zeke. His own version of Chicken and Earl.

"You gotta go, *where*? To see Mae?, Lilly? Earl? Can't be that, you don't see anybody anymore."

"I gotta take care of some business, out of Town."

C said, rote.

"Business?! *What business?* Grocery business? You don't have any *business*!"

C got angry.

"Hey, shithead, you don't know what business I have; not a fucking clue!"

He rarely addressed her in such crude terms. Carol immediately shot back, dripping sarcastic.

"You're right, I don't, I don't know anything about you, not really, so why don't you clue me in to this urgent business you have, which will take you out of Town, which apparently hasn't taken you out of Town since April, but now, suddenly does. How convenient."

C didn't answer; he was paying attention to Zeke, rubbing his face as he purred.

"How come you're not hanging with Earl as much? Marty said Earl thinks he did something wrong, said something wrong, but he's afraid to ask you, he thinks your gonna yell at him, or tell him you're not friends anymore. He's sad; he said you've been angry lately, not like you, not ever around, he...."

C cut her off.

"I think I'm gonna be going soon, real soon, for good, can feel it, just feels, like it does, when that happens. Just so you know, kind of a heads-up – if it happens, you should be able to cover the party – my ends done, and you can pick up the ball, if necessary. And don't go blabbing about it to Earl or anyone else, I'm just telling you, just in case."

Carol's eyes got wide, her mouth opened codfish, and she got an instant, angry piss.

"Are you fucking kidding me? Dropping this on me two days before? Nice....*real nice!*   And you're leaving? What the fuck you telling me for? I don't wanna know! Don't put that on me!"

"Fine, forget I mentioned it; see ya."

C tilted his shoulder to dislodge Zeke. Carol was incredulous, hands on her hips.

"So you're not even staying for the party? In two days, for Christ's sake!?   You are not even staying for Earl!? This is *unbelievable!*"

She barked, more of a yell. Zeke exited the kitchen in a hurry, to avoid the fray; no other cat was in sight.

He just shook his head and huffed at her; he didn't dignify the insult with a response. As he tried to exit the kitchen, on his way to the front door, she quickly blocked the way and just stared at him, her eyes demanding an answer.

Nothing.

She opened the top drawer, by the stove, and carefully grabbed two tiny rocks, covered in green lichens. She gently placed them in her open palm and held them up to his face.

"Do you know what this is?"

C just stared at her, blank, annoyed at the next *lesson*, apparently on its way. Annoyed that he already wasn't out the front door, on his way somewhere else.

"It's little pieces of *Couch Rock*, one of the most important things to Earl, ever. It's his *special place;* you know all about special places – right? And how much they mean? He gave these to me, because of you! He said if it wasn't for you, he'd never been able to even talk to me, or tell me about *Couch Rock*, or bring me there, to see it. He said it could be our *special place*, if that was okay, if I wanted it to be; do you have any idea how important that is to me? These two little rocks, that mean nothing to anyone else in the world, mean *the world* to me; do you have any idea how big a deal this is to him, and to me? And now he wants to take one back, and he's scared to ask me; I know he is, because he wants to give one of them to *you,* because he knows you know all about special places, and how important they are, and how important you are *to him.* He is who he is, who he is becoming, because of you; I can't imagine Earl ever being a better person, but he is, even better, because of you. He asked me *what would happen, if he were, you know, to maybe give you a piece of Couch Rock,* would I be mad? And do I think it would make you talk to him some more, like you used to, to make you happy again, and maybe not be mad at him anymore. He thought *Couch Rock* was that important, that it could make a difference, to you."

"I've never seen the *Couch Rock*, that's *your special place* with Earl, not mine. I'm happy for you and Earl, really – you seem like the makings of a nice couple; I wish you two the best, really do....*gotta go.*"

And he pushed through her dismissive, heading for the front door.

She looked at the back of him, in amazement.

"I can't believe....you are such a fucking, *fucking* asshole!"

As the front door quietly clicked shut behind him, all she heard was one word: *whatever*.

CHAPTER 273 - A LITTLE BABY IN BIG TROUBLE

Friday, October 6th; day one-hundred seventy; downtown, third floor, above the *Palace*.

He slowly turned the knob, as quietly as he could, his tongue sticking out, 'cause he was concentrating so hard, and heard the latch make a single, metallic click.

Too loud!

He stopped stone cold, but didn't hear a sound inside. So far, so good.

It was still dark outside, and although he should've been sleepy, he wasn't. He'd been awake for an hour, waiting forever for the clock to say five; it took *way* longer than an hour, that clock hand was way too slow, but he watched it, stared at it….the whole time.

As the door cracked, he saw the little gray head that was always so happy to see him, rubbing her cheek on the wood edge; the purr was a loud rumble.

"Shhh, *Chicken-Little;* you're such a good little girl."

He barely whispered, as he bent down on one knee and rubbed her cheek, and her chin. She jumped onto his shoulders, like she always did, and became the scarf around his neck. He gently stood up, not to disturb her; her purr buzzed his right ear.

He crept down the hall, his heart racing, trying not to make the floorboards creak, but they *always* did, especially when he stepped on them! He tried to tiptoe, he even remembered to take off his shoes, but it was no use - the more he tried to be careful, the more noise he made.

He was squeaking up a storm!

He missed his best friend so much. That's all he kept thinking, as he waited to see his head snug on the pillow, the blanket tucked up under his chin, smiling cause he was sleeping so sound. But as he turned the door jam, all he saw was a neatly-made bed. Cold and empty.

He hung his head, despite Chicken's purr.

Earl remembered what Billy taught him, when he was a cub scout, to check the toothbrush, and the towel, and see if the sink and shower were wet. Billy was smart about stuff like that, and Earl always paid attention when Billy told him all the tricks that the cub scouts learn. Earl wished he was a cub scout, but he could never do that, *never,* too many people he didn't know; that was way too scary. Plus the uniform would never fit, and his feet were too big for those little boots.

That was a long time ago, but Earl never forgot those sneaky cub scout tricks. And he ran down the hall, to the bathroom. Chick hung on, digging her claws into his shoulders, but Earl didn't mind, he never did.

And everything was lined up neat, in order, and dry: the toothbrush, the towel, the sink, the shower….everything. Not a drop of water.

He ran and checked the kitchen sink too....dry. And he saw the cat food and water; neatly laid out, two days worth.

And he got worried, because C probably never even came home; where was he staying? Who were his new friends? He must like them a lot, *way better* than him.

Earl's mind was racing, thinking of all the places they used to go, all the places C would go. But maybe he had a *new* place, a new secret place that he never told Earl about; of course he wouldn't tell Earl, because then it wouldn't be a secret! And he figured Cord didn't trust him anymore, since he slipped about Panama and told Lilly; he was sure C was mad about that, had to be, that must be why he wasn't around anymore, and they didn't do stuff together like they used to, and why he got new friends….all because he couldn't keep a secret! *Why did he tell Lilly about Panama! Stupid alcohol!* He had to apologize to his best friend, because C was his best friend in the whole wide world, and Ay was mad at him, and Earl knew C wouldn't be mad unless he had a real good reason, so he knew he must have done something *real bad* to C, like tell a secret; but, what if it wasn't that? Then he didn't know what it was! He thought and thought, but couldn't think of a thing he did wrong; he just didn't know, he wasn't smart about stuff like that, not as smart as C was. Maybe C didn't like him anymore 'cause he wasn't smart enough, and he figured it was too late to fix that; he was almost forty….in fact, his birthday was tomorrow!

Too late to get smart.

Earl was thinking too much, and when he did that, he started to fret, and then he did the best thing he could think….he started to run.

He scooped Chick off his shoulder, gave her a big kiss, then another, and then a third….he could never give her just one. She looked up at him with saucer eyes.

He gently laid her on the hall carpet, waved goodbye, calling her *Chicken Chimichanga….Chicken Cacciatore….Chicken Teriyaki* more of a sing-to-her than just talking; she seemed to like that. He loved that little girl, more than just about anything.

He promised to come back later to play string, and crossed his heart, which meant he had to come back, no matter what. That's what *that* meant – there was no messing around when you crossed your heart and made a promise – none at all. That was some serious stuff.

Earl slipped on his sneakers and off he went, out the door and down the staircase, two or three at a time, like a stampede of buffalo, or at least one big buffalo.

The feeling rushed over him all at once; he just *had* to find C, to tell him he was really, really sorry for whatever he did wrong; he knew he messed something up, he really wished he was smart enough to know what. His heart was racing as he slammed open the door, and spilled onto the dark, early-morning street in a full sprint, to find his friend.

Earl ran down Greenwich, a sprint in the murky early morning air. He was all alone, not a soul on the street. A low fog hugged the ground, rounding the sharp edges; everything looked a bit different, blanketed, tucked-in….they always did on mornings like this.

Earl ran swift through the clouds, and in minutes, found himself out of breath, at the base of the boat ramp. It was empty and quiet; no ducks, or geese or Aloysius or anything, just a gentle lap of the Autumn water on the gray-brown silty sand, where the ribbed concrete rails, the ones the trailer tires used to slip their boats into the drink, disappeared into the blackness of the Delaware. He looked upstream and saw two headlights cut the early morning mist, crossing the bridge; he could hear the tires rumble on the open metal grating, but he couldn't see the body, just disconnected light beams, crossing slowly from Pennsylvania to New Jersey. He stared in the direction of the bridge, and realized, for the first time this fall, he could see his breath. He tried to make smoke rings, but couldn't.

He looked around, left to right, and felt lonely.

Where are you?

He asked himself, but no luck. Maybe his mom would help.

But he knew she wasn't around; he could feel when she was somewhere else, not nearby. And she wasn't nearby, not now. Maybe she was still sleeping, or making breakfast; he always liked it when he sat at the table and watched her make breakfast for him and Lilly, all while Lilly was secretly kicking him under the table, or stealing his fork and licking it, or poking him in the arm, or in the side, or blowing stinky hot breath on his face, before she brushed her teeth; for being so pretty, she had the *worst* stinky hot breath in the morning. And she did all that stuff just waiting for him to squeal, to complain to their mom, so she could deny it, and get her mom to believe her, which she invariable did, or at least pretended to.

Then Earl would *really* get his, for squealing, later. Earl hated *later*, because *later* would invariably catch up with you – you couldn't run away from it – he tried and it never worked - and when *later* finally showed up, it was *always* bad with Bibby, if you were a squealer.

But despite all the taunts, Earl wouldn't give in, he would endure all the taunts and stink-breath, close his nose and just smile and look at his mom's shoulders, and arms, and back, fascinated at how they would change shapes and how her yellow sweater, it was his favorite, would wrinkle and move all over the place as she made the best eggs ever.

Every day they were the best eggs ever.

Earl was smiling to himself, shrouded in fog, thinking of his mom's eggs and Lilly's stinky breath, when he first heard the screech.

It sounded like a baby, a little baby in big trouble.

CHAPTER 274 - EARL KISSED HIM ONE MORE TIME, AND THEN AGAIN

Earl sprinted up the ramp, listening for another scream; that first one scared him but good.

Nothing.

He stopped short at the stub-end of Front Street, where it deadheaded at the boat ramp parking lot and scanned the scene. It was quiet, but it didn't feel safe; the fog hid whatever was out there.

He half-ran to the right, down Depue Street, for no particular reason. And that's when he first saw him.

It was a faint outline standing by the side of the road. But even in the mist, he looked super-sized, and mean, staring into the sky, up a craggy old ash. As he got closer, he saw it, there, in the first crook; it was a baby raccoon. Earl could see his eyes reflect in the haze of the amber streetlight; he wasn't moving, frightened to still. And Loki was growling at the base, his massive front paws against the trunk, claws ripping at the bark; stretched vertical he looked to be at least five feet tall, maybe more. His squared black head was *enormous*.

That's when Loki saw Earl.

He had a good memory, but the alpha in him made the memory moot, for he directed his venom at Earl, pushing off the trunk and assuming a stance that meant business, that meant Earl was the new target.

Loki lowered his head; a tuft of fur on his back, at the base of his thick neck, stood jagged and erect. He bared his teeth, slowly moving toward Earl in a deliberate stalk; strings of saliva dripped from his jowls.

The siren was off, but the red and blue lights illuminated the fog as the cruiser skidded to a stop at the intersection of Front and Depue, mere feet from Earl. Marty bolted from the cart out and quickly placed his hand ominously on the holstered gun, ready to draw.

"*Earl?* What the hell you doing out here?! Step back, slow, behind me."

Earl looked over at Martin.

"Don't hurt him Marty! He's not a bad dog, he isn't! He just keeps getting hurt all the time; all he does is get hit and yelled at, and I see 'em hit him with a big stick, and the man kicks him. He doesn't know what it's like to be, to have someone be nice...."

Nice just left Earl's lips as Loki speared him full bore, his jaw locking on Earl's thigh. Anyone else would have been flattened, and mauled, with the next attack being a kill bite, to the neck. That's what Loki was going for, what he wanted. But the blow by a two-hundred-twenty pound projectile simply knocked the three hundred sixty-plus pounds of Earl off balance, down on one knee. Before Loki could clamp down, and while Marty fumbled with the stuck snap on the holster, yelling: *fuck....fuck....fuck* while yanking wildly on his gun, which simply wouldn't yield, Earl had the dog wrapped tight in his massive arms, its mouth muzzled with the iron grip of Earl's single hand, just the same as the boat ramp, month's earlier.

And that quick, the threat was over.

Marty was down on one knee in the middle of the road, sweaty and exasperated, filling his lungs with air. He never did get that gun out of its holster....impotent. And by this time, had stopped trying.

"*Stupid fucking stupid gun; fucking....fucking....fuck!*"

2087

Was all he could come up with, as he repeatedly punched at the gun on his hip. And with the last punch, a lame half-attempt, more of a frustrated tap really, because he was spent after his adrenaline-fueled frenzy, the stuck gun holster snap simply popped open on its own, and Martin just stared at it.

Then he didn't; he ignored it.

Earl still had Loki locked in a cradle, squeezing him tight, but not too, because he didn't want to hurt him, or scare him. And Marty couldn't hear him, but he knew Earl was whispering and kissing the dog on the side of the snout, telling him everything was gonna be okay.

Martin let out a rush of air and shook his head.

"Earl, that dog's gotta go down, he's gonna hurt someone....bad! I know you don't think he's bad, but he is, he *really* is. Whether it's his fault or not, doesn't matter."

"Yes it *does* matter! Yes it **does** Marty! What if you got kicked and whipped with a big stick every day, huh?! Why can't he just have nice people take care of him? Why can't I take care of him? He'd get better, I know he would; he and I'd be best friends! Don't hurt him Marty, please don't hurt him!"

Earl hugged Loki tighter, in defense; the dog didn't make a sound, and didn't move – he was limp in Earl's arms.

Marty shook his head again.

"Lilly hates that dog, you know that; she'll never let you have him, *never.*"

Earl just looked at him; holding a two-hundred-twenty pound black monster-of-a-dog like it weighed next-to-nothing. And Earl was sad, and Marty knew it. And Marty could never take Earl's sad face for long. And sure enough, he gave in.

 "Okay, let me take him home, and I'll tell them this is the *last time;* he gets out again and I'm gonna take him away, and I'm issuing them a summons too, because…."

"*Don't do that Marty!* If you do, they'll just kick him more, harder, when you leave. They'll smile till you leave, but they're making-pretend! And don't say he did *anything* to me, just tell them you found him laying by the side of the road, sleeping."

"Earl, they're never gonna believe…."

"Okay, okay, just say he was running along the road and you found him and you asked me to help you get him home, okay? They know I can bring him home; I've done it before. And tell 'em he did *nothing wrong,* okay Marty, please? Please? *Please?*"

"Okay, okay, but I'm still telling 'em this is the last time."

"Okay, okay."

And Earl kissed him one more time, and then again.

CHAPTER 275 – WITHOUT A WORD, HE QUICKLY ROLLED UP THE WINDOW

Earl slid back into the cruiser; he was dry.   Loki didn't pee on him this time.

"They're gonna hurt him, Marty, I know it.   Even though what you told them, they're gonna…."

"I hope not; I'll keep a better eye on them Earl, promise. They're bad people, white trash *[Marty shook his head]*. But I promise, I'll take him away next time, for good, promise. Maybe we can bring him out to the farm."

"*Really?* Really Marty?! He'd **love** the farm, with all the barns and fields and hay and I could run all around with him and roll in the hay and stuff! He's a good dog, I know it!"

Marty just looked at him, wondering how Earl could see any good in that animal.

"How about we just keep him in the old hay barn, off the far corn field, down by the creek? He'd be happy there, right?"

Earl looked at him, incredulous.

"You can't keep him in *there* Marty, that's all by itself, by no one; none of the other animals would get to play with him. He's gotta be all over; he's gotta be free, that's the only way he'll be happy, I know, when no one's kicking and whipping him anymore, and ignoring him, and just rubbing and scratching his belly in the sun."

"And how do you know all this, huh; is that what you two were whispering about?"

Marty cocked his head, looking at Earl. But Earl looked down, at his feet, and shrugged his shoulders.

"Nah, I just know; some things you just know. And I was telling him I knew he was a good boy, deep down, and I loved him, and I was gonna take care of him some day, just him and me, friends. We could lay on a blanket together and everything, in the field out by the cows, and even take a nap together; I could use him as a big furry pillow! He's nice and soft, you know, if you hug him. I told him to be patient and don't hurt anybody and maybe we'll get to play together, you know, lots, lots and lots. He knows, he knows; he's just waiting."

Marty smiled at his friend.

"You'll bring him to the farm, and you won't let *anyone* hurt him anymore? You promise, *no matter what*…..promise?"

"I promise."

And Marty reached out and placed his hand gently on Earl's chest, on his heart, and did a little cross with his pointer.

"I promise."

And Earl exhaled a sigh of relief, a big one, with an even bigger smile, because he knew Marty didn't lie, especially when he talked like that, like he just did, in that tone, and *especially* when he did the cross! Earl knew that was some serious stuff, the most serious promise *ever;* that's what his mom always used to say - when you do the cross on your heart - now that was *serious* stuff, and Marty knew that. There were no take-backs on that kind of promise, no matter what.

And that's when Earl knew, for sure, Loki would be safe someday, and happy, on the farm. Earl just hoped it would be soon, real soon, so they could start playing. Loki had a lot of catching up to do.

"Hey, why were you at the ramp anyway; it's 5:30 in the morning? Jesus…."

"I'm looking for C; I miss him Marty, I think I did something bad, real bad."

"Bad? Like what? What'ya do?"

"I don't know, but it's bad, *real bad,* I just know it."

"Earl, come on, you didn't do anything bad."

"Well then why isn't C talking to me anymore? And he never runs with me, or plays with Chick with me, or tells me jokes, or secrets; it was the secret-thing, *I know it;* that messed it all up!"

"What secret thing?"

"I can't tell you, it's a secret! That's what got me in trouble to begin with! Stop asking me about the secret Marty!"

"Okay, okay, but I don't think Cord's mad at you, not *you.*"

"Okay, then why doesn't he talk to me anymore, and eat breakfast at Carol's like we used to every Saturday and Sunday morning, and why doesn't he live upstairs anymore? Huh?"

"He doesn't live upstairs? Really? He *moved out*?"

"Well, no, I don't think so, but he didn't sleep there last night. He left Chick all alone, and left extra food out, and his toothbrush was dry, and all that other cub scout stuff too, none of it; I checked it all out, you know, like a cub scout solving a mystery."

Marty just looked at him, and gave him a crazy-evil look.

"Maybe's he's living in the *Zombie Cave*."

"What?! The *Zombie Cave*! Which one? The right one, or the left one? The right-side one is *way* scarier! You think he's living there Marty? You think so? Really? No way! He's no zombie, and C would be a-scared of that *Zombie Cave,* both of them, right *and* left, and besides, the puppet probably goes there to hide in the dark, I bet, and C wouldn't be where the puppet is hiding, for sure!"

"The puppet? What puppet? Is that the secret?"

Marty asked, confused, which got Earl flustered.

"NO! But maybe that's a secret too! I don't know if that one's supposed to be a secret or not! Oh boy, now I'm *really* in big trouble; another secret gone! Promise Marty! Promise not to talk about the puppet to C or anyone else ever again….*ever!*"

"Okay, but what…."

"*PROMISE!*"

Earl screamed, his chest-heaving, shoving his pointer finger into Marty's face.

"Okay, okay, I promise; Jesus, Earl, take a pill."

Earl slowed to a mild hyper-ventilation.

"What pill? Will it help me find C?"

Marty shook his head; to be in that man's brain, what a trip.

"Never mind; I'm sure he's not mad at you. Let's just find Cord, okay Earl? He can't be that far. Where do you want to go? Wanna try *The Zombie Cave?*"

"What? No! He would *never* be in the *Zombie Cave*; C jumps like a little girl even when I just walk in his room and he doesn't hear me. He's been pretty jumpy, lately, when I see him, that is, which isn't too much, you know, but anyway, *no way* he's in the *Zombie Cave,* no way, especially with the you-know-what hiding in there *[Earl mimed a puppet dancing on strings – just doing that gave him the willies].* I don't wanna go check the *Zombie Cave,* neither one, right or left - no way, I don't wanna go there, he's not in there anyway….no way."

"Uh huh."

Marty said, smiling wry.

The last place in the world Earl would *ever* go on purpose would be the *Zombie Cave,* even if he *knew* C was hiding in it. If there *were* zombies hiding in the woods around Belvidere, and Earl was pretty sure there were, lots of them, the *Zombie Cave* was certainly where they would be hiding, Earl was convinced of that. And if C was there, he was a goner. Ay was probably *already* a brain-munching, eyeball-sucking zombie; even though he lost weight, he still couldn't run that fast - the zombies would have gotten him, for sure.

Earl was scared to death of that old railroad tunnel; there were two skinny tunnels actually, side-by-side, carved over a hundred-fifty years ago, even longer maybe, into a solid rock cliff, high above the Delaware River, upstream, just west of Town. The rails were long gone and a train hadn't seen those tunnels in a century....maybe longer.

None of them, Marty, Earl, Lilly, and no one they knew, as kids exploring, as teenagers drinking, even as rational adults, ever went in even close to far enough to find the tunnel end. The one on the left appeared to be sealed about seventy-five feet in from the entrance; an enormous pile of soil, littered with large rocks, rose three-quarters to the ceiling, blocking the way. At first blush, it seemed the tunnel ended there. But it didn't - it was a sneaky zombie trap to slow you down – Earl was convinced of it, because you could climb over it, if you were *really* dumb, and the tunnel continued on into the abyss, for how far, nobody knew; nobody ever chanced actually climbing over the pile and sliding down the other side, *nobody*….no way. And the tunnel on the right, that was even *scarier*, because it wasn't blocked, and seemed to curve and stretch deep into the rock, into the ink, forever. And no one knew anyone that ever went in deep, and ever came out to tell about it.

No one.

Even on the sunniest day, less than a hundred feet in, it was black as pitch. After a bit, with eyes adjusted, one could discern the faintest of shapes, all amorphous, with edges that bled to obsidian. It was then, up ahead, that you could see what appeared to be scattered mounds of scattered sizes, a mix of clay, slag and trap rock, cold and damp to the touch, with curious shapes thrust into them, overhead and mostly out of reach - appendages of some sort, that you couldn't really make out, and certainly wouldn't touch, if you could. As kids, they were convinced the thrusts were the bones and rags of clothing from people who went in too far, and never came out, buried in the trap rock mounds, as a warning:

Keep Out

As adults, they still weren't so sure.

It was dank and slimy on the curved rock walls, with a stale smell of must....Stygian. Faint trickles, drips and paddles of cave-water whispered just above and beyond eyesight. Calf-deep puddles were cast hodgepodge about the tunnels, pools that you couldn't avoid, because you couldn't see them till it was too late, and crooked rivulets formed in the gravel bed where the old rails once were, the water birthing from somewhere up ahead, but you could never collar where. Overhead, and slithering about your legs, cold breezes appeared from nowhere, with no warning, out-of-the-dark. It was frightening in the daytime, and forget about going there after dark. No one ever did, except maybe the zombies.

Fucking scary; always was.....*still* was.

For decades, anyone and everyone who knew of the tunnels hidden in the woods along the river simply called them *The Tunnel*. Even though there were two tubes cut in the rock, somebody long ago decided on the singular and it stuck; from that point on, they were always known as:

The Tunnel

Then someone, to this day no one knew exactly who, twenty years ago spray-painted big black letters on the crumbling stone entrance between the two rail tubes. Each of the letters was over two-feet tall, surrounded by a field of unwell yellow, splattered with a beryl-blue and blood-red border, which, in toto, spelled a single, flesh-creep word:

Zombies

And just like that, *The Tunnel* became known as, and morphed into:

The Zombie Cave

Now and forever.

"Okay, so no *Zombie Cave;* then where to?"

Marty quizzed.

Earl held up his hand, and counted off the places they would go, all the places he and Cord went, back when they went places, together.

The cruiser clicked into drive, and off they went.

The first was the worst, and Marty refused, but Earl insisted. C had to be somewhere, and that was certainly a place *no one* would look for him, especially Earl.

So off to the barn they went, into the bowels of *Jenny Jump*.

Martin rolled to a stop along the shoulder and kept the engine running; you still couldn't see the barn – it was early October, and the leaves hadn't yet dropped, and the dim of the new morning hung on.

"Make it quick; I don't wanna be here, or even be *seen* here….okay?"

Earl nodded, as Marty handed him his large flashlight; he kept it in a sleeve by the door. Earl quietly slipped out of the car, and soon disappeared amidst the brambles; he couldn't see it, but Marty heard the barn door slowly open, the rusty wheel riding a rusty rail. Although it really wasn't, since Marty was on edge, it seemed so loud that anyone in a quarter-mile could surely hear it.

"Christ Earl!"

Marty whispered aloud, as he looked all around, a nervous Nellie, swiveling his head, herky-jerk, to the sides and back, waiting for someone to walk up and ask *what's going on?* That had nothing but trouble written all over it.

As quick as the high-pitched squeal of the barn door started, it stopped, and all again was silent, except for some jays, and crows hiding somewhere, calling out now and again, talking loud amongst themselves. Martin strained to hear anything else, anything at all, but it was deathly quiet, and he felt the creep run up his arms.

"Come on Earl, Jesus; come on!"

Marty repeated aloud to himself, his fingers gripping the steering wheel tighter with each iteration. He found himself starting to sweat around the collar. It was still dead silent; he never heard the barn door shut – Earl must still be in there.

Marty couldn't get his mind off his sagging socks.

For some reason, all-of-a-sudden, Marty's loose socks started to bother him, and he had this intense desire, this need, to pull them up, high and tight. He bent over and tried to reach them, but he couldn't get his head past the steering wheel, and he rapped his temple on the dash, jabbing his hands wildly toward his ankles.

"Fuck!"

He finally grabbed a few-finger-hold of his right sock and pulled it up hard; he felt the worn cotton heel rip inside his shoe.

"Christ!"

He sat back up hard, his back slapping the seat, mad as hell at his stupid, fucking, ripped sock, and yelled to himself in the cab.

"Jesus Earl, come on!"

He said, craning his neck, trying to see through the wall of brambles and the early morning din beyond. *Great, now he had to go in and find him, with no flashlight* Marty huffed loud, annoyed, and turned to exit the car. That's when Martin screamed, a high-pitched yelp, like a little girl. There was Earl, bent over, looking at him through the open driver's door window, his head the size of a prize pumpkin.

"What the fuck Earl! What the hell are you doing, sneaking around the car? You scared the shit out of me!"

"You're a scaredy-cat, Marty."

Earl answered, with a bit of a smirk.

Marty blew a mouth of air.

"I'm not *scared*, I just ripped my sock! Why are you sneaking up on me? I could've shot you or something!"

"You can't even get your gun out of your holster, *Marty.*"

Earl snarked, which was met with a second Martin huff, through the nostrils.

"Why you sneaking around? Huh?"

"*I'm not!* I just walked over to the car and I didn't see you in here; I thought you left."

"*Left?* Where would I go? I was just bent over, fixing my….doesn't matter. I knew he wouldn't be here; get in….*let's go.*"

"Not yet. He's not in there, but I heard something rustling around in the dark; I saw it with the light, you know, the flashlight - it froze, like a deer, you know, but it wasn't a zombie or anything, it was just a cat. I tried to go pet it, but it ran away."

"Jesus Earl, stay focused! Forget about petting the fucking cat."

"I did, that's why I'm back out here; why's your sock ripped? I have to go down the road a bit."

"What?! Down the road for *what?*"

"It's a secret; you stay here, I'll be back."

"Enough with the fucking secrets, Earl. I don't care about puppets or zombies, but I'm not staying here; this, being *here*, is dangerous, for *both of us*, you know that; we *gotta go!*"

"*Don't leave Marty*, I'll be right back, and don't follow me! And anyway, the zombies can't get you, if you just roll the window up; they can't get through glass, *everyone* knows that."

Earl said as he turned and quickly sprinted down the middle of the road, before Martin could protest. Soon enough, he disappeared, melting into the linger of the morning mist.

And Marty huffed for a third time. He was supposed to be running radar on Water Street, which really meant sleeping in the car, in the dark, on Water Street; that was his favorite stint, hiding in the tall weeds. Instead he was sitting here, with a ripped sock and sweaty feet, which was annoying the hell out of him; he could feel his damp heel sticking to the leather inside his boot. He looked around, across the hood, at the thicket of weeds along the side of the road, pushed hard against the front and sides of the cruiser nose. Then he turned and looked out the back, and saw the same, weeds brushing the back of the trunk. It felt like he was being sucked into the woods, the mutant weeds pulling him off the road, swallowing him whole. His mind started to race; something *could* be standing right in those weeds, right next to the car, mere *inches* away, like a zombie for instance, and he would never see it, until it was too late.

Without a word, he quickly rolled up the window.

Not a single car passed the entire time Earl was absent.

"Nothing."

Earl said, out of breath from the run, as he plopped on the front seat of the cruiser.

"Where'd you go?"

Earl just looked at him, with *that* face.

"Oh, right, *secret*; can we go now?"

"Why'd you roll your window up Marty?"

Earl said, nonchalant.

Marty just stared at him with a blank face, and Earl stared back with the same; neither said a word. Then Earl gave him a quick uptick smile, so quick you would have missed it if you blinked, and just as fast his face returned to stone, to match Marty's.

They both knew the answer to that one....*zombies*. And that was the end of that.

Marty shoved the car in gear, and U-turned, aiming to get out of the weeds, and out of there, as quick as possible.

"Where to now Chief?"

Marty barked at Earl.

"*You're* the chief Marty; where do *you* think we should go? You're smart, like Ken and Sandy, about detective-mystery stuff like that; where do you think C is?"

"Well I coulda told you he wasn't out here, no way; maybe he's lifting at the gym, or over at Mae's."

"Okay, okay, then let's do that, *all* of that!"

And Earl began to fret again, rubbing his hand together nervous, wondering where his best friend could be. They hustled to Margies gym, but the doors were locked, the lights out. No luck.

They pulled into the Derby Lane cul-de-sac and idled at the curb; Mae was sitting at the kitchen table, reading, with Joe standing at the stove, cooking breakfast in his baggy, boxer underwear and a snug, all-white, ribbed guinea-tee, accentuating a small paunch of a belly, and the loose, wrinkled skin on his tiny, skinny arms. Earl was still afraid of Mae, so he made Marty go knock on the door. Earl could see Mae shake her head in the negative; when Martin saddled back in the cab, he said Mae hadn't seen C, not for weeks.

And now Mae was worried; that early morning visit just ruined her day. She knew Cord was gone, gone for good, and she would never see him again. Not seeing him, but knowing he was in Town, was nearby, was at least better than nothing, a security blanket in the closet....out of reach, but still in the closet.

But now he was gone, for good, and she felt empty all over again.

She got up and left Joe cooking in the kitchen. He followed in vain, asking never-ending questions as to what the police wanted with the *grocery boy* – Joe refused to refer to him as anything but that derogatory term – and was he finally going to jail, for good, where he belonged. But Mae never answered him, ignoring his taunts as she sulked down the hallway, slamming and locking the bathroom door on Joe, crying softly on the toilet, while Joe quietly, annoyingly, knocked and knocked and knocked, asking her to please let him in.

Marty drove over the bridge into Pennsylvania, out to the Tekening Trails, the ones that went to *Couch Rock*. He idled the cruiser in the lot while Earl ran hard all the way to the *Rock*, in and back, a full four mile loop through the woods; he never stopped, and it took him just over twenty minutes.

They drove on to *Georgia Pacific*, the *Palace*, *Sam's*, the boat ramp, for a second time, the *Shoe Tree*, the *Cemetery*, and even out to the supermarket, where Louie slept, and finally *Luigi's Rancho*, even though they never saw C actually ever go there. They went everywhere they could think; no Cord anywhere.

And then they gave up.

Marty dropped Earl off at the Park, apologized that he wasn't a better cub scout cum detective, and said he'd keep his eye out, and his ear to the dispatch radio, and would call Earl if he heard any news, anything at all. Earl hugged Marty, and then slowly walked, in defeat, toward the center benches and sat next to his mom, even though she wasn't there. He hoped she'd come, hoped she'd help him find his best friend ever.

Then he remembered what C once told him; how could he forget!

He got all excited, pulled a couple of crumbled *Animal Crackers* from his front pocket and downed them; they were broken into little pieces, and of course none had heads - Lilly had bit them all off, like always, but they tasted almost as good, just the same.

He thought of his kindred friend, squeezed his eyes shut and said aloud:

I wish....

And then he did.

2105

Earl remembered every detail, like always. It was one of his favorite stories. Actually, all of C's stories were Earl's favorites. But this one was extra special, because when he thought of it, he always thought of Carol.

He remembered Cord describing a beautiful lady, alone in a garden, and not just any garden, but a *royal botanical* garden, which must be a *really* special garden. He couldn't even imagine how special it must be. And the beautiful lady always stood beside a Wollemi Pine, whatever that was. C said she was always quiet, perched on her very own pedestal, looking to the ground, head cocked, just a bit to the left, eyes closed, as if deep in thought, just waiting for you to come see her. She *always* waited, no matter how long it took C to come and see her; she was patient that way, no matter how long it took for you to return.

She would just wait....*forever*.

And she was always interested in anything you had to say; she was a real good listener.

Her long hair framed a long thin face, disappearing past her shoulders, in a flow. She propped her hands in front of her, long delicate fingers barely touching, and she always held flowers, always different, but always red.

And C never knew her name, but that didn't matter one bit.

She was born in 1946, but she never seemed to age. She was as lovely today as the first time C laid eyes upon her. That's what he'd always tell Earl.

And she only said one thing:

And if you said it back, either to yourself, or aloud, and wished *real hard,* as hard as you could, maybe whatever it was, would come true. C liked to think so, and now, so did Earl, because he had a *real* big one: he wished his best friend would come back.

Earl squeezed his eyes shut tight, scrunching his face, and wished as hard as he could, thinking about that beautiful lady. But all he saw was Carol's face before him; she *was* that beautiful lady, and maybe she would be the one to answer his wish.

Then Earl thought about the *Wishing Tree,* the one C said was just a stone's throw from that beautiful Australian girl, forever standing silent in her Royal Garden. C said all you had to do was knock the *Wishing Tree*, just touch it really, or walk around it, three times forward, and three times back, and the Sydney spirits would grant your wish. Cord said it was a Norfolk Island Pine, but Earl had no idea what one of those even looked like, so he couldn't imagine it, to touch it, or walk around it; all he could think of was Charlie Brown's Christmas Tree - he couldn't get that sorry little tree out of his head, it was the only green tree that he could think of, and that certainly wasn't the kind of tree that had lots of spirits in it, to help his wish come true. But then again, maybe Charlie Brown's tree *was* the perfect tree; either way, it would have to do - that little tree was planted in Earl's head, so he touched it, ever-so-gently, so no needles would drop, and walked around that spindly little trunk, eyes squeezed shut and his head scrunched to his shoulders, three times forward and three times back, and wished as hard as he could, for his bestest best friend ever to come.

Slowly, he unsqueezed his eyes; before him, his wish was granted.

CHAPTER 278 – BEST FRIENDS DO THAT, WHEN NO ONE'S WATCHING

"Whatcha doing?"

"I was wishing, as hard as I could, but it didn't work."

"Wishing for what?"

"For C not to hate me, for him not to be mad at me; I think he found new friends. I musta told a secret I shouldn't have, or done something real bad, or maybe…."

Carol gently put her finger on Earl's lips.

"You didn't do anything wrong Sweetie, trust me. C is just….having a hard time right now, with a lot of stuff that has nothing to do with you. He loves you….very, very much."

Earl's eyes welled.

"You think?"

Carol smiled and answered simply.

"I know."

"Promise?"

"I promise."

Carol whispered.

"Where do you think he is?"

Earl fretted.

"I don't know, but he'll show up, especially if he knows I have two new ones of *these*!"

And with that, Carol pulled, from behind her back, a brand new box, unopened, of *Animal Crackers*. It was dangling in the air, like a first-prize, the whispy-white cotton string strap looped lazy around her slim finger.

"Oh boy, I bet they got heads and everything!"

"Yep, they even got heads, and they really like to be dipped in milk."

"*Really?* I never heard *that* story, and I've been eating 'em for years! How do you know that? Did they tell you? Was it a secret? If it was, don't tell me, for sure, because I'm not so good at secrets lately."

Earl put his head down at the last thought. Carol tucked her finger lightly under his chin and lifted it, to meet her beautiful face.

"It's not a secret. And maybe they did tell me, because they knew you'd like it. Let's go try it out."

And just like that, Carol went for it, without warning, and without asking, which surprised him, of course. And a warm rush coursed his body, which made his fingers tingle. But Earl didn't jump, and he didn't recoil, nor fumble about; he just stood there and let it happen. But he did peak around the Park, for stray eyes.

Carol smiled.

"No one's watching, promise; just you and me....*our* little secret, just you and me."

"I'm not so good at secrets lately."

Earl said a second time, dropping his head heavy, in defeat.

"I don't care who you tell; it's only a secret if *you* want it to be."

"Well, maybe let's just keep it a secret, just for now, between us. Is that okay?"

And Carol winked at him; the smile never left her face. And with that, two best friends walked side-by-side to the lion house, holding pinkies.

Holding pinkies....best friends do that, when no one's watching.

Earl refused.

He simply wouldn't walk past that closet; he would go the long-way-around every time, through the dining room and kitchen, just to avoid looking at them, or having them look at him. Even if the door was closed, as it always was, it didn't matter, because he *knew* they were in there, staring, and he was pretty sure they could see right through the door anyway. Earl wondered if they could see right through his clothes, right to his underwear! Thank God he was wearing underwear; and what if they could even see through them too?! That was very embarrassing, because, you know, he didn't even really know them that well. Just saying.

"Earl, would you please come over here! They're *not* scary, they're good! They're supposed to protect you; they can't do it if you don't let them."

"But why do they have *light* coming out of their eyes, and mouths! That's just not right! No one's supposed to have blue light coming out of their mouth, or red eyes; that's not the way it's supposed to be! And what about my underwear?!"

"*Your underwear?* What does the closet have to do with your underwear? Forget it – I don't even want to know *[although she really did].* And they didn't do the light thing, *I did;* I just thought it would look kinda cool, or something, when you opened the closet, you know, to hang up your coat."

"I never saw a closet like that! Staring back at you! Closets are for hanging, not staring!"

"I know, that was the point; I wanted it to be a closet like nobody ever saw before."

2111

"You win!"

Earl yelled.

Carol smiled; she loved when Earl got all-excited about something, no matter what, even closets.

"But I wouldn't have done it if I knew you'd never walk down the hall; come on, they don't bite."

"Then why are their mouths open? Huh?"

Earl wasn't buying it.

"You know, when I first bought this house, and stayed out here, alone, on weekends, I didn't have any cats, and no friends; I was all alone, and I was scared to death when it got dark in this creaky old house. So I used to do the *Hard Target Search;* seemed like I did it every night."

Earl looked at her cocked, forehead scrunched, clearly not knowing what a *Hard Target Search* actually was. But he found himself backing further away from the closet, just in case it had something to do with those creepy, glowing masks.

Carol sensed confusion in Earl's face, so she continued.

"Yeah, I guess you don't know what that is. Well, I'll tell ya. I would be in bed and hear something weird - like a creak, or footsteps, or something drop, or move around, upstairs in the attic, or downstairs, or wherever, and I would lay frozen under the sheets, waiting, scared to death, barely breathing and not moving a muscle, hoping that whatever was coming to get me, a burglar, or some sort of monster, or ghoul, or whatever, wouldn't hear me, or see me, and leave me alone. I know it sounds silly now, but it never felt silly when it was happening, trust me.

2112

And sometimes, if I laid there too long thinking about it, I would be *so* scared I would just, all-of-a-sudden, sit up in bed and yell, at the top of my lungs, so whatever scary thing or ghost or whatever was in the house would hear me. I'd yell the same thing, every time:

Hard Target Search!

You know, just to let them know I was onto them and the hard target search was coming, as if they cared, whomever *they* were, be it molesters or monsters.

I'm not even sure how I came up with those words - that phrase - doesn't really make any sense. What does *hard target search* actually mean? It really doesn't mean anything. But it didn't matter, somehow I came up with it, and it stuck. I'd get the big red flashlight, which I kept right beside the bed, and then proceed to turn every light on in the house, *every one,* all the while making all sorts of noise and talking to myself, way too loud as I tramped around the house, my heart about to jump out of my chest. I'd keep yelling the whole time: *Hard target search! I'm gonna find ya; not scared of you!* You know, to scare 'em. Never thinking that *they are* the monsters, right, they're the ones who *do* the scaring, not me. Do monsters ever even get scared *[Earl just shrugged his shoulders, because he had actually never asked a monster that question]*? I don't think so, especially of some scared-for-shit girl waving a flashlight around in her underwear. Plus monsters *know, really know,* when you're scared right? So I couldn't fool 'em anyway, because they can see right through all that yelling stuff. But I did it anyway. I swear I'd look in every closet, under every piece of furniture, behind doors, in the basement, in the attic, *everywhere,* every square inch of this house, every time."

Earl just looked at her, his head cocked and his eyes a bit squinty.

"What?"

He leaned into her, as if to share a super-secret, and whispered.

"Sorry, I don't wanna hurt you feelings or anything, but, you know, just saying, that's *kinda weird*."

"Hey!"

And she poked Earl in the side, which made him giggle.

"Anyway, you know what?"

"What?"

"I never found anything, *ever*, and all it did was exhaust me. So at some point, after a couple of years of non-stop *hard target searches*, I stopped getting scared, and when I heard the creaks and groans, I just rolled over and went to sleep."

And Carol looked at Earl, like he was supposed to get it – the moral of the story – but by Earl's blank stare, it was clear he didn't. So she filled in the blank.

"Anyway, the point of the story is, I stopped worrying so much about being scared, since nothing every really happened anyway, so you should stop being scared too, of the masks, or whatever, because it doesn't do any good anyway. Then, sometime later, I got these guys; you know, even though they may look scary, they're actually pretty cool, and they protect me, and the house, kind of like an insurance policy, so I don't have to worry anymore. But they know, Earl, they *know* if you don't trust 'em, and they can't protect you if you don't trust 'em….so you gotta trust 'em."

Earl whispered again.

"They don't look too trusty to me, and why are they hiding in the closet anyway?"

Carol smirked.

"Come on, don't be afraid; let me introduce them."

And Carol took him by the wrist and dragged him over to the closet. To her surprise, he quietly stood there, without squirming or fighting to run away. Suddenly, he seemed to be okay, staring at them. *Wow, that was easy,* she thought.

"See, not so bad."

"No, not bad at all; I kinda like 'em."

And as he stood there, Carol eyed him up, suspicious; something wasn't right. So she raised her hands and waved them a bit in front of his face. Nothing; Earl didn't move a muscle. She knew it! So she poked him again.

"*Earl!* Open your eyes! I know you're cheating!"

He let out an ooph, and found himself face-to-face with the three wild, wooden masks, splashed in vibrant colors, mostly blood-reds and lifeless whites, staring hard at him. They were set against the back wall in a vertical line, with a red and blue glow leaking from their feral eyes and ferocious mouths. And all he wanted to do was run. He started to hyperventilate.

"Okay, let's go!"

He yelled.

"Stop."

She breathed at him, as she gently squeezed his hand.

"It's okay, I got ya; nothing bad is gonna happen. Promise."

And the way Carol whispered the words, and held his hand, he felt safe – like he felt when his mom would comfort him, after a bad dream, or a bad scare. It felt *that* good.

So Earl stayed put, for now. Zeke, Hunter and Maguro were all on the stairs, watching the show; Big B was lying lazy by Earl's feet; Big B was always close to Earl. He didn't give the masks a bit of notice.

"Okay look, the top one, the smallest one; he's from the Ivory Coast, the mountains, on the west coast of Africa. I'll have to show you where that is on a map, unless you already know *[Earl shook his head a slow no; he never heard of the Ivory Coast, and wondered if it had something to do with soap]*. Anyway, he looks like he's made out of chocolate, doesn't he? His name is:

Protecting The Traveler

That's kinda cool right? I got him because I travel so much; he protects you from evil people when you're far from home. The people who carved him, they're called the Dan People."

"I *never* go anywhere, I *don't* like chocolate and I don't know anybody named *Dan*."

Earl said, and in one fell swoop, the first scary mask was history in his book; no need for anyone named Dan.

"Well, we might travel *together* some day; you and me, and then you might need him, right? Doesn't hurt to play it safe."

And Carol gave his big mitt a little squeeze.

"C and I are going somewhere, but it's a secret; don't try to make me tell you, and no poking, because I'm ticklish....and besides, I'm not very good at keeping secrets, lately anyway....not very good at all."

Earl shook his head, hanging it in despair as he spoke, and Carol smiled sad, and gave him a dry kiss on the arm. Surprisingly, he let it pass, without a flinch, which made her happy. Then she continued.

"Okay, okay; so where you going?"

She asked quick.

"Well, it's a long way, but....*hey!*"

Earl yelled, almost spilling the beans, so she poked him again, just because she wanted to.

Carol wanted to tell him more about the first mask, but couldn't remember the details, which made her mad. She knew there was all sorts of information on the tribe and the type of wood it was carved from and what the facial expressions meant; she knew it all at one time, it was on a little sheet of paper that came with the mask, and she was sure C would have remembered all that stuff – he reeled that nonsense off all the time, and it was impressive. But the paper was long gone, and so were the tidbits. But then she looked back at Earl, and realized he didn't give a lick about the type of wood or more stories about the face, all he wanted was *out* when it came to the Ivory Coast.

"Okay, what about the bottom one, with the white face, that one."

"That one's really scary! And his mouth's wide open! He looks all pasty and dead!"

"Well, it kinda is; it's called:

Punu - The Guiding Spirit

If I remember right, it kinda gets all the spirits of your ancestors together, and they come back and help people they know and love get ready for the afterlife, you know, when you die. That's from a tribe in another country in Africa, but I don't remember which one, or which country either; doesn't matter, I guess."

"Hey, maybe he knows my mom; she helps me a lot and she loves me a whole bunch too. But I'm not going to no afterlife, that doesn't sound very fun."

"You're right, we don't wanna go there. Hey, why are you in my closet?"

Carol scolded the mask. Earl waited for an answer.

Nothing.

"Okay, so far we're not doing so well. How about the last one, the one in the middle; it's a she....a Goddess."

"She's the scariest of all! I'm *really* afraid of her!"

Earl said, putting his head down, refusing to look at her.

Unlike the first two, backlit in blue, she oozed a red afterglow. She had bright white, burgundy and green bead-work, a tiny mosaic comprised of hundreds of beads, each no larger than a pin-head, set in concentric circles and swirls which blanketed her ominous face. She had dead-slits for eyes, painted black and barely open, with a corpse-like mouth that looked as one would when its last words were spoken. Red and charcoal fabric tassles hung from her ears and hair, framing her horrid face. She had a flat nose, and a too-long forehead. She couldn't be described as anything but ugly, and one could only imagine the color of her dead eyes behind the slits in her lids.

Carol sensed the dread, and tried to calm her friend.

"Don't be afraid of her Earl, she's a:

River Goddess

And she's *extra* special. She's actually a death mask, from Zaire; I remember that one. That's another African country, where it is, on a map, I mean, I really don't know. I wish I did, I should, but I don't. Anyway, she saves people from drowning; that's good right? No one wants to drown; that can't be very fun."

Earl wasn't convinced that scary mask could help you with *anything* except being scared, and certainly it couldn't save you from drowning - that was silly - how can she do that when you're in the river and she's up here, hiding in the closet? It made no sense to him, no sense at all. And he wasn't buying it, not for a minute.

"But then why is she a *death mask*, if she's supposed to save people? That doesn't sound too safe to me! Shouldn't she be a *life mask*, or a *save mask*? And why is she so ugly?"

Carol stared at Earl, then at the mask, and back at Earl.

"I never thought of that, any of that actually - good questions! I don't know the answers; why don't we ask her?"

"*No way!* I'm not talking to her! She's scary and ugly and dead! Can we close the closet now....*please*? Since I met all the masks? Hi masks! Bye masks!"

Earl's head was scoping his shoes, refusing to look at the blood-red glow of the Goddess, but she stared hard at him, through dead-slit eyes, her corpse lips slightly parted.

Carol smiled, happy that Earl made the effort. She nodded her head once in the affirmative and slowly clicked the closet door shut. With that, the three masks went dark.

Cloaked in ink, the *River Goddess* was deathly quiet, staring silent through the closed door.

CHAPTER 280 – IN THE GIRAFFE WENT, FOLLOWED BY A SEXY FINGER SUCK

Earl and Carol stood on opposite sides of the island, each dipping animal crackers in the same glass of skim milk. And they were getting toward the end of the box. Zeke was sprawled lazy on the island, a warm, gray fur buffer between them; Big B was curled at Earl's feet, as usual, partially draped over his left shoe.

Carol reached out a hand, and scratched Zeke under the chin.

"Remember when you wouldn't even look at me? And now you're in my house, just you and me, alone, eating cookies; how cool is that?

Carol whispered to Earl, but he didn't answer. He wasn't being rude; it was just that he was concentrating on timing the cookie withdrawal from the milk just right – trying to achieve maximum milk absorption without the hippo-cookie breaking and falling into the glass. It took a lot of concentration and skill, and Earl's brow was furrowed, eyes squinting, focused on the task at hand. Carol sensed the distraction, so she began to tread into more fertile territory, figuring he wouldn't run jackrabbit....yet.

"We're getting kinda low on animals to eat; so what're we gonna do next? Any ideas? *I got some ideas?*"

Unbeknownst to Carol, Earl was a good multi-tasker, and his radar went on high alert with that last slippery sentence. *Oh boy, this doesn't sound good* Earl thought to himself, as he slowly, carefully extracted the hippo, swollen to the gills, gorged with skim milk, but still in one piece. Victory was close at hand.

"You know, we could always go up to my bedroom...."

Carol whispered, the words dripping with sex.

Earl was moving the hippo slowly to his mouth, victory within reach, but the bedroom comment caught him off guard, and the herky-jerk of his hand split the hippo in two; the milk-soaked, ass-end crashed into the glass, making a kerplunk, as it sunk indignant to the bottom, lost at sea.

"Oops, sorry Earl."

Carol said mischievous, knowing *exactly* why that hippo-butt bit the dust. So she finished the end of her not-so-innocent sentence, as if the whole charade was benign from the get-go.

"….and lay on the bed and pet all the cats. You know they'll all jump on the bed with us if we go up. Wanna give it a try? Go lay on the bed together and pet the pussycats?"

Carol couldn't help it; she knew she was torturing Earl, but she was in a naughty mood, and figured she'd throw the line in the water, and see what she could reel in. But Earl recovered nicely.

"No need to go upstairs; we got lots of cats to pet right here! Look, I'm petting Zeke!"

Earl exclaimed, stroking Zeke much too fast and hard, which startled him, causing him to quickly rise and exit the island in a single leap.

"Or not...."

Carol said wry.

But Earl had Plan B, called Big B, at his feet. In a second, he scooped up his big friend, plopped him on the island, and rubbed his round, orange belly. Unlike Zeke,

Big Banana was going nowhere; he stayed by Earl no matter what, and was loving the belly rub to boot. Carol smiled at the end-around and shelved the bed-lay, for now.

"Okay, okay saved for now by Big B *[she scowled fake at Big B, putting her nose up to his – but Banana ignored her completely, purring as Earl rubbed his tummy]*. Then how about let's eat C's box of crackers; he'd never know."

Carol was still in a mischievous mood, and wanted to extend Earl's stay beyond the first box of cookies.

"No way! That wouldn't be right, would it? We gotta save them for C, don't we?"

And Carol looked at Earl's eyes shifting around the kitchen, and he cracked the slightest little devilish smile. And right then, she knew, Cord's *Animal Crackers* were goners.

"Earl! You're so bad! I was only kidding, we can't do that!"

Carol said, as she cracked open Cord's box, reached in, and handed Earl the first animal, another fat hippo.

And Earl giggled, and breathed a sigh, saved by Big B and one of C's hippos. *Thanks, C.*

"Maybe I can give C some of these instead."

Earl said, snickering to himself as he dug in his pocket and pulled out the tiniest crumbs of the animals crackers left in his pants, along with strings of lint, dumping them on the island. And with them, came the light-blue, two-inch *Post-It*, creased and pocked from being wet at one time, but now it was dry, with faded smears of mud, like it fell in the rain.

"What's that?"

Carol asked innocent.

"I don't know."

Earl said matter-of-fact, concentrating on the new hippo. And before he could say another word, Carol grabbed the *Post-It*, and began reading; it was faded black ink in a neat curly cursive only a woman would have.

Stop by Suzies

It said, in large letters across the middle, with an address, crossed out in circular pen. Carol squinted to read the destination:

4th at 12:30
No. 27

And all of a sudden, without warning, her face turned, and the words came out angry, and they came out ugly.

"Who's Suzie?"

And Earl stood up straight, dropped the hippo in the glass of milk, and he got that familiar stab in his chest, that sinking feeling that he was in big trouble, just like he felt whenever Lilly yelled at him. And he began to stammer, and nothing really came out.

"I don't know...."

And as quick as it came over her, Carol immediately felt shame, as she saw the fear in Earl's eyes; she knew that was a look that Lilly saw....often.

2124

She was devastated.

"Earl, I'm so sorry, I didn't mean to snap at you; I'm sorry."

And she put her hand on his; he didn't pull it away, but she could tell he was nervous, until he wasn't anymore. And in silence, he stuck his fat finger from the other hand in the milk, to retrieve the hippo, as Carol went to dunk a new cookie, at the same time. And that broke the ice. And this time her question was nice.

"Who is she Earl? And whatcha doing at 12:30?"

"Nothing."

"Well it can't be nothing. She asked you over for something, right? Where is No. 27 anyway?"

"I don't know."

And then Carol stood up straight, removing her hand from his. Not in a bad way - rather, in a *we-have-to-talk* serious way.

"Earl, I said I was sorry, and I meant it, I did....promise. I'm not mad, I just was curious, you know, what you were doing at her house, since I never heard you talk about a Suzie before. I don't even know who she is, and I like to know your friends. So, watcha doing?"

"I'm eating C's cookies and trying to stop dropping hippos in the milk, I guess."

Earl said slow, looking into Carol's eyes, and wondering if he got the answer right.

"I don't mean *right, right now,* I mean later, at Suzies. Why were you hiding the note?"

" I wasn't, I forgot to throw it away."

Earl said indifferent, as he reached for another cookie to dunk.

"Why are you throwing it away?"

"Because my mom said to. She always picked up stuff and threw it away, she *hated* litter-bugs! I'm no litter-bug, *no way*, but some people are, so I pick up after them, you know, when I'm walking down the street, and stuff."

Earl spoke, but didn't look at Carol; instead he was concentrating on his next cookie, a giraffe this go-round, trying once again to keep it in the milk absolutely as long as he possibly could, to soak up the maximum amount of milk, before the cookie fell apart. He was concentrating hard, his tongue out, for extra measure.

And as Earl performed the dunking, Carol looked at him hard, with a furrowed brow. Then she shook her head in the negative, and exhaled a half-chuckle, mostly to herself, as she finally figured the mystery.

"Earl, do you even *know* Suzie?"

"No, I told you I don't! I picked that up in the Park, by my mom's bench; somebody who knows Suzie is a *real litterbug!*"

And with that, the cookie broke in two and fell in the milk.

"*Aw, look!* The giraffe's head fell in! I really stink at cookie-dunking."

With that, Carol stuck her thin, delicate fingers in the milk, as if in slow-motion, swirled around, and captured the giraffe. In as sexy a voice as you can imagine, holding a milk-sogged cookie, she purred:

Open....

and Earl did as he was told. In the giraffe went, followed by a sexy finger suck.

CHAPTER 281 - GONE, AND NEVER RETURNED

"Watcha thinking right now?"

Carol quizzed Earl, as he stood at the island, petting Big Banana. She had her back to him, doing the few dishes they made. He was awful quiet, and seemed deep in thought. And she was thinking about Earl, and herself, the two of them – doing something together, as in, *really together*. It was a nutty, exciting, fun thought, and she hoped, maybe, Earl was thinking the same thing. She just felt it, so she sprung the question, knowing for sure they were like-minded.

"Um...."

Was all Earl got out. *She knew it!* she thought to herself. So Carol threw him a preserver; it would be easier for him to admit it, if she admitted it first.

"Okay, hold that thought, and I'll tell you what *I* was just thinking, right now. I'll go first."

And with that, she spun around excitedly and looked at him with loving eyes. She knew it was dangerous, to spill this, but since they were thinking the same thing, she went for it, hoping he wouldn't run, hoping maybe he'd admit it too. And she was thinking: *how cool that would be?*

"I was thinking about a picnic, on a blanket, bottle of wine, tiny grapes, some cool cheeses, some *Animal Crackers*, of course, some milk, some giraffes, and after we eat, lying on the blanket and taking a nap in the sun, looking up at the undersides of the trees, and the clouds, just you and me, and you.....and me."

And Earl just stared at her, lips slightly apart, like an epiphany. And she *saw it in his eyes*.

"I knew it! You too?! You were thinking the same thing?! Really?! How cool is that? Earl! How cool is that?! Tell me what you were thinking, all the details; tell me *everything!*"

And Earl wanted to lie, but he couldn't, he just wasn't very good at it, and his mom told him never to lie anyway; so he took a big, deep breath, and told the truth."

"I was kinda, thinking, you know, about radishes; they're really good! I was really wanting some radishes, you know with cocktail sauce, or cold butter, that's the best - a whole bowl of radishes, with cold butter spread on 'em! I got a real hankering….just saying."

And Carol stared at him, with a dumbfound look.

So he added a meek trailer.

"But I like picnics too….and radishes."

And Carol couldn't believe she could love Earl even more, but just then, she did. Thank God she found Earl; of all the years searching for the right guy, any guy who wasn't a louse, and nothing. A steady string of losers and leeches. Yet here he was, the whole time, a priority package, the *right* package, delivered to her front door once a month, with a smile and check in hand, for years. And she never gave it, or him, a second notice. Such were the cruel vagaries of life. Until Cord, that is, helped her open her eyes and see the incredible present right in front of her nose, all those years. She couldn't believe she was thinking it, considering what a total jerk he had become, but: *thank God for Cord.*

She smiled at the thought.

"Come on, let's go."

Carol whispered to Earl, taking him gently by the hand.

"Where we going?"

"To get you some radishes."

Carol said, through a sly smile.

"Really! I got a hankering, you know."

"I bet you do. I got a hankering too, but not for radishes."

And she raised her eyebrows at Earl, and tilted her head in that *you-know-what-I'm-talking-about* way. He quickly looked away, and started blabbering.

"Hankerings are the best, aren't they? I love saying that word: *hankering;* isn't that a great word? I'm not even sure where I learned it, but I'm glad I did! I could say it all day: *hankering, hankering, hankering!* Hey, what do *you* got a hankering for?"

Earl was so excited about saying the word *hankering*, he didn't realize he just asked Carol the one question he certainly didn't want to know the answer to. She saw the abject horror on Earl's face, realizing that one somehow slipped out, Freudian, for sure. So she just smiled wide at Earl and gently let him off the hook.

"Never mind. Maybe I'll get my hankering satisfied later. Go grab the butter, some napkins and a knife; we'll get the radishes and cocktail sauce at the store and eat 'em in the car, top down, kind of like a picnic - a weird car-radish-picnic thing, and drive around to root out where your best friend is hiding. I kinda miss him too, and have to thank him for something; what'ya say?"

"I think that's the best idea *ever!* Ever, ever, *ever [Earl was rubbing his hands together, fast, as he spoke excited]!* Especially the finding Cord part, and the picnic too, and we'll get some new *Animal Crackers*, okay? That would be the right thing to do, you know, that would be fair, since we ate all his, just saying. And the radishes, can't forget the radishes, 'cause I still got a *bad hankering!*"

In all the excitement, barreling out the back door, arms loaded with picnic supplies, and loading into the Ferrari, neither one noticed the solitary set of dead eyes, high above, shadowing their every move.

He had been sitting there, quietly, watching them in the kitchen, through the elliptical panes of the sink window, with cold, lifeless eyes. Perched atop the Methodist Church steeple, he stretched his immense black wings, soaking in the warmth of the Indian summer sun.

A gargoyle.

It was just the second time he visited, and once again, solo. And he was just as big as before, maybe even bigger. A real monster. The last time was April 21st, the day after the out-of-town bus pulled beside *Luigi's Rancho* and dropped a sole stranger roadside. The same day the stranger first darkened her front door.

The immense black vulture slowly rotated his head, left to right, tracing the candy apple roadster, top down, as it zipped around the corner and sped past the Park, toward the Courthouse. It stared hard in that direction, and continued to, long after the Ferrari had disappeared from sight. What it thought was a mystery, and would remain so....but whatever it was, it couldn't be good.

It let a low, extended hiss while folding its warmed wings, looked west and with a single mighty thrust, took flight over the Park, towards the Delaware; moments later, it was lazily cresting the river, riding a warm Autumn current of air, just south of the boat ramp. It

2131

gazed down at the river far below, circling tight and slow, as if in survey.

Suddenly, with a flurry of flaps of its enormous wings, it veered south, hugging the wooded western shore, tracking the rapids of the *Foul Rift*, on its way downstream, toward *Couch Rock*.

Not a soul witnessed the dance; a dress rehearsal for a play that may never see the stage. But then again, *It* knew better. *It* knew all along.

In a moment, the maleficent black vulture was gone, and never returned.

CHAPTER 282 – IT WOULD BE THE LAST TIME HE EVER SAW HER FACE

"I can't believe….you are such a fucking, *fucking* asshole! *Whatever.*"

He kept replaying the exchange, over and over, between him and Carol, as he kicked random leaves at his feet, more of a foot-shuffle, sitting on a rock, eyes down.

Fucking, fucking asshole.

He snorted and shook his head, pathetic.

At one time, Carol actually liked him, actually thought about sleeping with him, even if she tried to deny it now, which he knew she surely would. Regardless, it seemed a lifetime ago. And the mere thought felt dirty, because of Earl.

Neither one of them was the same person they were then; those people were long gone. Dead.

He *was* an asshole, no argument there. But he didn't care; he didn't care about her, or anyone, really.

Well, that was a pretty big lie. He still cared about Earl.

Truth was, C didn't know why he'd been in a funk. He was lonely and feeling sorry for himself; everyone else around him, most anyway, seemed so hooked-up and happy – so he guessed that was part of it.

Who was he kidding? He *knew* that was part of it, more than *part* of it.

And this feeling, this funk, wasn't new - it always came, wherever he went; if he stayed long enough, too long, it eventually surfaced. Dark periods would come like clockwork. Yet most of the time, wherever he was, he was alone anyway, and didn't really give two-shits about the people around him, so the funk didn't much matter. It was kind of a self-fulfilling prophesy; he wasn't so sure if it controlled him, or he it, maybe a bit of both. Another unwritten rule in a game he didn't understand, and had no choice but to play.

But this one, this funk, felt peculiar, for this place was at-odds with all the places that came before. Here, *real* connections were made….emotional ones. That didn't happen, wasn't supposed to happen, and it complicated things.

So this mess he found himself in was a healthy dose of self-pity, heaped atop the same old funk - a short temper coupled with an intense desire to be alone - a desire to be not-in whatever place he happened to be at the time, but rather, someplace else, far away….a new beginning. Another shot at at the next stop on the rail; another promise of better days.

He always seemed to be heading toward that new beginning, that new place, that would finally be the right place. For awhile, he thought he had found it here, in some forgotten backwater called Belvidere, but he was wrong. He wondered if such a place, for him, even existed.

And this feeling of flight, this was different than Jenny. When Jenny spoke, he *had* to open the box, play the game, and if the bullet didn't enter his brain, he had to go – there was no choice. Those were simply the rules; he didn't make 'em, they existed long before he did, and they weren't subject to debate.

They were just the rules.

And they were *always* the rules; as far as he knew, they had been in place forever, whatever *forever* really meant. *No beginning, and no end*; that was good as the explanation for *forever* ever got.

And he wondered if he alone played the game, or were there others? And were *their* games the same as *his* game, or were they different? If so, how? And why? He was pretty sure there were other players, although he had never met one, as far as he knew. It wasn't something you *announced*; the concept of the game didn't explain very well, when discussed aloud. Most people would just step back, slowly, and make a call. So you kept quiet; the players in his head kind of insisted on that anyway.

He wondered if there were just a handful, or dozens, or hundreds, or thousands of others trapped in the same game, or some variation thereof, wandering about, as lost as he was....a lost boy. He wondered how far back they existed; a millenium? Longer? Or was he really the first? The only?

He shook the thought from his head; it wasn't worth thinking about, because the answer wasn't coming, nor did it matter. He was stuck in the game, with no out; that was all he was sure about, the rest was nothing but hunch and a headache.

But one thing he *did* know; this fateful feeling that had been circling his brain of late, this funk, it *wasn't* Jenny; this was a different voice talking to him, from a different part, a distant part, buried deep inside his head....he wasn't sure exactly where it was, but it was usually dormant, until it wasn't. And he rarely acted on it; in fact, he *never* acted on it in the end, because it conflicted with her, and, sans an emergency that dictated flight, and true emergencies rarely happened, Jenny was the one who controlled if and when he left.

Those were the rules.

But usually, when this despondent feeling washed over him, drowned him, when this *other* voice called to him, Jenny followed soon thereafter, as if the two knew each other. Maybe they did. That's the way it had been anyway, the way it always seemed to work, when he felt the way he felt right now.

If any of that made *any* sense.

To him, it did, and that was all that mattered, he guessed, since he never had this discussion with anyone but himself.

Thankfully, he hadn't seen the hag again; he was a bit surprised by that, because he could still *feel* her, hiding just out of sight, right behind his eyes – that's how it felt – that's where it seemed she lived and patiently waited. And he knew she was always watching him, from inside his head. But she seemed to live in a different place than the puppet....a *new* place. And he felt, he somehow knew, that she could surface at any time, at will; she played by different rules than the puppet. And that thought terrified him. The puppet still scared him, for sure, but he had lived with the manikin for so many years, it was, for lack of a better term, a known entity, a known evil that he had come to grips with – and he accepted their need to coexist. The hag, on the other hand, was new, an unknown, an outlier, and the fright-factor with her was much worse.

Way worse.

He wondered why the hag showed, for the first time after so many years of playing the game, in *this* God-forsaken outback. Who was she, *really*, and what was *her* role, *her* place in the grand scheme? Was she new to the game, or had she always been there, simply hiding, and waiting? He wondered if Jenny knew the hag, or the hag, Jenny. And what was her name, if she even had one? And he wondered if either one knew the puppet, the crickets and the flies. Did they all live in the same town? On the same block? Or did they just live in different rooms, in the same house? What were *they* afraid of? Did they lock their doors? Did they all wear shoes?

He wondered.

The disparate thoughts jumbled and collided as his head rested in his hands, looking down at his old sneakers, ripped and full of holes, his only constant companion as he wandered the globe, alone. The sound of the river filled his ears, the pop and wash of the water over the boulders along the bank where he sat, on his new-favorite perch….alone.

Autumn had engulfed him, and the thought of the coming cold made him melancholy.

He was deep in the woods, off the scary part of Foul Rift Road, where the evil ball used to hang in the tree. It was gone now; where it went he had no idea. He was way behind the creepy houses, over the rail line, past a field of moss-covered boulders in old-growth forest, down by the water's edge, the Delaware, amidst the *Foul Rift,* facing the rapids he could always hear in the distance whenever he ran the loop, the one that Lilly had tricked him on that day during the summer, which also seemed a lifetime ago.

It was his new favorite place to be alone; he was good at that. And he thought more about leaving.

Leaving this place, Belvidere, was gonna be different. It had always felt different here. And strange things happened here, that had never happened before.

And he smiled a bit thinking about all the good memories he'd had since that Thursday, late morning, April 20th, when he got off the Greyhound. Christ, it had been almost six months; it felt like forever and the simple flip of a page, both, simultaneous.

And his smile soon faded; the more he thought about it, the more he realized his time here had run it course, his welcome worn. Mae was with *Tool-Box* – that thought still made him gag; Margery thought of him as baggage; Ji and Marty were an item – there was a time Ji liked him – he could have bagged her, even, but those days were long gone; Carol and Earl were spending more and more time together, mainly with Ji and Marty – a happy foursome, but Carol and Earl spent time alone as well. He knew for a fact Earl and Carol had gone to *Couch Rock* alone together, more than once, three times even, maybe more. And as for Lillian – well, that was best left alone.

And he stopped talking to Carol, the dead one, stopped going to see her; what was the point? The thought of that now, pretending to talk to her, pretending she was listening, that she was somehow *real*, and somehow cared, and somehow mattered, made him feel foolish. And he came to doubt he ever really communicated with her anyway, all just wishful thinking:

- *Kindred spirits,* and talk of angels, from the mouth of his best friend;
- *Open when you're ready,* written on boxes and letters;
- Tiny notes with the word *Help* scrawled on them, to help Lilly, that never really existed at all;
- Holding hands, guiding him through the dark, when bolts skewered his body, when he was as good as dead; and

- Drunken dart throws, piercing a map, and a river, at some bum-fuck backwater called Belvidere;

And whatever other pretend *miracles* he couldn't remember. Stupid, all of it.

With time, miracles tend to fade; theories, excuses, rationalizations seep in, they formulate and stick....they provide the *why* for why all of it never *really* happened.

Foolish, all of it. Just dumb.

He shook his head at all the time he wasted *talking* to her, thinking about her, some long-gone corpse he didn't know, buried decades ago in a half-marked grave, with nothing but a shit-spelter plaque from the down-the-street funeral home.

He needed new friends.

Maybe he could spend time with Buck, or Sam, or Woodie, or Moe. How about Frank, lounging on his stained sofa, sharing a rot-gut six-pack? Pathetic. Maybe he could just troll the high school and hang with Linda, from *Nonpareil;* he didn't even know she was spending a lot of time lately with Buck - that would have just added to the pity.

What he needed, badly, was Jenny, his fix, his one-way ticket out. And he did feel her, on the periphery; he knew she was close, and would come knocking soon.

He was ready for *soon.*

More thoughts jumbled and turned in his head, too many, as the *Rift* rapids rushed by, never-ending, paying him no heed. The smell of moist earth and mist from the river filled his nostrils. Cord's hand, a tightly clenched fist, was banging rhythmic against his thigh, but he didn't even realize it.

He breathed, deep and long, and after a minute or so, a calm entered his head; his hand unclenched and fell by his side. He was quiet; his head finally went quiet.

And he found himself practicing *Amazing Grace* aloud, just loud enough for himself to hear. He had been doing that a lot lately, at least when he sat on this rock, which was more often than not.

Why he sang that stupid song, he had no idea. He just did.

> *Amazing Grace, how sweet the sound;*
> *That saved a wretch like me;*
> *I once was lost, but now am found;*
> *Was blind, but now can see.*

And to his surprise, he didn't sound half-bad; he *was* getting better, much better. And it made him happy….a little happy anyway.   So he sang some more, a bit louder even, onto the second verse – he only knew the first three verses:

> *T'was Grace that taught my heart to fear;*
> *And Grace my fears relieved;*
> *How precious….;*

"Oh my God, Earl's right; that is just *awful!*"

A familiar voice, out of sight, somewhere behind him, cut him off, dead-stop.

The sight of running shoes, sleek, brand-new ones, with bright, lime-green soles, a stark contrast to the brown carpet of dead leaves beside the boulder upon which he sat, interrupted his *a capella*. He was surprised he never heard her sneak up on him; lost-in-song will do that.

Cord never raised his head; he just started singing again, lowering the volume, barely above a whisper:

How precious did that Grace appear;
The hour I first believed....

She half-heartedly kicked him in the shoe.

"Hey, cut it out; seriously, that's *so bad*!"

But he wasn't amused, or in the mood for banter, or meaningless games, with Lillian.

"*What?*"

Was all he said, annoyed.

Lilly stopped trying to make nice; if she tried at all - which was rare - she never tried more than once. To his rebuff, she became curt herself.

"You've been a jerk to Earl, and he's upset."

Was all she said. To which C didn't respond. So she kicked his shoe again, much harder this time.

"Did you *hear* me?"

"Stop fucking kicking me. And yes, I heard you, and I've heard; I'm not mad at Earl - if he's upset, have him talk to me."

Cord answered indignant.

Lilly didn't answer, and he just stared at her spotless sneakers, which didn't move. All he heard was the endless rush of the river, a cacophony of birds, and someone, far away, using a chainsaw.

But Lillian didn't make a sound.

He wanted to look at her, to see that beautiful face; maybe a tiny smile would greet him if he looked up, but probably not. But it didn't matter, even if she glared angry at him, which he figured she was doing right now, he knew he'd fall for her all over again, and he didn't want to give her the satisfaction, or him, the agita that invariably followed. He would soon be gone from this place, and he'd never see her again. And although she would be harder to forget, for sure, she too would eventually fade away like the rest, like they always did. And in time, he'd wonder what the fuss called *Lillian* was all about. For that reason, not looking at her, not seeing her, not engaging her, was better….it just was. The *forget* had already started, and he didn't want to go back to square one, not with Lilly; it was just too hard.

But he felt bad, her standing there, and him being a jerk, so he made a half-attempt at conversation, simply to end the awkwardness.

"How did you find me?"

"Not hard."

She snorted sarcastic.

He picked up his head and looked across the river, to the thick woods on the far bank, that stretched as far as he could see, upstream and downstream, along the expanse of the *Foul Rift.*

"Funny place to pick, to sit, all alone, in the woods."

She said, but he didn't answer; he was being stubborn again.   So Lillian crouched down beside him, and although he didn't want to, he saw her knee and part of her thigh and the tip of her finger. And he might as well have been looking into her eyes, because just to see her tan skin, her bony knee, made him feel a pang in his chest, exactly what he didn't want to feel.

He *hated* that he loved her, and he most certainly did.

"See that little beach, the tiny, thin strip of sand, the only sand along the far back, just downstream….and that white tree, splotchy-looking, growing out of the bank, near the beach, just upstream of the sand?"

C followed her finger.

"Right at the ridge, well half-way up, toward the top, it's hard to see from here, but that's it….it's right there; you can see a piece of it, just barely, from here."

Cord stared, and stared some more, and then he saw it, the river-end of it, tilted forward toward the water, like a table. It looked tiny, too tiny, from this vantage, but he was pretty far away – the Delaware was pretty wide, at this point.

"What is it?"

He said, innocent.

"You know what."

She said, not buying his act.

Of course he did. He was surprised he had gotten so close to it, on the opposite bank. There really were no landmarks, just the tiny beach, which was the only beach in either direction, within eyesight. That, and sketchy directions by Earl long ago, a different lifetime.

"I haven't seen you much; you've changed, everybody says so. So what's the matter? Why are you out here, alone?

"I've been alone so long, different wouldn't feel right."

He said, with a tinge of self-pity.

"Well what about Earl, and Carol, and Sam and Buck, and...."

"*And you?*"

He finished her sentence.

And Lillian desperately wanted to say: *Yeah, and* me, because that was the honest answer – that was the real *why* as to why she ran out here, looking for him. But she didn't, she was being stubborn.   So Lillian was silent, like she always was when she shouldn't be.

Cord figured that was the answer he'd get, no answer at all, and he was mad at setting himself up to be taken down a peg, yet again.

"It never lasts Lilly, it just doesn't; it never does."

He whispered, prefaced by a deep breath, and a long exhale.

"That's a cop-out! You're just scared! You could make it last if you wanted to. You could change it, you could easily change it, you could just do it....*just do it*! But you *choose* not to!"

She yelled at him, louder than necessary.

"It's not that simple."

"*Yes it is!*"

She yelled again, frustrated at his utter defeat.

With that, Cord looked up for the first time, and stared deep into her eyes. He looked at her in a way he had never looked at her before. And he could tell, she was listening.

"Really? It's that easy? Okay, then why don't you talk to your mom? Just try, *really try,* just once! Why don't you just leave this Town you hate so much; just get up and go, right now! Why don't you sing *Amazing Grace* – go ahead, let me hear it, right now, *just once*! Why don't you just extend you hand and be friends with the woman that Earl loves more than just about *anything* in this world, except maybe you? Run on over to her house right now and knock on the door and say *Hi, just want you to know, I'm happy you're with my brother and I wish you the best, both of you!* Simple, right? You can do it if you want; you could change it, you could *easily* change it…..*just do it!* Simple, right?"

And then Cord shut up, turned his head back to the river, to across the river, to *Couch Rock,* and stared at it, while the river passed by.

Lillian didn't answer, she just stood there; she didn't make a single movement, she didn't say a single word. Processing.

"Thought so."

He said sarcastic, then added.

"Let me know how that's working for ya, then you can tell me I'm scared, and call me a cop-out and tell me it's so easy to change."

He kept looking across the Delaware, waiting for what he knew was coming next.

And sure enough, within seconds of finishing the thought, it did. He heard the dead leaves rip and crinkle as she shifted her shoes. He heard her pick her way amongst the boulders and trees, cracking branches as she went. She made a lot more noise on the exit. Further distant, he heard the slag and trap rock from the old rail bed chaff, click and slide under her new, bright-green sneakers.

Then he heard nothing; she was gone, and he was alone again.

For a moment, he wanted to stop her, part of him, anyway, while he was listening to her getting farther away. He wanted to jump up and bring her back, to hug her, to apologize, to make up. But the part that didn't want to do that, the part that says this-is-how-it-always-goes, and-always-will, the part that felt sorry for himself….sat tight.

And in the end, that part won, like it always did. And soon enough, she was gone, and once again, it was right.

He reached under the rock, to a small, dry cubby beneath two boulders, the one he sat upon, and the one adjacent, and cracked open *1984,* to think about new ways to save Julia….always futile. He brought so many classics he meant to read, to start, but invariably, he always returned to *1984,* to read it just one more time.

But after just half a page, he closed the book and looked across the river, scanning the bank, looking for *Couch Rock*, and started to sing *Amazing Grace* again, for what reason, he had no clue.

And Jenny came to mind, oblique really, something a bit more than what would be considered a passing thought.

But it still got his attention; it always did, because she never showed for no reason. And for that reason, he knew she would be visiting, for real, soon. And he took some comfort in that, because in the end, he could always count on Jenny being there for him, being his friend, even if her visit ended with a bullet in his brain.

His thoughts tracked back to Lillian Liddell. He tried to commit to memory, how all the lines, shapes and features came together to make up her eyes, nose, ears and mouth. He wished he had a pad and paper, to sketch it, her face, but he didn't.

He concentrated hard, trying to commit her lines to memory. And wondered if this time, Jenny would be sure it would be the last time he ever saw her face.

www.ingramcontent.com/pod-product-compliance
Lightning Source LLC
Chambersburg PA
CBHW060615310726
48982CB00003B/573